Cape Mayhem

Jane Kelly

Plexus Publishing, Inc.
Medford, New Jersey

Second Printing, 2002

Published by:
Plexus Publishing, Inc.
143 Old Marlton Pike
Medford, NJ 08055

Library of Congress Cataloging-in-Publication Data

Kelly, Jane, 1949-
    Cape Mayhem / by Jane Kelly.
      p.   cm.
    ISBN 0-937548-41-3
    I. Title.
    PS3561.E39424C3   1999
    813'.54--dc21   99-33990
                                                           CIP

Printed in the United States of America

ISBN 0-937548-41-3

Cover Design: Lisa Boccadutre
Book Design: Patricia Kirkbride

Cover photo of the Turnbull house by Pat Palatucci

Dedication

To Linda, Nancy, Marilynn,
Ginny, Eleanor, and Pat

Acknowledgments

Thank you to Lou Elwell for sharing his memories, the Turk/Shapiro family for sharing their home, Lt. William J. McGough, Sr., for sharing his expertise, and the Bayer family for sharing just about everything.

Chapter One

"George." My own loudness startled me—and everyone else for that matter. Unexpectedly, I became the center of the group's attention. Make that the overt center of the group's attention. I'd been their covert focus since they'd figured out that I was visiting the Parsonage bed-and-breakfast alone. Apparently couples secluded for a romantic week in Cape May, New Jersey, welcome single women with the same warmth drug lords secluded for a summit reserve for DEA agents.

George, the co-owner of the B&B, responded to my outcry with a raised eyebrow and a concerned tone. "Meg, dear, whatever is wrong?"

"I...I forgot something." I rose with no idea where I was headed. "In the kitchen." I required privacy; the kitchen was the closest place to find it.

"You..." George accented the word with doubt, "left something in the kitchen?" As the proprietor of the bed-and-breakfast, he realized I had never been in the kitchen to leave any item behind.

"Yes. Yes, I did." I smiled at the assembled guests. They stared at me as if I'd just revealed my Ebola diagnosis. "Sorry. It just hit me. Silly, really. Come, George. Help me." I grabbed the man's hand and pulled him towards the door.

"Be right back," George called to his guests as I dragged him out of the room.

Inside an elaborate pantry area with floor-to-ceiling cabinets that I did not have time to admire, I came to an abrupt halt. The swinging door pushed George into me. He didn't apologize; neither did I. "Meg, what is the problem?"

1

I whispered my reply. "George, ix-nay on the talk about last night."

"What talk about last night?"

"You were teasing the Gimbels about their amorous adventures last night."

"So." He shrugged. "They're married. No scandal there."

"If those two are husband and wife, then Mr. Gimbel was not married to the woman he made love to last night." I ruled out bigamy.

"You're not making sense, Meg."

"This is a different Mrs. Gimbel than the one Wallace Gimbel checked in with."

"Meg, Ms. Daniels—sweetie, did you sneak out to a twenty-four hour liquor store?"

"Trust me on this, George. I'm sure about it. Don't you agree that Mrs. Gimbel got a little bent out of shape when you joked about last night's noisy lovemaking?"

"Claude tells me I overstep sometimes. I hate to admit it, but he could be right. She did seem a bit miffed."

"No, George, she was confused. She didn't know that Mr. Gimbel made love last night. Trust me and be a little careful." I paused only briefly. "Are you sure she *is* Mrs. Gimbel?"

"She always has been." He sighed. "Meg, are you trying to give me a headache?" He massaged his temples with exaggerated motions. "Let me see if I get this. Mr. Gimbel checked in with a woman who is supposed to be his wife. He made love to her..."

"Although she was supposed to be deathly ill," I interjected.

"Okay. Love works miracles. She is suddenly healthy." He stared at me hard. "So?"

"The woman at the breakfast table is a different person." My face contorted. "What I don't understand is: if Mr. Gimbel sneaked another woman in here, and I know he did, why does his wife recite the details of her illness?"

"Meg, you keep saying that this is a different woman. You don't know that."

"Yes, I do."

"You do?" His question challenged me.

"Yes, I do."

"And how do you know this?"

"Her ankles."

"Her ankles?" Under his breath he added, "This oughtta be good."

"Last night, all I could see of the woman was her ankles. I saw them two times." I didn't elaborate on how I happened to see the woman twice. "They were attractive, slim ankles. Go in the other room and sneak a peek at Mrs. Gimbel's legs."

George rolled his eyes.

"Now. Go." I gave him a gentle push towards the breakfast room.

I watched the swinging door make a smaller and smaller arc until it came to a complete stop only to be pushed back into a wide arc by George.

"Okay, Meg, you win." He released a deep sigh. "Where's the other woman?"

Guilt stabbed me in the stomach. Maybe I shouldn't have told George that I'd overheard the couple making love the night before. If I hadn't, George wouldn't have made teasing remarks at breakfast. If George hadn't made those comments, Mrs. Gimbel wouldn't have grown disgruntled. But I did and he did and, because we did, Wallace and Marvella Gimbel were going to have a rotten weekend. And, it would be all my fault. But then why should I care? I wasn't having a great weekend myself. The trip had skidded into a downhill slide as soon as it started—on Friday night.

Chapter Two

"Should have taken the television." I stared at the large, warm, antique, iron bed—empty because I'd locked myself out on the balcony. When I picked my prize (romantic weekend getaway for two in Cape May, New Jersey, or 26-inch TV), selecting the trip to the picturesque resort made sense. Who knew that by January first I would have lost one boyfriend and his replacement and retained no hope of finding romance before the prize expired at the end of the month? I'd taken the complimentary limo ride to the Parsonage bed-and-breakfast alone. Well, not completely alone. At the Thomas Edison rest stop on the Jersey Turnpike I moved up front with Larry my limo driver and new best friend. Larry had a lot of the qualities I liked in a companion: an open mind, basic values, and no need to criticize my life choices. I offered him the opportunity to prove that he was a good listener during the two-hour drive down the Garden State Parkway. But now, as I started to shiver in the frigid air, Larry was long gone. He was back on the road, and there was no one to let me into the bridal suite.

Before I left New York, the weatherman on Channel 4 projected that Friday night would be one of the coldest in twenty years. Just my luck, the guy was right for once. If he had made such accurate forecasts on a regular basis, I might have believed that the night was unsuitable for taking in the view from the balcony. But no, I had to step outside where the gentle surf fled a late-rising moon; I wanted to sample the fresh salt air. What a feast for four of the senses! Unfortunately nature endows us with five senses. The fifth was the problem. The ability to feel allowed the frigid air to torment every part of my body, to override the enjoyment of the other four, and persuade me to go inside after five seconds on the balcony. Good idea—but I couldn't.

Why? Literally, because a small metal latch had fallen shut and locked me out of my room. I, however, did not fault the mechanics of the lock. I had other targets of blame—several targets—my own stupidity not being one of them. Okay, number one I blamed the Channel 4 weatherman. Number two, I blamed George Hilburn, the proprietor of the Parsonage. Last but certainly not least, I blamed the occupants of the room next to mine—the room I eventually discovered was occupied by Marvella and Wallace Gimbel.

I was stranded on a twenty-four inch wide balcony that wrapped around a bay window with floor-to-ceiling glass panels in metal frames. Ignoring what I'd heard about the cold spell, I'd stepped onto the balcony in search of fresh air to settle my queasy stomach. That's the part I blamed on George Hilburn. When he realized the winner of the romantic weekend getaway had checked in alone, George, co-owner of the B&B, had insisted on welcoming me into the drawing room for three sherries-worth of his life story. Only after I got into bed did I realize that three sherries was two beyond my limit. That night my stomach had tides as strong as the ocean across Beach Avenue. I had hoped the air would still the waves of nausea. I was right. What I didn't know was that my quest for air would lead to bigger problems.

I leaned back to search for an escape route upward. That was when the wind lifted the skirt of my nightgown and slipped the lace onto the pointed spear of the wrought iron railing—stopping my motion, exposing my flesh, and spinning my head. I was not playing the voyeur. I had no choice. My eyes peered onto the balcony of the room behind mine.

In the moonlight, I saw two figures. The couple looked not at all like the acrobatic team that kept me awake with their amorous

adventures—but more like a Victorian mirage. A man held a woman
in his arms like a baby. He kissed her gently, almost furtively. The
blanket wrapped around her blew gracefully in the wind. The
woman's bare feet dangled in the cold night air. Nice image. I'm sure
I would have found the couple's embrace more touching if I weren't
being strangled by my clothes at the time.

By the time I extricated myself from the railing's grasp and
resumed breathing normally, the couple had vanished. I whispered, spoke, and finally screamed, "Help!" to no avail. I couldn't
shout louder than the wind howled. I searched for a loose item to
throw at their window—in vain. All the decorative detail was
attached to the outside of the building. The couple would be no
help; I was on my own.

Holding my skirt, I leaned back and surveyed what I could see of
the inn. I hoped to discover a light in a window but the house was
dark. Except for the sudden and persistent yelps of a neighbor's dog,
I identified no sign of life in the area. I calculated the odds that the
canine with the soprano bark was a rescue-trained St. Bernard bearing brandy. That was a bet I wasn't about to make. Searching for
more realistic options, I studied Beach Avenue. Not a person or car
budged. I didn't have time to wait. I had to take action.

The turret on the northeast corner of the house reached from the
ground to the third level. I was on the second floor. The porch on the
first level, however, extended several feet beyond my balcony at a
forty-five degree angle. I had no choice. My route to safety was via
its roof. Once on the ground I could find an unlocked door or window. If that failed, I could ring the bell and announce my stupidity.

I sighed. Why had I conjured up so many phony ailments to avoid
gym class? A fair amount of jumping and climbing would be
involved in negotiating the path to freedom—and warmth. Even getting to the other side of the wrought-iron fence required agility that
I did not possess—and the weather didn't make the task any easier.

The iron was so cold to the touch that the metal burned my bare feet and hands. I thought of the advice my friend Cheryl's Swedish cousins gave her when sending her out on a walk: don't lick the railing. Cheryl was twenty-eight at the time.

Licking the fence was the furthest thing from my mind as I curled my toes around the metal. The icy round iron rod felt as sharp as the dagger-tipped *fleur-de-lis* whose points etched small designs onto my inner thighs as I moved from a hanging position inside the railing to a hanging position outside the railing.

Suspended thirty feet above the ground in the night air, I cursed the couple in the next room. If they hadn't kept me awake, I would have been sound asleep on my feather mattress. The couple's lovemaking was apparently influenced by too many trips to the Ringling Brothers Circus—and had as many acts. When I'd first heard the woman's groans, I assumed her wailing related to the illness she had broadcast at check-in—although short of a gunshot wound or an accidental amputation I couldn't imagine what malady would prompt such howls. Eventually I realized that hers were not cries of pain. She had apparently experienced a miraculous recovery and subsequent equally wondrous events. She didn't keep her elation to herself.

"This is no time for recriminations," I told myself. "Keep moving." Actually what I said sounded something like "K...K...K...Keep m...m...moving." I reached out one foot. The porch roof was rough—tough on the feet but good for traction. I gained my balance and took a single step. Although my body remained upright, I had the sensation of pitching forward onto the ground below. As I waved my arms in the hopes of remaining vertical on the roof, I resembled a dancer on one of those 1960's dance shows. Tonight on Hullabaloo, Meg Daniels does the Freddie—albeit not very well. However unattractive the technique, it worked—to a point. I was still on the roof but no longer upright. Cautiously, I turned so that I could back down on all fours.

At that point the thought occurred to me that I'd neglected to place any blame on Andy Beck. If my former, kind-of boyfriend hadn't moved to a tropical paradise, he would have been in the bridal suite to rescue me. Then again, if he'd been in the bridal suite, chances are I never would have stepped outside.

But I did—and getting back in wasn't going to be easy. The rough roof surface I savored for traction dug into my hands and knees. My cotton nightie offered no protection—from the roof tiles or the weather—although the Victorian trim coordinated nicely with the building's gingerbread. From a more practical perspective, the most I could ask of the nightie was that the volume of fabric would serve as a parachute in the event of a fall. As I backed down the roof, the man in the moon and I flashed each other similar faces. Modesty was not an issue. I'd have gladly shown any body part to a potential rescuer.

If only the couple in the next room had a quieter love life. I was probably more annoyed by the reason the woman kept me awake than the simple fact that she kept me awake. After all, I was the one in the bridal suite. Unfortunately, I was also the one with the pitiable romantic history. I'd resorted to holding a pillow over my head to mute the lovers' sounds—in vain. The pillow didn't help. Thumping noises seemed to come from all over their room. When I heard the couple opening champagne—one bottle for each of them—I'd hoped the alcohol would knock them out. It didn't—but drinking did make them feisty. I overheard their arguments. Well, I didn't actually hear their arguments. I heard sentences like: "Did you have to erg mooshu you ate?" and "I suppose you earn millions of duodenal ulcers?" I think the meaning was lost through the wall—or as I learned later, the recently renovated fireplace.

I called my mind back to the task at hand—wallowing in my misfortune could wait. And, things were actually looking up. I fell in love—with Victorian architecture. Actually I fell in love with brackets—no longer useless ornamentation to my eyes. Holding on to the rain gutter, I lowered my feet to grasp the elaborate wood carving with my toes. The gutter I gripped threatened to pull loose from the house. The decision to move quickly was not a difficult one. On the brackets I found two bars each large enough for my grip. I grabbed them. While remaining curled in a fetal position, I calmed my breathing and surveyed the path to safety. All I had to do was extend my legs until they touched the railing. Using the porch column for balance, I could jump onto the shiny porch surface that I hoped would prove less slippery than it appeared.

I slid down the column, jumped eagerly and executed a perfect, if somewhat noisy dismount. Pulling myself erect, I raised my eyes to heaven and issued a long sigh of thanks and relief. The declaration moved skyward in a white cloud—my breath. As I lowered my head I gazed directly into an unfamiliar face at the library window. I was so happy to see a person I didn't even flinch. I smiled. When the door didn't open, I understood. The party on the inside had to be somewhat surprised to discover me. I said calmly, "Please let me in."

Chapter Three

"Should I open the door?"

I couldn't hear the man—the one I expected to save me—very clearly, but I swore I'd read his lips correctly.

"That would make it easier." If I didn't need open doors for entrances, I would have beamed myself into the bridal suite.

"Of course. We'll be happy to offer assistance." He spoke over his shoulder. "Lulu. Hurry. I need help." He pointed to the front door.

The man who met me at the inn's main entrance was beautiful—or at least his face was. Because he was dressed all in black, his translucent white skin and large dark eyes were all I could see in the dimly lit hallway. If George hadn't installed a nightlight, the head would have appeared to float in the darkness. A black-haired woman with equally fair skin and dark eyes peered over the man's shoulder. Whoever Lulu was, she didn't seem at all surprised by my arrival. She stepped around the man and grabbed my hands. "Her skin feels natural but cold."

I eyed her with a quizzical expression but didn't protest. Her massage was warming my hands.

The man made the introductions. "I'm Neil Cummings and this is my wife, Lulu. Her maiden name was Richter."

I attempted to paste an interested expression on my face as I nodded. Why would I possibly care about her family name when my level of discomfort was approaching 8.0—if I used the scale named after her clan.

"We're extremely happy that we were here to help you." Neil's tone was preternaturally calm. Why did he talk to me as if I were a nitwit? Simply because he found me standing on the porch in a cotton nightgown in the middle of the night in subzero weather?

"She's shaking, Neil."

Why wouldn't I be? "It's cold out there."

"I hope we didn't keep you waiting. We had responded to a noise at the rear of the building. I thought...we'd thought...we'd found...heard something in the back of the house. How long have you been waiting to get inside?"

I shrugged. "It might have taken me five minutes to descend to the porch."

"Descend?" Neil's voice lost its eerie hushed intonation and took on an edge of excitement.

"Yeah. I locked myself out of the bridal suite. I had to climb down from the balcony. I almost fell off the roof."

"When did that happen?"

"I told you—about five minutes ago."

"Tonight?"

No last Tuesday. I suppressed that answer. Instead, I remembered who had opened the door for me and replied politely. "Yes. Tonight."

I knew my expression tipped him off; I questioned his sanity. Could he actually think I'd been standing outside in a thin cotton nightie for hours, or days, on end? Once again I held my tongue.

"Neil. She's a guest here. She's staying in the bridal suite." Lulu released her grip on my hands. "Didn't your husband hear you?"

"Oh, I don't have a husband."

"In the bridal suite?"

"Anywhere," I explained. "I won this trip. My boyfriend...you see, in late November...well, he moved...he said he'd be back in the spring but..." I determined from the expression on the couple's faces that neither of them cared that Andy Beck had gone to the Caribbean to take ownership of a new sailboat on which I suspected he would drift away from me. What did they care that the man I desired was living with beautiful scenery, beautiful weather, and beautiful women—or that I thought all three would be irresistibly seductive? "Never mind, it's a long story…the bottom line is that there is no one is in the room to let me back in."

Neil's face that had been so white glowed red. He demonstrated no interest in my love life—or lack thereof.

I studied the couple. They were dressed similarly as either second story persons or residents of lower Manhattan. I gave them the benefit of the doubt and concluded that their uniformly black attire was simply evidence they were from New York.

"Have you stayed here before? Do you know where they keep the extra keys? I need to get back into my room." Chattering teeth punctuated my sentence.

"We've stayed here before. I don't know where they keep the keys, but we have broken in…to our own room…of course. Let me help you." Despite his kind words, Neil's demeanor was suddenly cold as the night.

Observing that my clanking teeth made enough noise to wake the dead and my shivering cut my height in half, Lulu suggested that Neil hurry. "She needs to be into a warm bed."

Neil's behavior was no longer solicitous, but I perceived that he felt some sense of responsibility towards me. Why, I didn't know—nor did I care—as long as his guilt feelings worked in my favor. He grunted that I should follow him—and I did—up the stairs like a puppy.

As he worked the old-fashioned lock with one of the many prongs of his Swiss army knife, I asked a favor, "Do you think that we could keep this…you know…between us? And Lulu?"

He seemed relieved. "I won't tell if you won't tell."

"Trust me. I will not be repeating this story."

The lock snapped and I thanked him. With an oddly formal nod of the head, Neil turned and rushed down the steps.

Chapter Four

I awoke with the sun. It was January. Luckily the sun didn't rise too early—but it was still sooner than I would have liked. I struggled to open my eyes, only to be overwhelmed by flowers. Pink flowers. Roses. Tulips. Flowers so elaborate that nature could not have created them. They were everywhere. Papered on the wall. Painted on the furniture. Woven in the rug. And that didn't take into account the upholstery, drapes, or linens. I was drowning in a sea of florals. Even the six globes on the chandelier were covered with pink posies of an unidentifiable genus. The solid white paint on the wooden fireplace couldn't conceal the flowers carved throughout. The blooms appeared to be offerings to some sort of deities whose eyes stared past me as they performed their duty: supporting a thick mantel topped with heavy cut glass vases full of, what else, pink flowers. I saw by the pink porcelain clock decorated with deep pink flowers that the time was not yet eight roses o'clock.

Early, but not too early for the couple in the next room. They were fighting—or if they weren't, they needed to work on their people skills. I didn't know what was worse: overhearing their noisy lovemaking or their noisy fighting. At least as I lay in bed listening to their arguments, I didn't feel that I was missing out on anything.

The couple's angry interactions guaranteed that I was wide awake. Once fully conscious, I viewed the room's decor more favorably. Like the rest of the Parsonage, the bridal suite was a Victorian love fest. Although the decor seemed more geared to summer, the alcove would make a fine place to cuddle up with a good book—and let's face it, romantic weekend getaway winner or not, that was all I had to cuddle up with. After a tumble off the mattress and onto the carpet—taken while wondering why if earlier generations were so short they required such tall beds—I curled up on the chaise lounge nestled in the large alcove. Surrounded by the windows that had denied me entry the night before, I found the sun provided warmth for comfort and light for reading.

Before settling on the chaise, I pulled out a pre-breakfast snack. A half-pound of vanilla fudge would hold me until breakfast was served. I'd arrived late the night before, but not so late that I couldn't run into the Fudge Kitchen on the Promenade while Larry sat across Beach Avenue with the engine idling. I got my foot in the door just as the lights were about to go out inside. I banged on the door with a woolen mitten on my fist and a frantic look on my face. "Pleeeeeease," I mouthed. "Just fudge." When it comes to fudge, I can get downright pushy.

I know what you're thinking—that I planned on using fudge as a substitute for sex on my romantic weekend. You could not be more wrong. I planned on using shopping as a substitute for sex. I would have made the trip to the fudge shop even if David Duchovny had been waiting for me at the B&B—though if he had been, I probably would have bought a full pound. Since the actor was otherwise occupied that weekend, I restricted myself to half a pound—and planned to return the next day for another.

As I relaxed in the warmth of the morning sun, I nibbled and ignored my book in favor of perusing the text on the candy box. Seemed the fudge could be frozen indefinitely. Yeah. Fat chance the candy would ever see the inside of my freezer. If everything went according to plan, this fudge wasn't going to see the sun set.

Warm and comfy with mystery novel and sugary treat in hand, I was enjoying my romantic weekend prize.

I'd visited Cape May several times over the past few years with an old boyfriend who was best forgotten. Those trips could have been termed romantic if one considered catching up on professional reading, writing and answering e-mail, and talking on a mobile phone romantic. David did. All in all, my solitary weekend in Cape May promised to be as romantic as any I spent with David. Plus, the conversation would probably be better, and less taxing than whatever was being said in the next room—where suddenly, and to my delight, a cease-fire had erupted. A reprieve. I enjoyed the quiet and delved into my book—chewing faster as the suspense mounted.

I was figuring out that all was not as it initially seemed with the disappearance of a young parson in a small English village when the noise recommenced. The couple in the next room exhibited a diverse repertoire. They debuted a new variety of hubbub. No calls of ecstasy. No cries of anger. It was the sound of sadness. Of pure unadulterated despair. Sobs and sniffles that elicited not kindness but gruff rebuke. Whatever made the woman cry was not appreciated by the man. His tones were not angry but they were firm.

I climbed out of the chair and ambled casually to the end of the room where the sound was loudest.

"You owe moisture here," I heard the male voice say.

"Bubble above you." The female responded through her tears.

A door slammed. I jumped. The conversation stopped. Eventually, the crying faded away.

The next sound I heard—growling—came not from the next room but from my stomach. I checked the clock on the mantel. Elegant gold hands signaled the time to put down my mystery novel and get going in order to reach the breakfast room in ten minutes. I was dressed, to a point, and out the door in eight.

Chapter Five

At the top of the stairs, I came face-to-face with my male neighbor. Knowing a bit more about the man than I wanted to, I blushed. The man's face was also red but I attributed his flush to the outside temperature. Apparently, he had just come inside. I felt the cold emanating from the same heavy topcoat I'd seen him wear when checking in the night before. One hand clutched a fedora; the other grasped a camera.

I took a good look at the man I had only glimpsed the previous evening. Associating the tall, yet squat, bald, yet hirsute man with the groans of the previous night was a stretch. There was no accounting for taste. On the other hand, I hadn't gotten a good look at the woman. There was no guarantee that she was any prize, although I did recall she had nice ankles.

The man greeted me warmly. I noticed that as he spoke his eyes became coated with tears. He made an obvious attempt to suppress the emotion with an apology. "My wife felt sick during the night. I hope we didn't bother you." He appeared genuinely concerned.

"No," I lied.

"She kept having relapse after relapse."

Relapse was not the word I would have used. Lacking the nerve to make my comment out loud, I said politely, "I hope she's doing better."

"Oh yes, much." The man's voice quivered. "She's resting. She had a rough night. She hallucinates when she vomits."

His comment fell into the ranks of more than I needed to know—especially on the way to breakfast—where, I explained, I was headed. I backed towards the stairs.

"I think I'll see if my wife is up to eating." He disappeared into his room leaving me with the distinct impression that I—not he— had been dismissed.

I headed to the bright porch where I'd been told the morning meal would be served. The only thing that greeted me in the elaborately decorated conservatory that served as a breakfast room was the aroma of fresh baked goods. That was fine with me. I wasn't looking forward to facing Neil and Lulu in the light of day. So far, so good. The room was empty—aside from a man who showed little interest in acknowledging me but plenty in reading the *Atlantic City Press*.

"Morning, Meg." George's demeanor was maniacally cheerful as he burst into the room. The reflection of the sun off his teeth was blinding. How could anyone smile so broadly? So frequently? So sincerely? What remained of my memory told me we had consumed a fair amount of sherry together. How had George escaped unscathed?

"Claude, say hello to Meg Daniels, the winner of our romantic getaway weekend." As Claude offered a perfunctory handshake and a wan smile, George explained. "Claude Middleton is your other host for the weekend. Unfortunately he's been cooped up too long. He's losing his social graces. We don't usually fraternize with the guests."

Although I'd known George only twelve hours, I was sure he was lying—at least on his own behalf. Maybe Claude didn't spend much time bonding with the paying customers, but I bet George traded Christmas cards with every visitor—starting with the first.

The two made an odd couple that had perfected their dance. George the extrovert, soothing the guests; Claude the introvert, punctuating the conversation with pained expressions. An odd, but extremely attractive couple.

George Hilburn had won the lottery on almost every feature. Straight nose—neither too narrow nor too broad. Wide mouth and generous lips—neither too thin nor too full. Lush head of sunbleached hair that promised to be hanging from his head for many years to come. I hadn't seem many eyes as blue—or as bright—as George's. They gave him a perpetually happy expression. George's style was conservative—just left of preppie—but with a change of clothes, he would have been as comfortable on the beach at Malibu as he was on the beach in Cape May.

Claude Middleton was not so classically handsome but he was far from unattractive. Long nose, long face, long hair, long body, long legs, long fingers. If I had to describe Claude in one word that one word would be "long." Claude was distinguished and well-dressed in a Brooks Brothers classic style. His lush and carefully coifed hair, brown with the most subtle traces of gray, saved his conservative appearance from veering towards dull.

"Let me get you some coffee." George virtually bounced across the room to the elaborate sideboard lined with even more elaborate china. A large silver samovar served as the centerpiece.

"George, no coffee, thanks. I take my sugar and caffeine in cola. Got any?" I prayed for a positive response. I needed something cold, bubbly and laced with caffeine.

"Whatever you need, and believe me I mean whatever you need, we will find for you." George pointed to a chair with a high back carved in a cherubs-picking-fruit motif. With a broad wink, he disappeared leaving me face-to-paper with Claude.

Claude, the least congenial of men, now hid behind yesterday's *Wall Street Journal*, perfecting a dour expression that he revealed only when turning the pages. I jumped when he spoke. "When will Mr. Daniels be joining us?" Claude did not remove his eyes from the newspaper.

"No…no Mr. Daniels…there is none…only me. I should have let you know." I sounded apologetic.

"No problem. We'll introduce you as the winner of our relaxing weekend getaway. I am, however, curious as to why an attractive woman, as you indubitably are, is spending a romantic weekend alone. Narcissism run amok?"

"Boyfriend run amok." I explained how I had won the weekend and lost the boyfriend—and his replacement.

"You could have brought a female friend. Any companion might spare you George's efforts to fix you up."

"He wouldn't."

Claude folded the paper and made eye contact for the first time. He stared at me with brown eyes so dark that I could barely identify the irises. "You've known George for almost twelve hours. He told me you spent time together last evening. Do you believe there is anything that man wouldn't do? A young, and if you don't mind my saying so, pretty blonde arrives on our doorstep alone on a cold, bitter night. It's more than a romantic like George can tolerate. Subtly, he'll wheedle all your vital statistics out of you and go to work."

"Let me make it easy for him." I described myself. "Unattached. Five-six. Blonde, but not by birth. Thirty-three." Technically. Until Sunday.

"Weight?" Claude asked with a sly grin.

"Within the insurance standards."

"Eye color?"

"That you have to ask indicates my problem. Kind of green. Like an old army jacket."

"Hobbies?"

I sighed. "Not lately, but I swear I'll pick them up again. I used to skate and ski—water and snow. I let my outside interests go when I got overly involved in my last job. But I am determined to become a more well-rounded person."

"Clearly, a woman who knows what she likes—although that will make absolutely no difference to George. Trust me on that." He shook his head. "So tell me, Meg, what is it you do?"

"Nothing, actually."

"Well, that represented my best stab at polite conversation." With exaggerated deliberation, Claude crossed the longest legs I'd ever seen off a basketball court.

I was surprised that he made me laugh. "I'm in transition."

"Fired?"

"Not that lucky. I have to get through this without severance." I explained how the summer before, finding my life in danger, I had made a pact with God that if I were saved I would change my life and do good.

"You were previously doing evil?"

"I worked in marketing."

"Ah, sufficiently evil. Killing the English language in overly hyped brochures and advertisements."

"Marketing is not that bad."

"You can't fool me. I worked in marketing and public relations for twenty years. Rising at six in the morning to catch the train to New York to get an early start on persuading people to buy things they didn't need and couldn't afford."

"What got you out?"

"Interesting choice of words, Meg, my dear. I suppose a midlife crisis did it."

"Well," George reappeared and slid a bottle of coke and a carved crystal tumbler filled with ice in front of me. He sank onto the chair next to mine. "I'm happy to see that you and Claude have hit it off."

There was a strong element of surprise in his tone.

George sighed. "Our late arrivals, the Gimbels, include an ailing wife. I feel bad. They come here at least six times a year—although not usually in January. I've never seen her so bundled up."

I'd never seen anyone so bundled up. I'd noticed the couple coming up the stairs the night before. The woman had her coat pulled tight around her, her collar raised, a scarf tucked around her neck and across her mouth, plus a wide brim hat pulled down around her ears.

She should have been as careful with her feet as she had been with her head. I recalled wondering what protection nylons and thin black flats were against the cold.

"She seemed in pretty bad shape and we haven't heard a word. I hope she didn't die." George sighed.

I gulped the coke before I commented. "Trust me, if she died overnight, she went with a smile on her face." I returned to guzzling my caffeine supply.

George turned to Claude and snapped. "I told you that fireplace was a problem." Apologetically he spoke to me. "It's not that the walls are thin. Early this month, we had work done on the fireplace in your room and ever since then, those two rooms..." His next remark was for Claude's benefit, "one of which I might mention is the honeymoon suite." He returned his attention to me, "Those two rooms have shared more than their occupants may have cared to."

"Well, like I said, my assumption is that she made a miraculous recovery."

"She certainly seemed under the weather last night. Poor Mrs. Gimbel." George shook his head emphatically before engineering an abrupt change of direction in the conversation. "So, Claude, did I overhear you telling Meg about your midlife crisis?"

"Not really. Thought I'd leave that to you." Claude glanced at me. "George believes in full disclosure. I've gotten used to it. He'll provide you with all this information in some way over the next three days. He might as well convey our entire life story in one large brain dump. Now, if you'll excuse me, I've heard this tale before." Claude reached for another newspaper.

"Claude can be so secretive. Me, I don't believe in secrets."

"I believe that's why we were forced out of our jobs." Claude's voice came from behind the *The New York Times*.

George sighed. "Last night I told you a lot about myself, but I suppose you'd like to know a bit about Claude and me. We're gay, you see."

Claude interrupted. "George, the woman is sitting on a tufted back chair in an antique-ridden Victorian mansion owned by two middle-aged men in lavender. I think she knows."

"One middle-aged man and one thirty-something. And besides, my sweater is aubergine." George corrected Claude before he turned my way. "Anyway, we bought this place eight years ago." Thus began a synopsis of Claude's history and the couple's life together since meeting ten years earlier. Although George's description was fairly extensive, his account didn't quite reach the level of detail that he had used when narrating the story of his own life. I didn't learn when Claude had chicken pox, whom he first fell in love with, or where he lost his virginity. (Answers for George: six, Billy Baxendale, and a 1969 Volkswagen beetle.)

George's narrative was cut short after ten minutes by the other guests—the first arrival heralded by a high pitched yelp followed by prolonged giggling. I crossed my fingers and prayed that I was not about to encounter Neil and Lulu in the light of day.

Chapter Six

A couple stumbled into the breakfast room wrapped in each other's arms and clothing that I couldn't recall ever being stylish, hip, or preppy.

"Claude, Meg." George paused for emphasis. "Meet the Blandings."

"Yes," the woman giggled, "the Blandings. Just like Myrna Loy and Cary Grant and that dreamhouse."

"Hardly." The single word came from behind Claude's newspaper.

"Yes, Barely." George covered quickly. "Little pet name he has for me. He thinks I hardly do anything. He hides behind that paper and I think he's barely breathing." George walked behind Claude and gave him a slap that was more than a love pat.

The Blandings settled at the table next to ours. In lieu of the fruitcup, Mrs. Blandings nibbled her husband's lower lip. He responded in a similar fashion. Minutes that felt like hours passed before Mrs. Blandings wrestled her lips free from her mate's. "This is our first time in Cape May." The female Blandings didn't speak as much as giggle her sentences. "We've heard it's extremely romantic."

The very word romantic must have aroused her husband because the twosome launched into another public display of affection. The force of her husband's kiss raised the glasses off Mrs. Blandings' nose. I wasn't particularly comfortable watching movie stars engage in similar behavior onscreen; the Blandings, no Hollywood pairing, were far too close for comfort.

"I trust you slept well." George offered the Blandings one of his bright smiles.

"Oh we didn't mind being awakened." Mr. Blandings kissed the tip of his wife's nose.

"I hope that little dog barks again tonight." Mrs. Blandings flashed a broad wink at her husband.

"I hope he barks more. Three times was hardly enough."

I, for one, had had enough—of the Blandings' show. The couple found each other not only attractive but entertaining as well. Their little exchanges, physical and verbal, were well rehearsed. The couple had performed their shtick for a number of audiences. What kind of group encouraged them to continue the act? I was growing bored. I was growing annoyed. Okay, I was growing jealous.

"It's like they won cutest couple in high school or something," I grumbled.

"I wonder who lost." Claude spoke from behind yet another newspaper.

As Mr. Blandings studied his wife, I studied the adoration on his face. He must have seen her with different eyes. What I saw was a woman frumpy in every respect. Nature hadn't bestowed beauty on Mrs. Blandings and she managed to do the least with what she was given. In spite of her physical shortcomings, she drove her husband wild. I vowed to use the weekend to study her technique—if I could overcome my embarrassment at witnessing such intimate events. I averted my eyes.

My gaze found a tall, blond man standing at the doorway to the breakfast room. Not a guest, I suspected, and not Robert Redford— although that was the tougher call. He slipped out of a fleece-lined leather bomber jacket as he took in the room with large brown eyes that narrowed as they lit on each of the guests. He studied me briefly but carefully before letting his gaze linger on the Blandings. I feigned interest in the novel that until he appeared I might have found genuinely interesting.

"Claude. Good morning." The man strode across the room and thrust a hand between the newspaper and Claude's face. When he smiled, I realized the man exceeded any classification of handsome; he was charismatic. Even Claude responded. He glanced up from his *Philadelphia Inquirer.*

"I had a feeling we might see you this morning. When did he have time to call you?" Claude folded his paper and gestured for the man to take a seat at our table.

"What makes you think George called me?"

"My IQ." Claude nodded in my direction. "Meg Daniels. Let me introduce a friend of the family. Hank Bergman."

"Pleased to meet you." The man with the wide smile thrust his hand towards me.

As I took it, I realized the hand had recently spent a considerable amount of time outside. The skin felt frigid. Made sense. The man had the look of someone who had spent more time outdoors than in, more time moving than sitting. His hiking boots hinted that my supposition was true; the details of his physical appearance confirmed my theory. His skin was wrinkled from too much sun and the tips of his hair still displayed the bleach job the sun had done the summer before. He had a lean but strong physique that he had dressed for emphasis in jeans and a white T-shirt covered by a dark shirt with the sleeves rolled up. Each item of clothing was just a little tight—I assumed by intent.

"Oh, I see you two have met." George's enthusiasm for all aspects of life appeared limitless. He bounded out of the kitchen with energy that bowled me over at ten yards. "Isn't she all that I promised? I told you she had that great just-got-out-of-bed look."

I was going to protest that I had just gotten out of bed but George lunged forward and wrapped an arm around my shoulder. "And Meg, isn't Hank a hunk?"

"He called you. I knew it." Claude didn't look at either man.

"He asked me to come over to check out the engine on your dinghy. He did happen to mention that you had a most attractive guest." My eyes met Hank's, flitted away, and met his again. I felt embarrassed but interested. What else did I have going on?

"Yes." Claude cleared his throat. "In mid-January there exists no higher priority than to ascertain that the motor is in tip-top shape. Any moment now the temperature could soar into the high twenties and we'll yearn to go out for a spin."

"Claude, you're embarrassing Meg." George ignored—or simply did not acknowledge—his role in my humiliation.

I wanted to protest that I wasn't a charity case—that I didn't need to be fixed up—but George's enthusiasm was infectious—as was Hank's smile. I sputtered. Hank, apparently accustomed to George's matchmaking tactics, remained composed. He dug into breakfast as he told me a bit about himself—on the occasions George let him get a word in edgewise.

Hank worked for the county—in what capacity he didn't specify. He was very divorced—whatever that meant. He liked to hang around the Parsonage because he wasn't much of a cook and he actually liked these guys. I read between the lines that Hank did not number a lot of gays among his close friends. "And these fellows take advantage of me, " he concluded, "by having me fix anything with a motor. So," he leaned forward, "tell me about yourself."

An overly-anxious George answered, "Meg is from New York."

"New York, New York, huh? The town so nice they named it twice." The words, and the whistled lead-in of the Kander-Ebb anthem came from the mouth of a fit but oversized redhead who seated himself at the next table. The exuberant gentleman introduced himself and his wife as the Pankenhursts, Will and Nanette. He announced that they'd come from Baltimore—although Mr. Pankenhurst's accent indicated he might have emigrated from Texas—possibly within the last week.

Will Pankenhurst wore polyester pants and a sports jacket in the banner colors of the seventies—orange and brown. I figured he was older than he appeared, assuming he'd first worn the outfit when it was in style. If he were waiting for his clothes to wear out before he replaced them, I wanted to tip him off that they never would.

Mr. Pankenhurst's demeanor was as loud as his clothes. Mrs. Pankenhurst on the other hand didn't fit the morning person category. In loose fitting sweatclothes she might have slept in, she rested her head in her left hand and clung to her empty coffee cup with her right. Given her husband's height and girth, the petite woman faded into his shadow.

On the other hand, Mr. Pankenhurst appeared wide awake and wanted to know everything about everyone at breakfast. Only later did I realize how little he had revealed about himself.

Chapter Seven

Over breakfast, I learned that the couple in the room adjoining mine were named Wallace and Marvella Gimbel. When they entered the room, Will Pankenhurst immediately lost interest in the rest of us and redirected his attention their way. Or at least, Mr. Gimbel's way.

Like Nanette Pankenhurst, Marvella Gimbel was no fan of morning. Her clothing denied its existence. Her navy satin suit and matching pumps with four-inch heels were more suited to the cocktail hour. Not that the woman was up to partying. Mrs. Gimbel didn't even feign interest in the group—or food. She settled onto a high-backed chair next to her husband's. Rather than pulling the seat into the table, she sat with her back against the glass wall and planted her stolid legs in front of her side by side. Maybe a relapse had killed her appetite.

After the initial greetings, Mr. Gimbel apologized for any inconvenience his wife's illness might have caused the other guests. "Mrs. G. was so sick last night. She was up and down all night."

She wasn't the only thing going up and down in that room. I spoke only to myself.

Mr. Gimbel handled public relations for the couple. If Marvella Gimbel cared to comfort the group, she gave no decipherable indication. Despite her illness she had taken the time to pouf the front of her hair into a pompadour and sweep the rest into a chignon in back. From her coloring, I guessed that she was a natural redhead. Unfortunately, her current shade of dark red was not found in nature. Just as unfortunately, she made up her face to match. Despite the interventions, traces remained of her beauty. Bad hair and bad makeup couldn't hide it; only her seemingly perennial scowl constituted a fair disguise. Although I calculated both Gimbels were well into their fifties, I guessed a makeover would shave ten years off the age Mrs. Gimbel admitted. The same could not be said for her husband. He had the look of a man who appeared—and felt—old for most of his life.

Wallace Gimbel addressed the group. "We apologize for any odd noises. I hope Marvella didn't disturb anyone." He called to me. "Especially you, Meg, that is your name, right? I understand you're a grand prize winner and our neighbor in the bridal suite."

"Yes, I am but no...no...her bad health...no, it didn't disturb me." I wasn't lying. Whatever ills had plagued Mrs. Gimbel had not contributed to my inability to sleep. Traces of a coy expression were visible on my face. Mrs. Gimbel did not miss my glance in George's direction. When George's eyes met mine, she did not miss the ironic glance he flashed at me.

"Excuse me, Miss..." Mrs. Gimbel turned my way.

"Meg. Meg Daniels."

"I hope my illness didn't disturb you."

That was when George started acting up. He cleared his throat meaningfully—a tone I hadn't heard since my sophomore year of high school. I shot him a look that said "shut up."

"Because I wouldn't want to think I ruined your romantic getaway..." Ms. Gimbel continued.

"Relaxing," I interrupted, "relaxing weekend getaway."

"Yes. Yes. Relaxing weekend getaway. I'm sorry if we disturbed you."

"Please don't worry about it."

"So we didn't keep you up?"

"I...I...I wake up every night."

Mrs. Gimbel appeared perplexed by my demeanor but Will Pankenhurst didn't give her time to question me further.

"What was wrong?" Mr. Pankenhurst asked Mrs. Gimbel. The guy was full of questions—all of which Mrs. Gimbel eagerly answered—in more detail than seemed appropriate for mealtime. Mr. Pankenhurst greeted each revelation with a long whistle.

Tragically for the rest of us, Mr. Gimbel encouraged his wife's recitation of her medical conditions. She listed her symptoms with clinical detachment. Headache. Body aches. Dizziness. When she reached vomiting, my interest in the miniature muffins waned. Will Pankenhurst, however, maintained a high level of enthusiasm—both for her narrative and the pastries. The Blandings displayed sympathy—and a growing interest in being alone. I thought it was time they left for their room but, unfortunately, the couple did not find socializing and foreplay mutually exclusive activities.

Next to me Hank had a bemused expression pasted on his face. I glanced across the table to catch sight of an appalled Claude. I waited for his pointed barb—in vain. His message to the chatty guest was only visual. She remained oblivious to his stare. More than subtle visual signals were required to silence Mrs. Gimbel. She had a story to tell and by God she was going to tell it—despite George's best efforts to change the subject.

When the phone rang, George whispered, "thank heaven," before he rushed to the sideboard and picked up an extension—an old yellow princess phone and an odd intrusion in the otherwise meticulously decorated room. "Hello. No. No." He paused. "No. That was my answer last night and it is my answer today. No." He sighed. "You're right. She could have but she didn't. Gotta run. Sorry."

In the meantime, I fixated on Mrs. Gimbel's ankles. The woman was retaining all the water she needed to cross the Sahara. Her ankles were twice the size that they were the night before.

"Now, Mrs. Gimbel, why don't you share with us your secret for a quick recovery." George's tone was teasing as he returned to the table.

Mrs. Gimbel did not understand her host's exaggerated wink.

"Romance is the name of the game here at the Parsonage, except in poor Meg's case, and a little bird told me romance is what cured you."

"Time is what cured her." Mr. Gimbel grumbled.

"I don't understand this conversation." Mrs. Gimbel was irritated.

"That's because my partner has very little sense when it comes to polite social intercourse." Claude's voice was comforting, yet I noted the stab in his choice of words.

George didn't sit still for the criticism. "Claude, don't be an old fuddy-duddy. We're in the romance biz here at the Parsonage. We shouldn't be ashamed when the atmosphere works and creates medical miracles."

Marvella Gimbel remained bewildered.

"I'm afraid Mr. Hilburn is under the impression that my romantic prowess knocked that illness out of you." Mr. Gimbel patted his wife's hand.

"Why would he think that?" Mrs. Gimbel's reaction was far more serious than the conversation mandated. George's comment may have been inappropriate but his inflection was playful—pretty much like George himself. She'd been a guest at the Parsonage before. She should have known what he was like.

"He's kidding you, Marvella." With effort Mr. Gimbel made light of George's remarks. "George is just kidding you."

"Why?"

Mr. Gimbel didn't have an answer and apparently George felt no obligation to supply one. The group grew increasingly uncomfortable. Hard to believe that Will Pankenhurst's quizzing of Mrs. Gimbel yet again about her illness saved the day. She answered his questions, but her halting speech and furrowed brow told me her mind was elsewhere. That was when the nature of her discomfort hit me.

Chapter Eight

I felt relief when the breakfast room emptied—for two reasons. First, the conversation about maladies past and present ended (Mrs. Gimbel held the lead in a perverse competition as the morning's match concluded), and second, I'd survived breakfast without running into Neil and Lulu. With any luck, the couple had checked out.

"Did all the guests come to breakfast?" I made a concentrated effort to sound casual.

"No. You haven't met Neil and Lulu Cummings. Very hip couple from New York. They never make breakfast." George leaned close and whispered. "They're nocturnal. They've stayed here before. We rarely see them in the daylight. Claude suspects they are vampires." He shrugged. "But I keep telling him to remember they're downtown types." He turned abruptly. "Oh, no you don't." George held Hank in his seat. "We have to talk. We have a puzzle to solve."

"What recipe for mischief were you two cooking up in the kitchen?" Claude interjected.

"Yeah, what was going on in there?" Hank flashed that incredible smile. "I had to sit here staring at Claude's paper—and listening to conversation better reserved for meetings of the American Medical Association."

Claude folded his newspaper. "Even though I've known Meg only briefly, or perhaps because I have known Meg only briefly, I must say that I found her behavior a bit unusual—if not bizarre." He nodded at George. "From you I expect such misconduct, but Meg appeared, at first glance anyway, to be somewhat more circumspect in her manner than you."

"I can explain," George offered, but he didn't. He turned to me. "Go ahead. Tell them."

So I did. The suspicions that sounded so strong in my head sounded so feeble on my lips. On that point—and only that point—Hank and I appeared in agreement.

As I launched into my explanation about the Mrs. Gimbel's check-in and her attire, I focused on Hank. "The woman was totally bundled up. You name it, she wore it. Long coat, hat, gloves, scarf across her face." As I provided details as to how I'd moved from that initial observation to my final conclusion, I caught myself leaning a little too far forward, smiling a little too broadly and laughing a little too loudly. What was wrong with me? Hank appeared old enough to be my...my much older brother.

He viewed me—or my theory—with amusement. "And I would care that another woman was here because...?"

"Today the Gimbels wanted us to think this Mrs. Gimbel was the same person."

"Why would anyone come to a crowded place where they are known and get up to no good—whatever that might turn out to be?" Hank didn't bother to hide his skepticism.

"For exactly that reason," I argued.

I hadn't expected Claude to jump in on my side but he did. "If he were to become a suspect, we would be his alibi."

"Suspected of what. Alibi for what?" Hank found our claims entertaining.

"We thought you could tell us." George leaned forward in anticipation.

Under the table Hank's knee brushed against mine and lingered for a moment. I didn't know if the contact was intentional. I glanced in his direction. If he noticed, he didn't let on.

George's contorted features reflected his confusion. "Why would he switch women in the middle of a weekend?"

Claude answered. "Now there's an appropriate question for Hank."

Unrattled, Hank simply flashed his smile. Again, his leg grazed mine. Did he realize?

I leaned forward and forced the men to give me their attention. "I simply wonder why this morning a different woman is describing her arrival last night and trust me, this is another woman."

"And you know this because..."

"Her feet. Actually her ankles. The woman I saw in the hallway had beautiful slim ankles." I only referred to seeing the couple check in. Why mention the balcony? "Remember I told you that when arrived she was all bundled up—except she was wearing black flats like a dancer. Mrs. Gimbel doesn't appear to be the plain black flat type."

"And I, for one, would hate to see her in a tutu." Claude affected acute dismay.

Hank leaned forward. "You say that this woman is an exact duplicate of the guest who checked in—except for her feet?"

"I could be an exact duplicate except for the feet." I turned towards George. "You checked them in. If you had never seen Mrs. Gimbel before how would you describe her based on her appearance last night?"

"Well, it's hard to say. She was all bundled up because she didn't feel well."

"How tall was she?"

"Hard to say. She was all hunched over. She wasn't feeling well, you know."

"She made that perfectly clear. Last night and this morning. I mean she bored us to death with that story."

Hank dismissed my suspicions. "Right, she had details. Doesn't that convince you? Her story was the truth."

I shrugged. "The detailed description convinced me that she wanted us to think her story was the truth. I think she was well rehearsed."

"Anything else?"

"She sneezed last night. When she passed my door, she sneezed."

"I don't believe that sneezing is an offense in the state of New Jersey." Hank stared at me with an amused expression.

"She kept talking about her stomach flu. Why does a stomach flu make you sneeze?"

Hank played devil's advocate. "Maybe she sneezed while she had the flu. Maybe she has allergies."

Okay, I had to give him those points. Nonetheless, I upheld my theory that the woman sneezed for my benefit—an embellishment not in the script. The real Mrs. Gimbel couldn't know about the sneezing. She didn't include any mention of nasal congestion in her recitation of symptoms. "Even though no detail was too small for her to include."

"And based on these observations, Meg has concluded that Mr. Gimbel substituted a different woman in his room last night." Despite his effort to sound skeptical, George's voice betrayed excitement.

"I'd swear to it." I glanced from Claude to George and back. Although I avoided Hank's eyes, I felt them boring into me.

George directed his comments to Hank. "She could be right. We might have a mystery—right here in the Parsonage." He considered the possibilities. "But why would Mr. and Mrs. Gimbel agree to sneak another woman into their room." He paused before answering his own question. "Oh right. I get it."

I explained why I ruled out group sex—and my motive wasn't to avoid envisioning the couple involved in any nontraditional intimate acts—although that was a perfectly valid reason. "I don't think Mrs. Gimbel was there. Mrs. Gimbel knew her husband had another woman in the room; that didn't bother her. She's willing to impersonate that person. But George makes a harmless innuendo about lovemaking and she sits up and takes notice. I am a woman. Trust me on this one. She was jealous."

Hank leaned back in his chair and stretched his legs under the table. His left one brushed my right as he moved. He cupped his hands on the top of his head. "Are you reporting a crime?"

George answered my puzzled expression. "Hank is an investigator for the district attorney's office."

My stomach fell. I didn't mind gossiping—but getting the police involved was another thing. My only goal was to make sure George didn't step in it again. Wasn't it? I grew silent.

Hank took the floor. "Let's say Mrs. Gimbel was really sick. Mr. Gimbel wants to have a little fun on the side. He gets his girlfriend to pretend she has Mrs. Gimbel's symptoms. She fools you into thinking she's Mrs. Gimbel. You folks have no idea that another woman has been here. Therefore, you can't slip and tell Mrs. Gimbel. Gimbel has his fun. Then he sneaks out with one wife and in with another. Why would he ever expect that other guests would be making snide remarks about his love life at breakfast?"

George nodded. "We wouldn't know if one woman went out and another came in." He sounded dejected. "What do you think, Meg?"

I sighed. "What Hank says makes sense—even though Gimbel still ran the risk of George talking about her health at check-in." I sighed. "Hank's proposal is as logical as any explanation." Logic. I hated logic. I was more of an intuition kind of girl. But given my growing discomfort with having thrown the ball into play in a game with a cop as an unexpected participant, I was willing to accept Hank's theory.

"Of course, Hank describes only one possibility." George faced the cop. "Make a few subtle inquiries." His intonation made the project sound like fun.

To my surprise, Hank did not dismiss George's request out of hand. "Are you fellows serving lunch?"

"We can." George was eager.

"A hot lunch?"

"Steaming."

I got the impression George would promise anything to guarantee Hank's involvement.

"Okay. I'll see what I can do."

"What do you think you'll find?" George was breathless with excitement. "What do you think happened to the other woman?"

"That's obvious." Claude paused until all our eyes turned his way. "They killed her." With that he disappeared behind the *Cape May Star and Wave*.

Chapter Nine

Because the wind-chill factor had yet to climb into positive digits, George offered to drop me in town. Dressed in Michelin-man chic, I rolled down the steps to meet him.

"Meg, dear, you make an interesting fashion statement."

"I'm warm." Since we were still inside, I was actually roasting.

Claude threw in his critique. "I'm sure George didn't intend to demean your sense of style. It's simply that as I recall when you arrived you were quite svelte. Now, a mere twelve hours later, it appears that you might have trouble arousing the Pillsbury Dough Boy's interest."

"He's a dough boy, not a dough man, and I don't think we should think of him in sexual terms." Instead of discussing the dough boy's love life, I explained my layer system—starting with a Jockey undershirt and ending with a Gor-Tex parka. I described five layers in between. I didn't fill them in on the stocking, sock, legging, jean, sweatpants compilation I counted on to keep my lower extremities warm.

"But you've rendered yourself essentially immobile." Claude pronounced the word to rhyme with "smile."

Given the unlikely event of an emergency, I was willing to trade mobility for warmth. I waddled down the hall after George. He led me through the conservatory where we'd had breakfast, the pantry where I dragged him to gossip, the kitchen where I supposedly lost an unidentified object, and past a back staircase to the Parsonage's rear entrance. A lattice fence and tall shrubs gave George and Claude's personal patio privacy from the guests' prying eyes. We went down three steps into what in spring and summer George assured me was a lovely garden, past an elaborate gazebo, through a wrought-iron trellis to the parking area. Hidden behind a row of bushes, parking consumed fifty percent of the back yard.

I paused under the trellis for my first daylight view of the Parsonage's exterior. The Parsonage had been built as a house, not a hotel, but an awfully big house. I couldn't imagine a family whose members the building would not accommodate—and I did consider the Osmonds when reaching that conclusion. The inn got its name from its previous owners, who, with tongue planted firmly in cheek, had named the establishment based on the house's occupancy for several years in the early sixties by a radical religious group. The faith was based on worship of a messiah from Trenton through whom a diverse group of characters—including St. Thomas Aquinas, Blackbeard, and the baker who had provided bread to the court of Louis XVI—communicated with Americans during the Kennedy Administration. There was apparently little record of what they said—except "Move to Washington." The group had subsequently relocated twice. Apparently, historic figures were not aware that there was both a Washington D.C. and a Washington state in twentieth-century America. Rumor had it that remnants of the group still lived near Walla Walla, Washington—a site chosen because Lord Byron found the alliteration lyrical.

The structure boasted the finest Victorian credentials. An acroterium adorned every gable peak. A pendant hung from every dormer. A bargeboard trimmed every inch of roof. Even the wrought-iron railing around the widow's walk was overwhelmed with gewgaws.

"If you see a spot where we might cram one more item of architectural detail, let us know. Nothing succeeds like excess." George mocked himself undeservedly. The house was beautiful and tasteful.

If the Parsonage was a bit overdone that was only because the era's style dictated an overabundance of ornamentation.

"I'd like to learn more about the architecture—in the summer." I cut short my study of the house and turned toward the parking area.

Somewhere a dog protested our intrusion as we made our way across the gravel. The crunching was louder than the barking. "That poor dog, Doogie. He gets upset whenever anyone comes into our parking lot." George explained. "He tries to be ferocious but instead of barking, he yelps."

"What kind of dog is he?" I asked, expecting some tiny breed.

"A Great Dane. I don't know what happened to his vocal chords. That oversized puppy could sing in a boy's choir. And Doogie *knows* there is something odd about his bark. He may start out aggressive but he backs right down. He's the type of dog that carries an extra set of house keys in case burglars have a hard time getting in." George yelled at Doogie with uncharacteristic harshness. "Shut up." The dog did—immediately. George sighed. "Always works."

Most of the spaces in the Parsonage's lot were full. Matching the guests with their cars seemed easy. Most likely the Pankenhursts had driven Cadillac's largest model with the Maryland plates. Neil and Lulu must have driven the New York car, the compact with the sign announcing that no valuables remained inside.

"Is that your Mercedes?"

"I wish." George shuffled into the wind. "That's the Blandings' car. Mr. Blandings' midlife crisis, wouldn't you bet? The Gimbels are driving the minivan. I drive the jeep."

My eyes were glued to the minivan. I wouldn't have paired the Gimbels with a forest green WindStar. "Are you sure?"

"Meg, I bought the car myself. I should know."

"No." I shook my head vigorously. "Are you sure the Gimbels are driving the minivan?"

"Positive. I always ask at check-in."

George's gaze followed mine. He stopped on a dime. "Do you think we should search their vehicle?"

"For what? An extra woman?" I kept moving. I was more interested in getting inside George's car.

George caught up and leaned close—at least as close as my layered clothing allowed—and whispered, "How about a body?"

Not that I expected George to find a corpse but what was the harm in sneaking a peek? "When you come back you might park next to the van—although I don't think there is much possibility of seeing through the dark windows."

With a promise to spy discreetly, George deposited me at the north end of the Washington Street Mall. I rolled out of the car and bent my arm as far as possible to wave good-bye.

"Don't forget to return for lunch. Hank's coming. Remember."

"George, doesn't this flagrant attempt at matchmaking embarrass you?"

"Meg, honey, nothing embarrasses me." He paused. "Although today your outfit comes close." With a wave he hurried off to do his errands.

Lost in nostalgia, I stood at the head of the mall thinking about my first love. My first but, unfortunately, not my last unrequited love.

His name was Lou. Lou Turner. I fell hard for Lou. Sure I knew he was much more sophisticated than I. He was ten; I was six. Let's face it, he was into double digits. Lou was a man of the world. He went to public school. I was six and about to be a second grader at St. Athanasius School. To my mind, Lou knew everything. Attending St. Athanasius, I'd spent most of the first semester just learning to spell the school's name.

Lou and I worked together at his flower stand....table....stool. Actually, Lou worked but you know in those days behind every successful man there was a woman....or in this case a naive second grader. I supported his efforts largely by staring at my boss with adoring eyes. I use the term boss lightly since no money ever changed hands—just a few wilted roses. All in all, however, Lou was good to work for. He let me get him sodas, run home to pick up his lunch, or watch his flowers while he made a quick trip to the comfort station.

At the end of my two-week stay, which coincided with the end of the summer, Lou presented me with a Cape May diamond necklace. To a six-year old, the Cape May diamond, a highly polished piece of quartz—that I knew Lou had found in the waters around the sinking concrete ship at Sunset Beach—was as exciting as any stone Tiffany's had to offer.

I pretended not to know that Lou had found and polished the stone for Kimberly Bryant. Unfortunately, Lou and Kim's love did not out-last the time required to polish the stone. It takes a lot of tumbling to turn a piece of smoky stone into a shiny jewel. I could have told Lou that Kim was trouble. She was, after all, an older woman. She'd already turned eleven and felt she'd left Lou behind. She rejected his gift and his love.

I, on the other hand, wore the necklace everyday—and night—until Sister Joan Frances seated Dan Nadler next to me. I came to understand the dangers of long-distance relationships. Having transferred my ado-ration, I slipped the diamond into my jewelry box. I still fingered it occasionally and thought back to those summer days on the mall. Days a lot warmer than that Saturday. It was too cold to reminisce.

I started down the mall head down, hands in pockets. That was when I saw him.

◆ ◆ ◆

I didn't actually set out to follow Mr. Gimbel. My intent was a systematic search of the antique stores on the mall. I was determined to find a Victorian lamp for my desk—an "eliminate the middle man" birthday gift. The plan was simple. If I had a boyfriend, say the recently departed Andy Beck, I would spend $100 on his birthday gift. Andy in turn would spend $100 on my birthday gift. I planned to take the sum I saved on his gift and spend the money on a present for myself.

Then, Wallace Gimbel surfaced directly in front of me. In his heavy wool overcoat, fedora, and dark sunglasses, his image was less last night's reclusive celebrity of the 1950s and more a gangster—of any era. I recalled Claude's conclusion. As unlikely as the possibility seemed, what if there had been a murder? What harm was there in keeping an eye on Gimbel? Besides, there were only two directions on the mall; I had no choice but to tail him. Okay, maybe to avoid passing him I had to reduce my speed a bit and develop an interest in store windows that at seventy degrees Fahrenheit might have been truly interesting but at ten degrees lost much of their appeal.

Mr. Gimbel did not appear to be in a hurry. He sauntered from store window to store window. He clutched a camera in his right hand but demonstrated no interest in snapping photos. I couldn't figure out what he was doing. There was no sign of Mrs. Gimbel. He might have been waiting for her; he kept glancing at his watch. Finally, with a minor display of frustration he took off down the mall. I was contemplating pursuit when a splash of orange across the street caught my eye. The face barely visible in the oval hole created by the hood was familiar. The shock of red hair that protruded was unmistakable. Will Pankenhurst.

The Parsonage guest loitered suspiciously in the doorway of a T-shirt shop that had closed for the season. I moved into the doorway of the Making Waves gift shop to watch the tall man slide casually into the entrance of Laura's Fudge, also closed for the winter. I tried to follow his line of vision but couldn't identify the object of his gaze.

I glanced back at Pankenhurst. He started down the mall. I stepped out of the doorway, turned, and watched his reflection in the store window until his fluorescent parka disappeared behind a fenced enclosure memorializing Cape May fishermen lost at sea.

Standing in front of a clothing store window, I sneaked a glance but didn't see the figure in orange. The next look I stole down the mall caught Will Pankenhurst mingling with several intrepid tourists. He strolled aimlessly and then stopped again. As he stepped aside to peer in a window, I saw a figure in front of him. Mr. Gimbel.

Will Pankenhurst was tailing Wallace Gimbel.

Chapter Ten

There had been a time—I think it was the day before—when I'd liked winter. I used to defend the much maligned season. As I opened the heavy lead-glass door to the Parsonage, I wondered why. Older people used to tell me, when you are older, you'll hate the cold. I'd snickered. What did they know about me? Maybe nothing, but they certainly knew something about getting old.

By the time I walked the few blocks from the town center, I was shivering so hard that my back hurt. Instead of five-foot-six, I stood three-foot-three. My skin was plasticized by the cold. I couldn't imagine what color my face was, or that I would ever smile again— not that I would ever want to smile again but that I would ever be capable of smiling again.

I'd made the walk in record time. No strolling the streets at a leisurely pace licking an ice cream cone—so desirable in the summer. No stopping to study the architectural detail—so mesmerizing in the summer. No hesitating to envy the relaxed outdoor diners so plentiful in the summer. I'd do all those things later—in the summer.

Obviously my layering system didn't stand up to the cold snap. I wondered if NASA had a layering system that would stand up to the cold snap.

As the door to the Parsonage closed behind me, George popped into the hallway. He jerked his head to summon me to the breakfast room. Apparently, he mistook my shaking for a nod; he disappeared into the conservatory. I stored my newly purchased lamp in a corner and scurried down the hall. It wasn't that I was in a hurry. I'd lost the ability to take broader strides somewhere on Columbia Avenue.

Hank and Claude were seated at the table where we had breakfast. Claude read the *The New York Times*. Hank exuded the glamour of a movie star.

"Okay, Meg is here. Now we can talk." George took an empty seat and directed me towards the last chair at the table. I still demonstrated some serious shivering as I settled onto the seat. "Are you cold?" George's question—stupid to anyone who disputed the "there is no such thing as a stupid question" philosophy—would have angered me if he hadn't asked it in such concerned tones.

I simply exaggerated my shaking to indicate yes.

"Then you must have tea. I don't care if you like it or not. I'll get it."

"We should never underestimate the danger of the cold." Hank rose from his chair. He helped me from my parka and instructed me to lose at least three layers underneath. The group waited while I yanked off my boots, slipped out of my cardigan, pulled an Aran sweater over my head, and removed a sweatshirt.

I spoke for the first time—through teeth that still chattered. "It's really cold out there."

"Well, I suppose someone has to state the obvious on these occasions." Claude's words were cold but his expression was warm.

"Really, really cold." I retorted. My body convulsed as if punctuating my statement.

If I weren't so chilly and if the massage weren't so warming, I might have questioned Hank's motives as he tried to rub heat back into my extremities.

"Hank." George interrupted when he returned with my tea. "Show Meg what you found."

Given George's contrived behavior, I expected a major announcement. With a flourish Hank produced a photocopy of a newspaper clipping. A photo showed four people. Two of them were clearly Mr. and Mrs. Gimbel.

Unable to stop my hands from shaking, I lowered my cup onto the saucer—causing a terrible clatter. The trembling didn't make the caption any easier to read when I picked up the newspaper photo.

"Let me." Hank held the clipping in front of me.

"Okay, so they are who they said they were. We never doubted that. George and Claude could ID them. That isn't the issue."

"We could have gone to the library and done that." George made no attempt to hide his disappointment. "You should have ordered Mrs. Gimbel's driver's license."

"I have no reason to." Hank sighed. "Will you folks please stop trying to pin a murder that never happened on upstanding citizens of Atlantic City."

"The Gimbels are from Atlantic City?" I had never asked.

Hank answered. "He runs a hotel there—casino and all. He's a big deal. Comes here to get away. His wife keeps their apartment in New York and I do mean she keeps the apartment. Woman was loaded from birth. Big-time wealthy. I think they use his salary for pin money."

George sighed. "I'd love to live that way."

"You didn't find that out in the library." Claude's comment was more to the point.

"Maybe I used a few confidential sources." Hank flashed those teeth. His smile was devastating. "Just in case Mr. Gimbel was the kind of guy one would pin a murder on—which by the way, he does not appear to be."

"What hotel?" George remained stuck a few thoughts behind the rest of us. Hank's answer impressed him. "Even I know that place." George described a major resort hotel with hundreds of rooms, a popular casino, and a wide array of entertainment. "Maybe you two should check the situation out. You know, see if Mr. Gimbel had a girlfriend who's missing—or something."

Hank responded with a wry smile. "We, two?"

"Well, it's Meg's case, so to speak, but you are the pro. Claude and I would like to help but we have work to do."

Hank stared at George. "Right. We drop by the hotel and ask if a woman is missing or if anyone found a body." Sarcasm dripped from every word. "Or maybe we start a casual conversation, 'Say, Wallace Gimbel murder a lot of people around here?'"

I volunteered. "I know a little bit about investigating." I explained that I was acquainted with a PI. I didn't define acquaintance. "I can think of a cover story. I won't get caught. The Gimbels are not leaving Cape May, I don't think."

"And why would you do this?" Hank seemed sincerely perplexed.

My face displayed the same puzzlement when I attempted to answer. Was a foray into detective work an homage to Andy Beck, Private Investigator, my recently lost love? Possibly. Was it an excuse to spend time with Hank? Probably. Was it because I had nothing better to do? Absolutely. The weather—standard winter weather if you spent the season in one of the warmer corners of Antarctica—made me change my plans. I'd planned to brush up on Victorian architecture and furnishings at the Emlen Physick museum—and I'm sure I would. In the summer. The thought of making that walk this weekend was as appealing as running the Ididerod without a team of dogs—or a sled. I chose to verbalize a more noble motive. "If I'd come to a bad end, I would want someone to check the situation out."

Hank rolled his eyes. "And how do you suppose to accomplish this mission?"

George had the answer. "You're the cop. You do that type of thing all the time. You do it. Meg will go along for moral support. Won't you?"

I shrugged. "Sure."

Hank sighed. "You are right on one point. I do ask questions all the time—when there is a crime. We have no crime."

"Those are not the same ankles." I was emphatic.

"Maybe she's retaining water."

How did men find out about the water retention problem? And, why didn't they get the story right? "That woman would have to drain the Panama Canal to change the size of her ankles that drastically."

"Then let the Panamanian police handle the case. It's out of my jurisdiction."

"Well, then, how about the Cape May Canal?"

Hank responded with a dismissive shrug.

George argued the virtues of a nice warm ride on such a cold day. "You can't stay outside. Why not have a little fun inside? And where better than Atlantic City?"

"George hates Atlantic City." Hank spoke to me in a faux aside. "Says so all the time."

"What do you mean? That town is full of fun," George protested.

Claude eyed Hank skeptically when the cop gave in to George's demands.

"What can a little trip hurt? It's the weekend. If we have a case, I go to the chief on Monday. Actually, Monday is a holiday so you folks have an extra day to advance your cause. If you don't produce any evidence, the worst that has happened is that I've taken a ride with one of your lovely guests."

God, Hank was smooth. Somehow the nauseatingly sweet words did not make me sick when coming from Hank's mouth. Of course, when a person looked like Hank, not too much he said sounded sickening.

"Do be careful, Meg." I was shocked by Claude's solemnity.

George jabbed his mate in the side. "Of course, she'll be careful. Plus, she'll be with Hank. What could possibly happen?"

I heard a long "hmmm" emanate from behind the *Times*.

As I ran upstairs to drop off several layers of clothing, I reassured myself that I would be fine for two reasons. First, Hank was a cop, and secondly, he was a friend of George and Claude. Somehow, it slipped my mind that I had known the men for only twelve hours.

Chapter Eleven

I restricted myself to one extra layer of clothing for the trip to Atlantic City. The reasons tourists visited the town in January did not include sunning on the beach. I didn't expect to be spending much time outdoors. George nodded approvingly at my attire. Claude eyed my décolletage and suggested a scarf. Hank simply studied my décolletage. I buttoned my cardigan.

As Hank and I descended the highly polished stairs, I was happy to discover that without the extra layers and the sweatclothes, I no longer waddled. "I'm sorry if George pressured you into this." I made the statement without an addendum offering to back out.

"George knows I would have said no if I didn't want to go." With his left hand on my lower back, Hank guided me through the iron gate and closed it behind us. "Most weekends I say no."

"You mean to say George is always dragging you over to entertain his unescorted female guests."

"Not always. A lot of times that house has more couples as guests than the Newlywed Game. No action for me. Other times there's a wide selection. A pair of girlfriends. A sorority house full of middle-aged women. Then it tends to get ugly. There aren't that many eligible men around. I feel like a pork roast with an apple in my mouth. On the up side, I manage to eat better than I can cook and today I get to take a ride with you." The earnest expression in his eyes was tinged with playfulness. "That sounded smooth, heh?" He flashed a set of pearly whites at me.

A little bit too smooth for my taste. I didn't share my thought with Hank. I just smiled. He opened the door to a black Porsche and held my arm as I slipped into the passenger seat. As he started the car, I filled the dead air with conversation. "So do you think my story about the other woman is nuts? I mean murder wasn't my idea. Claude came to that conclusion."

"When you know Claude better, you'll understand that he was only fanning the fire. He doesn't believe that theory for one moment."

"So you do think my idea is nuts."

"Nuts? Nuts is a strong word."

"Ridiculous?"

"Ridiculous is unpleasant, don't you think?"

"So."

"How about overreaction? That's a good word. So we invest an hour or two in putting your mind at ease. As I said, I'm happy to do so."

I spent the minutes while we wove our way through Cape May and out to the Garden State Parkway grilling Hank on his personal history. He answered willingly if not enthusiastically. College graduate. Married at twenty. Father at twenty-one. Divorced at twenty-five, twenty-nine, and thirty-five. Bad husband. Great father. "She's the most important thing in my life. Her name is Shannon. She's smart, beautiful, and really good to her old dad." He flipped down his sun visor to reveal a picture of a blonde whom I imagined was college age—at least in the photo. Hank's daughter was beautiful in the same healthy, outdoorsy way her father was handsome. She'd inherited his deep brown, penetrating eyes.

Unwilling, or unable, to endure the silence, I chatted about the clear blue sky. The day was one of those winter anomalies, when the bright sun and blue sky belie the reality of the outdoors. If the temperature had risen a mere seventy degrees, Saturday would have made a great beach day. If Hank found my observations interesting, he didn't let on. His smile could at best be described as polite.

"Did you come to Cape May a lot as a kid?" Hank's tone told me he wasn't particularly interested in my answer. I pretended not to notice his lack of attention.

Growing up, I'd spent very little time in Cape May. It was, however, quality time—sponging off a family that reunited their Midwest and New Jersey factions in Cape May once a year. Every August the Turner family—of which my first love Lou was a member—gathered in a house with modest Victorian pretensions but enough bedrooms to hold not only a big family but their friends. By the tenth year I think they had long forgotten which attendees were actually family. No blood relative, I came to the reunion on a regular basis. Some of my fondest memories involved the house's antique farm table in the kitchen, elegant mahogany table in the dining room, and big wooden table that was pulled into the backyard for long, leisurely dinners that began in the afternoon sun and finished long after sunset. The Turners liked to eat—and luckily cook.

"No kid could really relax in Cape May." I explained about the Turner family and the sisters of St. Joseph.

"Excuse me? The sisters of St. Joseph?" At last I'd caught his interest.

"The schools I went to were staffed by the sisters of St. Joseph. You know they have a big retreat house at Cape May Point." Hank was aware that the order owned a huge retreat house that—although once set several blocks from the beach—was now beachfront property. Needless to say, those who knew the story harbored suspicions about the nuns' special relationship with the Supreme Being. What Hank wasn't aware of was why this would matter to a kid.

"Well, when you were in Cape May you were always in danger of running into one of them. Maybe one from your school. Maybe one who taught you."

"And that would be bad?" Hank didn't bother to hide his smirk.

"Consider what a frightening proposition that might be for a kid. Running into your teacher in July or August. We weren't that enlightened when I was young."

"I can't imagine the good sisters would have been too relaxed either knowing you were following them on vacation."

I'd never looked at it that way but Hank was probably right.

◆ ◆ ◆

"Since I didn't get the hot lunch I was promised, whatta you say we stop to eat. Been to Wildwood lately?"

"Not since the day I threw up on the Tilt-a-Whirl."

Hank swerved quickly to make the exit. "No one gets sick on the Tilt-a-Whirl."

"Not true. They had a hose handy to clean me up. I couldn't have been the first."

"They had to hose you down?"

"Yeah. Should I wait until we're eating to fill you in on the details?" I answered my own question. "No. The story is too fascinating. During college I spent the summer in Sea Isle City. I..." My jaw snapped shut the instant I saw the minivan. "That's Gimbel." I pointed at the WindStar that passed us going the opposite direction.

"Meg, do you know how many green minivans are registered in New Jersey?"

I recited the license number. "I took the liberty of memorizing the tag. The plate is one of those old blue ones. Let's follow him."

"Why on earth...?"

I had no logical answer. "The more we know, the better. Right? Besides, if we based today's outing on logic, we wouldn't have gotten into the car in the first place."

"Meg, on a scale of one to ten, I've assigned your complaint..."

I interrupted. "I did not file a complaint. I gossiped—the situation snowballed."

"Okay, I have assigned your...theory a feasibility factor of 'one' on a scale of ten. One doesn't warrant surveillance."

I shrugged. "How's my complaint...uh, theory...ever going to rate a 'two' if we don't apply ourselves to the investigation."

Hank grumbled as he made a U-turn, "Okay but if we end up with a restraining order slapped on us..."

"We won't if you're careful. Don't let him see us."

Hank smirked. "Good idea. Odd that law enforcement never thought of that."

"No need to be snide."

We followed Gimbel to Route 9 where he headed south. Gimbel was an amazingly cautious driver. Never once did he allow the speedometer to move above the speed limit. If the limit dropped from 50 to 40—so did Gimbel—immediately.

"He's law-abiding to the point of being ridiculous. Hard to believe that a man who won't speed will murder." Hank downshifted angrily.

"You wouldn't speed either if you had a body in your car."

The cop scrutinized me out of the corner of his eye. "Is that a statement of fact or another example of reckless speculation?"

"Reckless speculation." I didn't dissemble.

Hank told me that was his assumption. I shrugged.

"I'd prefer to follow a stolen car at high speeds." Hank's agitation was beginning to worry me. It didn't take Sherlock Holmes to detect he was frustrated with the low speed chase. "I hate to disillusion you Meg, but I think we're following him to the Parsonage."

The longer we trailed Gimbel the more convinced I became that Hank was right. "Maybe the key is not where he's going but where he was. He went to Wildwood. Why would he go to Wildwood?" I reacted as if the man had made a day trip to Anchorage.

"It's not an out-of-the-way spot. I can think of lots of reasons."

"Name one." I waited. "Okay, okay." I stopped Hank after the fifth. "But I still think it's odd to come on a romantic weekend in Cape May and then sneak off to Wildwood without your wife."

"Sneak?"

"Well, he..."

"How do we even know he went to Wildwood? Consider all these stores. He might have needed any one of a million things."

"Yeah." My intonation betrayed my doubt—and disappointment. Why? I wondered. What had Wallace Gimbel ever done to convince me he was guilty of anything at all?

Chapter Twelve

We followed Gimbel back to Cape May—to the Parsonage as Hank had predicted.

"Good call, Hank," I congratulated the cop as we cruised by the parking lot where Wallace Gimbel climbed out of his van and, camera in hand, trudged towards the front of the B&B.

Hank shrugged. "It's my job. The only thing that bothers me about this wild goose chase is that I never got to eat. Let's grab something at the Ugly Mug."

The Ugly Mug was a local landmark that I had visited over the years without taking the time to understand fully the protocol of the mugs hanging on the ceiling. A now phased-out tradition provided that frequent visitors purchase a mug to use while drinking at the tavern. Between visits the customers' numbered mugs hung from hooks on the ceiling awaiting their return. Those facing seaward signaled that the regular had raised his last glass—or was now drinking from that big beer mug in the sky.

The restaurant was bustling, by January standards. Unlike many of the Jersey shore towns, tourists came to enjoy Cape May's charms in any type of weather.

Well, almost any type of weather. The town was as empty as I'd ever seen it. Yet I was not the only tourist—even in January, the slowest month and the only respite between New Year's and the Valentines/Presidents' Day weekend when parking spaces were easy to come by, rooms were available without reservations, and the locals enjoyed a breather from entertaining. By February, the streets, mall and shops would again be full of tourists.

Hank found us a seat. I noticed that he took a chair next to mine—not across the table. I also noted that his arm brushed mine frequently as we settled in.

We hadn't yet ordered when Nanette Pankenhurst sauntered back to the bar from the direction of the ladies' room. "Coming on a romantic weekend alone, I believed that I would be the guest experiencing the least romance." I nodded at Nanette. "Mrs. Pankenhurst and Mrs. Gimbel are giving me a run for my money."

I eyed Nanette Pankenhurst. She didn't appear at all happy about the situation. The lines curving from the corner of her lips indicated she hadn't been happy about much in a very long time. The wrinkles marred an otherwise pretty face. I made Mrs. Pankenhurst over in my mind. Highlights to hide the gray creeping into her brown hair. Makeup to accentuate deep green eyes. Facelift to remove those mannequin slots around her mouth. Okay, we could skip the facelift and spend the money on clothes. Nanette Pankenhurst had no discernible fashion sense which, given the attire of the other guests at the B&B, appeared to be an asset. Mrs. Pankenhurst favored the unisex look of sweatsuits that a bright shade of pink did not render feminine—let alone sexy.

"Let's ask her to join us." I made the suggestion because of the woman's sad expression. Okay, I had an ulterior motive. Why was her husband following Wallace Gimbel? I wanted to know. No use explaining my reasoning to Hank. I didn't believe he would appreciate my uncovering, or—as he might say—creating more intrigue.

Nanette Pankenhurst seemed pleased by the invitation—possibly because it was delivered by Hank. She didn't seem quite as happy to see me. She settled with marked difficulty on the seat directly across from mine and flashed a exaggerated smile—first at Hank and then at me and then at Hank. After three attempts at a coherent sentence, Nanette gave up verbalizing and concentrated on drinking. Apparently, the Ugly Mug was not her first stop of the day. "I'm not much of a drinker." With that she emptied the glass she'd brought to the table and signaled the waitress for another. "I'm sort of a social drinker."

I nodded that I understood. I figured she was a really sociable person.

Nanette sniffled and—without being asked—admitted immediately, "I'm not having a good time. Will isn't paying any attention to me. I thought if we came here—a romantic locale—things would be different. I think they're actually worse." Her voice escalated and broke. Tears found their way through the thick powder on each cheek leaving a trail like two very slow skiers on new snow.

"Where is your husband now?"

She stared at me with a empty expression. "Oh, Will. He's at the Parsonage—bonding with Wallace Gimbel—or trying to."

Aha! I wasn't surprised.

"My luck, Marvella Gimbel is under the weather and Wallace has time to kill. So, Will is filling his time."

"Mrs. Gimbel is sick again?"

Mrs. Pankenhurst's bobbing head provided an affirmative answer. "Seems like a emotional problem to me. That one is a little loony. Always picking on her husband—blaming him for something— everything." She sipped her wine. "I guess I'm mad because I hold her responsible that Will isn't spending time with me."

"We husbands sometimes get a little caught up in male bonding— unconsciously, you know." Hank's demeanor was soothing.

She shrugged. "No, I wouldn't know. I've never been married." Slowly she raised her eyes and peered at us over the rim of her wine glass. "Oh, oh." Deliberately, she lowered the glass to the table. "I wasn't supposed to let on. I'm not really Mrs. Pankenhurst."

I wasn't shocked. She could barely pronounce the name.

"We'll call you Nanette then." Hank's tone was reassuring. He expressed no interest in prying but Mrs.—that is, Nanette—wasn't finished talking.

"Will paid me to come with him."

Hank shrugged. What did he care? He didn't work vice. "We don't frown on you for that. Everybody's got to make a living."

Nanette appeared puzzled. "Oh." She pulled herself up straight in her chair. "I should be offended. You think I'm a hooker." She laughed. "At my age, I'd be starving. Know what I mean?" She winked at me conspiratorially.

Why wink in my direction? Nanette had at least ten years on me.

She chuckled. "Hooker. God, I'm flattered. No, I'm his secretary. I'm Will Parker's secretary." Once more she eyed us sheepishly. "Oh, oh. I wasn't supposed to tell. Will Pankenhurst is really Will Parker."

Hank shrugged yet again. Nothing odd about a man who runs off with his secretary using a pseudonym.

"Oh God. He'll kill me. Don't let him know I told you."

"Don't worry." Hank patted her hand. "It's unlikely that I'll run into Mrs. Parker."

"Mrs. Parker?" Once again Hank had confused Nanette. "Who's Mrs. Parker?"

"Well, I assumed..."

"Oh, you think Will is married. No way. He's too much of a ladies man. Married!" She affected a jaded laugh but the expression in her eyes was wistful. "Will! I wish he were the type."

I expected Hank to ask why, if he wasn't married, Will Parker had paid Nanette to stay with him under an assumed name at the Parsonage. But Hank didn't ask.

Nanette didn't give him the chance; she began to ramble. "He doesn't love me. He doesn't even like me." She patted my hand. "I understand how you feel all alone on this romantic weekend or whatever they call the trip you won. No one wants me either."

Why bother protesting? I wasn't going to change her opinion of me. "How long have you worked for Will?" I asked.

"Sixteen years and six months."

"How long have you been in love with him?" Hank took a long slug of beer.

"Sixteen years and five months. Maybe a little longer." She finished off her wine. "I need another drink."

I figured she needed another boss. Hank figured she needed a ride to the Parsonage.

I studied the cop as he helped Nanette into her coat...her hat...her scarf. She even needed help with her gloves. She especially needed help with her gloves. On her first few attempts, those finger slots eluded her. Nanette gazed at Hank with wide, adoring eyes as he fit each finger into the right spot. She took his arm and he walked her to the exit. He dazzled her with that smile. I bet that by the end of the ride, she wouldn't give a hoot about Will Parker.

By the time Hank returned to the restaurant, I'd eaten half my lunch. Hank bit into his sandwich and finished ahead of me.

"I promised Nanette we would keep her secret. I can't see any reason to tell Claude and George until they, the Pankenhursts...Parkers ...whatevers, are gone...although I'll find out what Will is up to before I decide for sure. I did coax out of her that he's using an alias because he suspects that something untoward...that's the word she used...is going on in the business. They both work in the accounting department of a marketing consulting firm."

"It could have something to do with Gimbel..." I was going to tell Hank what I had seen that morning, but he cut me off.

"Meg, Meg, Meg, Meg, Meg. Everything in life doesn't have to do with Gimbel."

"Fine." I crossed my arms across my chest. Let him find out for himself.

Chapter Thirteen

My guess? The decorator wanted us to believe we were being transported to Venice by the moving staircase. In reality, the escalator deposited us in the lobby of an Atlantic City hotel. The intent of the decor was clear. Okay, the Venezia signs were one clue. The striped shirts, white pants and straw hats on the staff at the bell desk was another—especially since the dangling ribbons displayed the hotel name: *Ecco Venice*. If I'd depended on the murals on the wall, I never would have figured out the motif. Perhaps one of the owner's relatives, clearly one who had never visited Italy, fancied a career as a painter.

The escalator left us in a lobby as crowded as on the July 4th weekend—or the *quattro de luglio*. "Boy, people just can't wait to lose their lire, can they? Or are they losing Euros now?" I shook my head. "Maybe while you're asking around, I'll find a video poker machine..."

Hank interrupted. "I thought we were on a mission." He didn't bother suppressing his sarcasm. "I might need you. I want you to stay here. Don't do anything rash. Don't do *anything*." Hank's demeanor was paternal. Was it the fact that he was older or that he was a cop that made him sound dictatorial?

Whatever the reason, I ground my teeth in protest. "But I'd like to help," I said sweetly—or as least as sweetly as I ever say anything.

"You can help by finding an empty gondola and sitting. Do nothing. I will make a few discreet inquiries."

Hank didn't notice that I made no promises. "*Ciao*." I waved weakly as he headed for the back offices of the hotel. I took off my parka and cardigan and still felt warm seated in one of the many fake gondolas adorning the lobby. With my bulky clothes, I looked clumsy and out of place. Most of the other patrons had already checked their coats—or lost them at the crap tables.

Sitting in the lobby, I felt much farther from Cape May than forty miles. The distance couldn't be measured—in metrics anyway. I'd climbed into Hank's Porsche in another world, another time. A trip to the late nineteenth century had landed me smack in dab in the hubbub of the twenty-first century. Not that the decorators wanted me to figure that out. They had the sixteenth century in mind—okay, a neon sixteenth century. It didn't take me long to grow bored although interpreting the decor did take some time—and effort. I identified two major contributors to the theme. Venetian glass, for one, although I didn't recall everything in Venice being purple. The other motif centered on canals with a heavy emphasis on gondolas: Life-size gondolas to offer seating and miniature gondolas to cruise the mini-canals. I tried to figure out whether the gondolas or the gondoliers were motorized. In either case, the boats cruised the man-made waterways with a speed that surpassed romantic.

Canals cut across everywhere and customers had to climb up and down bridges to move from the hotel to the casino to the restaurants. The multilevel design created hundreds of little waterfalls that provided a pleasant background when the loudspeaker wasn't blaring. Make that *would have* provided a pleasant background if the loudspeaker ever stopped blaring.

The people-watching in the hotel lobby was far less interesting than in the actual Piazza San Marco—where I doubted the main fashion statement was semiformal gym clothes. On the bright side, there were no pigeons—or, more importantly, pigeon droppings. The weather was consistently beautiful under a fake sky across which a fake sun traveled to create a fake sunny side and fake shady side of the fake Piazza.

Bored, I wandered to the casino—down cathedral-aisle hallways, past cathedral-shaped vending machines that dispersed similarly shaped soda, candy and cigarettes through elaborately carved doors. I stood at the casino entrance and eyed the cocktail waitresses. I got the theme right away. Hooters Venezia. The uniformly attractive women were all identically attired in leather lace-up boots that fended off flood waters, striped shirts that highlighted tight midriffs, and shiny black hotpants that encouraged big tips.

I wove my way back to my gondola docked in a shallow pool in the hotel lobby. I knew I could help resolve the mystery, and that I should help. After all, I was a key player in the development of the case...theory...rumor...whatever. Plus, I'd learned a little about investigations hanging out with Andy Beck, PI. Why let that training—casual as the instruction was—go to waste?

I considered what assistance the concierge might offer. From a distance the couple—I assumed related by work only—who manned the desk appeared officious. I edged closer and heard in their tones the unstated footnote "Of course I wouldn't be caught dead there" added to each statement "I think you would like this restaurant." They would be no help. The front desk was out of the question. Registration was far too busy. Then I noticed the bellstand. Despite the heavy check-in, the staff appeared to have time to kill. Seemed most of the arrivals were happy to lug their own bags to the elevator to save a few lire for the gaming tables.

After eyeing the group to see who might be most sympathetic, I sidled up to the youngest of the crew—Teddy, according to his badge. I considered that he might know the least, but calculated that he would be most willing to share what he did know.

"Ciao, Teddy. Do you know *Signore* Gimbel, the manager?" I spoke quietly but smiled broadly.

"Are you making fun of my outfit?"

I wasn't off to a good start. "Not at all. I'm into the whole motif, that's all. I thought you might know Wallace Gimbel."

His nod, so deep his face momentarily disappeared under the brim of his hat, was accompanied by apprehension.

"This is embarrassing. I'm supposed to deliver a package to his girlfriend and I can't remember her name." I strove to look pathetic; my outfit gave me a head start.

"You mean his wife?"

"It doesn't matter to me what he does. I mean his girlfriend. I could be wrong but that was what they told me. When they gave me her name—the one I forgot—they told me to come here, to the hotel." I snapped my fingers. "I know. She works here...I think."

"You can't remember her name?"

I shook my head.

"If you knew her name..."

"I only know that she's his girlfriend. Look I could get in trouble..." I was ten years too senior to bat my eyes at the guy. I stuck with pathetic.

"You mean Celia?"

"Yeah that could be the woman. Delia?"

"Celia. It's gotta be Celia Chaney. She dances here."

"Yeah. That sounds familiar. Celia. Do you know where she is?"

"She's not here today."

"Where can I find her? I mean I'll end up in deep..."

The bellman seemed a fool for my pathetic act. "Wow, is your timing bad. If you find Celia, let us know. She didn't show up for her gig last night and the entertainment manager is pissed to say the least. She just got promoted out of the chorus. These days if she doesn't show, it's a problem. Two weeks ago no one would have cared. Cared very much, that is. Now when she's a no-show..." He shook his head. Apparently words could not describe the problem her absence caused—or at least the words in Teddy's vocabulary couldn't.

My stomach dropped at the same time my heart rose. I might actually be right—something bad had happened. "How do you know all this?"

"My friend Eddie worked last night. I met him to go to a couple of clubs after. He told me that Tom Russo, that's the entertainment manager, had him running all over town searching for the bitch." Teddy averted his eyes. "That's what he called her. Anyway, that's how I know."

At that moment, I noticed Hank making his way across the lobby. I thanked the bellman and left him to cater to the needs of a couple who, unless they were spending the calendar year, had definitely overpacked.

"Well?" I asked as Hank took my arm. Without slowing his pace, he propelled me towards the boardwalk.

He spoke quickly—the same way he walked. "Gimbel has been seeing a woman named Celia Chaney. Dances here. At least she was a dancer here. When she comes back, she'd better have a good excuse for her absence last night."

I said nothing.

"She didn't call. She was not supposed to be out of town. Her alternate did the early show yesterday as planned. Celia didn't come in for the second show." He glanced over his shoulder. I followed his eyes to Teddy, who was juggling luggage tags and the phone. "By the way, I thought I asked you to do nothing."

"I was chatting with the bellman." My tone asked why Hank was making an issue of harmless chit chat. "That's all. And he mentioned that if I was looking for someone who might be called Gimbel's girl-friend, that person would be Celia Chaney."

"He brought the topic up?" Hank made a statement that his incredulous tone turned into a question.

"Don't worry. I was discreet. I pretended I had a package to deliver."

"Where is it?"

"Oh yeah." It had never occurred to me that I asked the questions empty-handed. "What's it matter, anyway? I didn't mention my name. I don't know these people." I caught his scowl. "Besides, you're the one who says there's nothing going on."

"Yeah." He murmured. "That's right...I did say that didn't I?"

Chapter Fourteen

At last I understood Hank's willingness to support my investigation. "I need Taylor Pork Roll. Never come here without grabbing a sandwich. Tastes better when someone else makes it. I know a stand. It's a little bit of a walk." Hank took off fast on legs considerably longer than mine. As he charged into the cold air on the Boardwalk I hesitated by the door to the casino, pulling on various items of inner and outer clothing.

"You don't crave Venetian caramel popcorn, Venetian custard, Venetian taffy, or Venetian funnel cake?" I waved at a row of concessions.

"Are you always this snide?" Hank didn't slow his pace.

"No," I scurried to keep pace with the cop. At least rushing kept me warm. I hoped Hank didn't notice I was sweating. "I appreciated the decor. It's just when I was in Venice I must have missed the funnel cake—and the mountains."

"No mountains in Venice?"

"Not right there in the town."

"I wouldn't know. I haven't been all over the world like you." He was defensive.

"Hey, I'm not making a value judgment—except for the decor in the casino. You and I are different; we've lived differently; we've spent our money differently. You haven't been to all those places but you have a house, a car, a boat, and I haven't got a house, a car, a boat…or a pot to piss in for that matter. You did different things with your life." I let a sneer creep across my face. "Like planning your weddings."

"That's snide. Don't you have friends who've been married more than once?"

"Twice more than once." I reminded Hank of his marital history. He peered at me with narrow eyes.

"That was snide. I admit it. I do have acquaintances who have been divorced five times—well, one person but she had to repeat one of the husbands to get the tally that high. I guess someone like me, who has trouble finding one person they're willing to hold hands with, can't understand how anyone can find three people to marry."

"And, don't forget, divorce."

I shrugged. "I guess accepting that outcome does make the search easier." I tried to hide that I was growing winded but the task was difficult with every breath displayed in the cold air. I prayed the Taylor Pork Roll stand was on the next block.

"What do you have against marriage anyway? When you were a little girl didn't you ever dream about a wedding?" Hank's brown eyes studied me briefly, but intensely, before returning to his search for pork roll.

"A wedding? Sure. My friend Nancie and I spent hours planning our weddings. Then I found out what happened after the honeymoon. Cooking, cleaning, paying bills. I like family life—as long as I'm the kid. I don't want to be responsible for...for...for anything." I changed the subject. "Did you ever have a big wedding?"

"All three times." He smiled. "I liked weddings. Still do."

"And three times your family posed for photos, made toasts, bought gifts..."

He shrugged. "The marriage was a first for each of the brides. I think they deserved a blow-out."

He stopped so suddenly I passed in front of him.

"What?"

His expression was frantic. "It's gone. The stand. It was here." He wandered forward as if numbed by the loss. "I swear the stall was right here." The new concession sold Chinese food.

"This guy sells hot dogs. Why don't you ask? Maybe he has pork roll."

I should have done the asking. In Hank's hands, the request came out more like a demand than a question.

"No Taylor Pork Roll." The proprietor shook his head emphatically.

"You should have Taylor Pork Roll."

"No Taylor Pork Roll." Getting his tongue around the words appeared difficult for the recent immigrant.

"Have a hot dog." I nudged Hank with my elbow and smiled at the vendor reassuringly.

"I don't want a hot dog."

"Have a hot dog. You upset the guy."

"He should be upset. I want..."

My look interrupted him.

"...a hot dog."

Hank ate as we strolled up the Boardwalk. Eating slowed his pace, creating a good news/bad news scenario. I could keep up with him but I could also feel the cold. On our return we walked into the wind. Hank seemed unperturbed by the weather conditions. I tried to mimic his nonchalance and failed.

Hank's mood improved after he finished eating—although he repeatedly made the point that a hot dog would never replace Taylor Pork Roll. By the time we cut through the hotel lobby, he appeared cheerful. He even waved back when Teddy the bellman broke away from chatting with a friend and waved enthusiastically at me.

Chapter Fifteen

Our walk to the car and our drive to the Garden State Parkway passed uneventfully. That was why I was shocked when Hank suddenly gunned the engine and took off down the highway.

"What the...what are you doing?" I glanced at the speedometer. I hoped my eyesight was failing.

"I think we're being tailed. I want to make sure. Don't turn around." I started to rotate in my seat.

"You don't take orders very well, do you?"

"Never really had to take orders," I paused before adding, "sir."

"Don't get sarcastic. This may have nothing to do with your silly little escapade."

If Hank thought my little escapade, as he called it, was so silly, why was he knee-deep in the adventure with me? I didn't ask. I sulked. Or tried to. Sulking was relatively difficult in a car doing ninety-five mph on the Garden State.

"Is it that blue Honda?"

"Yep."

I monitored the car's movements in the side mirror.

Hank slowed. The Honda slowed. Hank sped up. The Honda sped up. Hank passed a bus. The Honda passed a bus. Hank lingered behind a camper. The Honda lingered behind us.

"Yep. He's with us all right." Hank sped up once again.

"Any idea who the person is—or why anyone would follow us?"

"Not a clue—unless, of course, your bellman's phone call had something to do with our situation."

Like I could pick the one person out of a staff of 1,000 who had a vested interest in Celia Chaney's fate! If I had those kind of powers, I'd be back at the casino using my gifts on the progressive slots.

"Hank, how is this chase going to end?" Visions of Fox TV specials played in my head.

"Don't worry. I've got this under control." He downshifted and roared past a church van.

When Hank picked the wrong toll lane at the Great Egg tolls, the car slowed and waited for us. "If he thinks I'm going to pass him, he's nuts. We'll fool this jerk and get off at the next exit." But the driver, after carefully signaling, pulled off onto the shoulder where he sat only until we passed.

"Look in my direction." Hank gazed past me for a peek in the car.

"Know a fellow, early thirties, dark hair, fairly handsome guy, that might want to follow you?"

"They all do, Hank."

"Yeah, right." He checked his rearview mirror. "Here he comes again. Don't look." After passing two SUVs and a sports car—all of which were exceeding the limit, Hank dropped to fifty-five—coincidentally the currently posted speed. "He's still with us." Hank slowed again but the car didn't pass.

Hank resumed a normal speed as we approached an open rest area. "Nice day for a picnic, heh?" I prepared for the worst. Hank put on his blinker and veered onto the ramp.

"Nice work—with the blinker and all."

"Snide" was his only response.

The Honda didn't follow us into the rest area but chose to pull onto the right shoulder for a view of the picnic grove.

"Whoever he is, he's no pro." Hank flashed an insincere smile at me and nodded at the collection of wooden tables hosting no other visitors. "I don't know, Meg, maybe it's a tad cold for a picnic."

"Hank, it's a tad cold for ice fishing."

The cop pressed the gas pedal to the floor and merged with traffic. I didn't check for the other drivers' reactions. Maybe they didn't find it odd that Hank chose to occupy the 1.3 car length space between the Trailways bus and the minivan.

Less than a minute after I'd inquired about airbags we rounded a bend doing sixty-five. Hank, with what I considered insufficient notice to me and surrounding vehicles, slammed on the brakes and swung the car onto a poorly paved road between the north and southbound lanes. As the Porsche rotated 360 degrees I performed an involuntary test of the seatbelt with my full body weight—as well as a complete, albeit rapid, review of the thirty-four years of my life. The car screeched to a halt; I simply screeched. Without missing a beat, Hank pulled along the row of pines to our north. My body slammed back in position just in time to see the little blue Honda speed past us without slowing.

"Hurry, we'll lose him." I was into the chase.

"Meg, you forget. He's following us. Losing them is what you do when they are following you."

"But didn't we need to know who the guy was?"

"Don't worry, Meg. I think we'll have another opportunity to meet him. For one thing, I got his license number." He squeezed my knee. "But for now I think we'll let him go, take this exit and use the back roads to Cape May."

Chapter Sixteen

Hank and I burst into the Parsonage. Well, I burst in. Hank followed circumspectly, being careful to wipe his feet and close the door behind him. I charged into the drawing room where George had entertained me the night before.

Although unfamiliar with the history of design, I realized that I had traveled to the long reign of Queen Victoria. The room reflected a fondness for ornamentation that I hoped was matched by a fondness for housework. I viewed the furniture's intricate carving with admiration—not because of the artistry but because of its cleanliness. My first reaction had been clear: Who dusted this place?

In muted shades of green and gold the room made a perfect winter retreat. Flocked velvet striped wallpaper adorned with heavy-framed oil paintings. Lush velvet drapes secured by thick gold braid. Elaborately carved chairs and sofas covered with heavy velvet. The soft glow from a gilded chandelier completed the image. In jeans, T-shirt, boots and parka I felt underdressed. I assumed that any visitor to the room since 1917 had felt that way. I assumed they had been.

As I'd come to expect, Claude was ensconced in his chair—the spot next to the fire. "Well, if isn't Nick and Nora come for a visit." Claude peered at us over his reading glasses and *The New York Times*. "Asta taking a leak?"

"Don't be vulgar." George scolded his mate as he emerged from behind a sofa with a duster in his hand.

I rushed to a growling, not roaring fire, and warmed my front and then my back. After a quick round of charades to verify that the

Gimbels were not currently in residence, I blurted out, "Celia Chaney."

"God, not you, too." George made a show of his exasperation.

"What do you mean?"

"A man has been calling here for the last day or so asking for Celia Chaney. He must have rung ten times."

"Did you take a number?"

"Why would I? She isn't here."

"Next time the guy calls, I'll talk to him. If I'm not here, get a number." Hank settled into the chair next to Claude's and reached for a section of a local paper.

Since Hank gave no indication he would be offering an explanation, I did. "Celia Chaney is Wallace Gimbel's girlfriend. Celia Chaney is a dancer—I assume with beautiful ankles and feet. And," I paused for effect, "Celia Chaney is one other thing."

George leaned forward anxiously and Claude lowered his paper.

"Celia Chaney is missing."

"Meg, you're a genius." George patted me on the back.

Claude asked, "How long has she been missing?"

"Twelve hours."

"Twelve hours. She could have gotten in the wrong line at McDonalds." He disappeared behind the *The New York Times*.

"I thought you read the *Times* this morning." I was shocked to hear the comment come out of my mouth—and in a somewhat belligerent tone.

"Not the obituaries."

"Let's get back to Meg's missing person." George was excited.

"Now, George." Hank insisted on interjecting logic into our conversation. "Celia Chaney did not show up for work on Friday night as expected. She was not at home when her employer tried to reach her. That hardly means she's missing." He cleared his throat. "On the other hand, Celia Chaney is five-foot-nine."

George and I turned to him expectantly.

"If she were going to imitate Mrs. Gimbel she could not afford to wear high heels. Even in flats she had to stoop. My guess is that Marvella Gimbel barely reaches five-three."

"Aha." George and I nodded in unison.

"Has Gimbel ever brought Celia here?" I asked George.

"He's been here many times. Always with his wife."

Claude cleared his throat to catch our attention. He lowered the paper. "You know, I may have mentioned this to George at the time, but I quite literally bumped into Mr. Gimbel once on the mall in the autumn. It was a Sunday and he was carrying two coffees. He seemed embarrassed to see me—I assumed because he wasn't staying with us. He said how sorry he was that we were booked when he called. He was staying at the Evergreen House over in Cape May Courthouse. We had an opening but I don't recall if it was because of a cancellation. I never checked to see if his story was true."

I latched onto Claude's thought. "Maybe he wasn't with his wife. So he stayed elsewhere."

George's eyes opened wide with excitement. "We can drop by and talk to Sara and Jack." He explained to me. "They run the Evergreen House." He planted his hands on his hips. "What else can we do?"

George's eyes turned to Hank. He, rather than Claude, hid behind the newspaper.

If Hank wouldn't propose action, I would. "You have access to the rooms."

George nodded eagerly. "Sometimes I do the rooms on weekdays in the winter. On weekends I usually check them. During the summer we have help and in winter I have heavy duty cleaners in once a week because someone, who shall go unnamed," he nodded at Claude, "never has time to help out with housekeeping duties."

Claude let out a long, low sigh. "I keep busy. Shall we return to Meg's point?"

"Actually," Hank posed the question I'd been dying to ask, "what *do* you do around here?"

Claude remained behind the paper. "Perhaps you've noticed that it's warm and comfy in here? Who do you suppose installed the new furnace?"

George assented. "Claude is a whiz with those major repairs."

"The guests always have clean linens and fresh muffins, do they not?"

George answered again. "He does those chores."

"Don't our guests walk on lovingly refurbished hardwood floors?"

"Okay, okay." Hank put an end to Claude's recitation. "I now understand your incredible value to the B&B. It's just that I never see you out of that chair."

"When I do work, I work quickly."

"Have you been in the Gimbel's room yet, George?" I returned the conversation to the matter of the missing woman. "Did you notice a pair of black flats in the closet?"

"Black flats. You must be kidding. I'm gay, remember? If we were searching for gold lame or red sequins, maybe I would have taken note. But black flats?" George shook his head in disgust. "Anyway, I haven't been in their room since they arrived. Agnes cleaned this morning."

I had no idea who Agnes was but didn't stop to ask. "I can think of two things you can do. First, ask Agnes if anything appeared out of order in the Gimbels' room this morning."

"I'll be discreet." George uttered the words with conviction.

"And, I think it would be a good idea for you to check on the room…and maybe you could notice about the flats."

"Aye-aye, sir." He saluted.

"And make sure the pink flowered bag is still there."

"The flowered bag?"

"The Gimbels checked in with a small flowered, quilted bag—mostly pink."

"I didn't..."

I interrupted. "Mr. Gimbel carried the bag up the steps himself. I noticed because the sight of Wallace Gimbel holding such a feminine item was fairly incongruous."

"Oh, that's absolutely cause for suspicion." Claude's delivery was droll. "He is much more of a paisley type. Don't you think, Hank?"

"Absolutely. We've got him now." The two men snapped their newspapers in unison.

George and I ignored them and headed for the door.

"Meg." Hank stopped me. "You might want to take this." He pulled a five-by-seven photograph from the inside pocket of his jacket.

"What is it?" George called from the hallway.

"Celia Chaney's head shot?" I answered with a question.

"See, Ms. Daniels. You underestimated how much you needed me in Atlantic City. I am the professional, you know."

"You're proving it. Time and again, you're proving it."

I studied Celia's five-by-seven photo. The face that stared back was pretty in an ordinary way and devoid of emotion in an extraordinary way. Although her muscles forced the woman's face into a smile, there was no joy in the cool blue eyes. Staring from the photo, Celia seemed to observe me—critically.

Celia thought this was her best shot? I'd never been a producer. I'd never met a producer. I'd never knowingly ridden in an elevator with a producer. I felt strongly, however, that if I were a producer I would never select the photo of a woman who appeared to disapprove of me before we'd met.

I had the urge to put an end to the caper. Celia Chaney was just plain unlikable. Then intellect overrode my emotions. It wasn't fair to judge Celia by one picture—even if it was worth a thousand words—all of them seemingly unpleasant. Besides, I had nothing else to do.

"What do you think?" I flashed the photo in front of George.

"Nice enough looking girl."

"Think so?"

"Meg, what do I know? I'm gay."

"I don't think I like this woman."

"Meg, don't be silly. What can you tell from a picture?"

Chapter Seventeen

Jack and Sara Beaumont ran a bed-and-breakfast in Cape May Courthouse—the county seat of Cape May County and home to the county courthouse, the county prosecutor's office, and the county jail. I had been in the town only once before when eighteen-years old. I didn't mention that visit to George since I had been acquitted and my records expunged.

We left Cape May and followed a road through the pine forest. George assured me the route was "just a little out of our way" and headed across the farmlands. There were enough deciduous trees among the pines that it was easy to see a figure in the woods. I swore I saw Mr. Pankenhurst disappear among the trees. "It was. I swear!" There was no denying the excitement in my voice.

"That man sure looked like Will Pankenhurst." George was thoughtful.

"How many people have fire-engine red hair and wear a bright orange parka that makes them resemble a mobile, if not particularly fast moving, forest fire?" Not many.

"But Meg, we don't suspect him of anything."

"We suspect everyone." I didn't explain that Mr. Pankenhurst was using an alias or that I'd believed Mr. Pankenhurst was following Mr. Gimbel that morning. "You think it's normal to park your car in this desolate area and disappear into the woods."

"Well, going in the pines at any time wouldn't be an option for me, but I'm not much of an outdoorsman. This behavior might be normal for Mr. Pankenhurst. Plus, being from Baltimore, he might not know about the Jersey Devil."

"I don't think the Devil prowls in the daylight hours. Plus, technically this pine forest isn't part of the Pine Barrens. There's probably a housing development and a strip mall fifty yards through those trees."

George wasn't convinced. "I don't think monsters know enough to check the state and federal records to determine what area is protected—or to keep bankers' hours. But even if the Devil does, he might travel or put in a little overtime now and then." George let his jeep coast down the road slowly. After fifty yards we spotted a Cadillac. The sedan bore Maryland plates and a strong resemblance to the car in which the Pankenhursts had arrived. The vehicle was pulled far off on the shoulder and tucked under the branches of an overhanging tree. George slammed on the brakes. My eyes begged him: don't let this opportunity pass.

"It won't be good for business if word gets out that I follow the guests."

I waved my hand at him. "Who will ever know? I won't tell."

George required very little coaxing. We abandoned George's car near the hidden sedan and ran toward the spot where we'd last seen Will Pankenhurst. George made great time because he was obviously in peak condition. I strained to make adequate time—only because I saw no point in prolonging any outdoor activity that day—even if the trek into the woods was my idea.

Evidently, our prey had descended into a ruggedly carved crevice and followed a shallow stream bed crusted with frost into the pine forest. We slipped down the bank and followed Will Pankenhurst, or rather traces of Will Pankenhurst who, luckily, was both sloppy and clumsy. Evidence of his passing was everywhere. Will Pankenhurst was a threat to the environment but easy to tail.

Our progress proved slow and difficult. The cold was numbing. Branches poked at our faces. Soft earth underfoot unbalanced and toppled us. Splotches of ice were just as treacherous. "Could he possibly know where he's going?" George was growing tired of the chase.

I smiled hoping my enthusiasm would be contagious—not fatal.

"Maybe he needed to take a leak." George's enthusiasm for the hunt was waning.

"He's gone half a mile. Don't you think that's excessive modesty?" I kept moving forward despite a growing fear. What if Will Pankenhurst was a pervert of some sort—a kidnapper, a murderer? What if we discovered something horrific? Foolishly, my concerns were limited to what we might discover—not what might happen to us.

We were gaining on Will Pankenhurst. I recognized his whistling. The theme from "Shaft." Suddenly, the shrill sound shifted to the left. I grabbed the hem of George's parka and pulled him to the ground. Twenty feet in front of us, Will Pankenhurst scrambled up a low ridge of red clay, mutilating trees and bushes with a vengeance. It took five attempts and a fair amount of cursing before his feet disappeared over the top. He mumbled as he moved away.

"Where are we?" George asked.

We scaled the ridge with considerably less difficulty than Will Pankenhurst but not without sliding backwards in the crumbling surface several times. George followed me as we eluded the clutches of sharp branches and soft sand. We sneaked forward to a position behind a row of fat pine trees. The lights were on in the dining area of a local bar—not one I knew or had any desire to know.

The establishment was housed in a building that looked as if it had stood in the sandy turf for years but was unlikely to last the afternoon. It was the kind of place that didn't invite a stranger to stop and sit a spell. It was the kind of spot that tourists sped by on the New Jersey roads labeled by three digits. It was the kind of dive that without parked cars in the dusty lot appeared to have gone out of business a decade before. I was willing to bet that the front of the building boasted a neon sign with at least one letter dangling or dark.

Why would Wallace Gimbel frequent such a place? And, more importantly, how did Will Pankenhurst of Baltimore possibly know how to find a good view into the back of the restaurant? And was the outcome—watching Mr. and Mrs. Gimbel drink cocktails—worth the effort? Apparently so. Seemingly impervious to the cold, he settled onto a fallen log. From his jacket pocket, he pulled a pair of binoculars that seemed highly unnecessary given the view George and I had.

"This did turn out to be odd." George whispered.

I nodded and shivered but not from the cold. Something really was going on at the Parsonage. Who ever expected I would be right?

Chapter Eighteen

The inn that Jack and Sara Beaumont ran was smaller than the Parsonage but just as meticulously decorated, inside and out. The painted lady boasted at least five shades typical of the Victorian era. I wanted to study the exterior in more detail—in August—if the weather didn't turn too hot. In the meantime, my main interest was getting inside.

Jack and Sara flung open the door and welcomed George and the stranger—me—with effusive greeting and hugs. The couple invited us into a huge country kitchen full of the warm glow of a hot oven and the sweet scent of baked bread. As they worked a duet preparing tea, I wondered. Were all the B&B's in the area run by ex-models? Both Jack and Sara fit the profile. He was tall, dark, and handsome; she was tall, blonde, and gorgeous. And gracious.

Until we'd settled into the comfort of their kitchen, I hadn't given a thought to how we were going to approach the topic of Celia Chaney. George and I had no prepared script.

"My God, George, what happened to you?" Sara checked out the dirt smudged on George's dark khaki slacks and then smiled at me. "I don't think I've ever seen George looking less than perfect."

"Meg and I had an adventure. I'd never been into the Pines before. Next time I think I'll stay on the road." George clutched his teacup for warmth.

"Oh, Meg, are you one of those fillies who appreciate our flora and fauna?" Jack seemed happy to think I was.

"I've been into the Pines a few times." I didn't mention that one of those times was after I had been dumped and left for dead. "They are quite interesting." I mugged to communicate to George not to elaborate about our latest visit. He responded with contorted features and a shrug.

"Next time I'm going in the spring, summer, autumn, whatever...not winter." He shivered theatrically. "Anyway, we just wondered if you knew someone." He nodded at me. "Meg, show them the picture."

I pulled Celia Chaney's headshot from my jacket pocket and handed the photo to Sara.

"Yeah." She stretched the word as she studied the picture. "I recognize her. Didn't she stay here, Jack?"

When she passed the color portrait to her husband, Jack nodded immediately. "I wasn't likely to forget this one. She was a frisky little colt. She checked in with an older gentleman..."

"Wallace Gimbel?" George asked eagerly.

Jack pondered the name. "That sounds right. Doesn't it, kitten? He was a big gorilla of a guy..."

Did Jack view every human in the context of the animal kingdom? How would he describe me? I was afraid to know. Jack went on to give me an accurate description—in human terms—of Wallace Gimbel.

"Oh, I remember." Sara nodded emphatically. "He was called away on Saturday afternoon, and she had a guest." Her emphasis on the word guest told me the visitor was male. "He was handsome. Dark hair. Around thirty."

"Yes, a virile young stallion. Looked like a thoroughbred. They both did, really. She rushed him in and out...no pun intended. Gimbel returned before dinner."

"I thought having that fellow here took a great deal of guts." Sara's tone indicated amazement not admiration. "Not only because she pulled this trick off so brazenly in front of us...but because Gimbel had gone to a meeting down at a local dive about twenty minutes from here." Jack named the bar where we'd seen the Gimbels earlier.

"Meeting? What kind of meeting?"

Sara shook her head. "I don't know. Unscheduled. He got a phone call..."

"From a real baboon...I took the call." Jack interrupted. "Scared him, don't you think, bunny?"

"I don't know if he was scared or not but he certainly moved fast enough."

"Like a gazelle." Jack laughed. "And so did she. She had that young fellow here in moments. He must have been waiting around the corner with a cell phone. Courage of a lion, that one had."

I would have described her audacity more crudely—but then, I lacked Jack's encyclopedic knowledge of zoology.

Chapter Nineteen

"Hank, thank God you're here. This story is getting more complex." George ripped off his coat as he flew into the drawing room. "Meg, tell them."

"Them" was Claude and Hank seated in matching armchairs looking all the world like denizens of an exclusive men's club. They eyed George and me as applicants whose very appearance induced thoughts of the blackball. George and I didn't care. We told our story. Actually, I did.

When I'd finished, Claude reacted first. "Excuse me, are you telling me you stalked one of our guests."

"Stalked?" George was outraged. "I would never stalk. This was surveillance."

Hank intervened. "If they have to testify, I say they take the position that they believed Mr. Pankenhurst to be unfamiliar with the terrain and that they felt his life might be in danger."

Claude was not amused or pacified. "This caper seemed funny only a few hours ago, but now your behavior is verging on the ridiculous."

"Not so ridiculous. In town this morning, I thought I saw Mr. Pankenhurst following Gimbel. I was right." I turned to Hank. "Do you think he knows Celia Chaney?"

"We can't just ask him." George's contorted features betrayed his puzzlement as he sought an approach.

"I agree. You two can't." Hank's tone was mocking yet, I liked to believe, encouraging. "Let me see if I can come up with a connection. You two should lay low for awhile." He eyed George. "You must have something better to keep you busy."

"Yes." Claude's voice was no longer angry. "You must have strangers to stalk. By the way, lest you accuse me of being less than supportive of your investigative efforts, while you were gone I did my part. I spoke to Agnes. She said she noticed nothing unusual about the room the Gimbels occupied last night—but she really hadn't been searching for anything. I myself did a room inspection and did not, after an admittedly quick perusal, locate either black flats or a pink flowered bag."

George sought my reaction.

"Hardly conclusive, but Claude's findings in no way counter our conclusions. We are definitely onto something here. I'm going to my room; I'll think about it."

"No." It was Hank who spoke. "Stay here with us. We've been so busy chasing and being chased, I haven't really gotten a chance to know you."

Claude lowered his paper just far enough that I saw his raised eyebrow. I glanced from his eyebrow to Hank's smile. There was no contest. I settled at the end of a Victorian sofa. Hank moved from his chair near the fire to the opposite end. "So let's hear all about Meg Daniels."

What a coincidence! One of my favorite topics. So I talked. Was I telling Hank too much? Too much! He knew the guest list at my high school graduation party by heart. I took an occasional breath, but he would fill the space with open-ended questions that I would answer— never briefly. His brown eyes reacted to each comment with enthusiasm. Hank certainly wanted me to believe he found the story of my life exciting. I'd lived it. Trust me, my life wasn't that exciting.

Chapter Twenty

About forty minutes into my life story, I had relapsed into the delusion that I like cold weather. I can't explain or defend the notion. I hadn't come to the shore for a weekend indoors— although given the weather a revised plan might have been in order. I cut short the story of my life at age thirty, made my excuses, and climbed back into all my layers.

Even though I'd missed all the tours at the Emlen Physick house, I considered a trip to the gift shop. Certainly, that would count as a cultural activity. I was visiting America's Oldest Seaside Resort, a town that was in total a National Historic Landmark. Absorbing a little culture was in order—even if that culture was absorbed in a store.

I kept reminding myself of the need for cultural redemption as I wound my way past architectural gems without a glance. I overshot— a major mistake on the increasingly cloudy day. I approached the mansion from the north. The last tour was lingering on the lawn. Well, maybe lingering was the wrong word. The small group was huddled in front of their guide—a woman I'd bet grew up in Alaska. She gesticulated wildly—and happily—pointing out posts, brackets, dormers and other architectural details that made the building a Victorian treasure. Only one member of the group seemed unimpressed by architect Frank Furness's efforts. Marvella Gimbel! There was no mistaking the hair color that peeked out from under the Hermes scarf.

Mrs. Gimbel had turned away from the group and if I weren't mistaken was weeping quietly into a tissue. I moved closer. I was right. She was crying. Suddenly, she broke away from the tour and teetered across the lawn in a pair of her usual high-heeled shoes. I slowed down to avoid overtaking her.

I had a choice. Follow Mrs. Gimbel down Washington Street or locate the entrance to the gift shop. It didn't take me long to reach a decision. I fell into step behind Marvella Gimbel. I didn't want the tour members to think, make that know, what a philistine I was. There was no way to get to the gift shop without passing them.

Following Mrs. Gimbel on foot was a lot like following Mr. Gimbel in a car. Not overtaking required hard work. We'd gone only two blocks when a green minivan with the old blue Jersey plates tore around a corner and sped down the street. Just as he passed Mrs. Gimbel, the driver slammed on the brakes and skidded to a stop— directly next to me. My eyes met Wallace Gimbel's only briefly before he threw the van into reverse. He skidded to a stop next to his wife, threw open the door and snarled a command which she obeyed. She climbed into the passenger seat. The door fell closed as Gimbel lurched into drive. I pretended not to notice as the van passed me but I felt Gimbel's eyes bore into me.

Nothing suspicious about walking down the street, was there? Even as I vowed to keep away from the Gimbels, I knew I wouldn't. I needed a little excitement in my life. Oh, no. What had my life come to? I thought following a middle-aged couple around Cape May was high adventure?

I turned toward the beach. I waddled down Beach Avenue to the Promenade. Despite my extra clothing, the air was a painfully cold— even colder because of an invasion of gray clouds. Out beyond the clouds, shafts of sunlight stretched to the sea, but there was no sun to warm me as I took a sentimental walk down the Promenade.

Aside from hiding the fact that I wasn't a Turner, my main job at the Turner family reunion was organizing skeeball tournaments in the arcades on the promenade—although the Turners called the macadam strip the Boardwalk despite its obvious lack of wooden boards. After two decades, I still hadn't converted all the Turners to skeeball, but I was making great strides—especially with the youngest generation that remained too unsophisticated to differentiate between the joys of an old mechanical game and the thrill of an electronic playstation.

As I passed the arcade that had been closed the night before and, I feared, for the season, my mood lifted. Skeeball! The arcade was open. Of course, a sign in the window had advertised the same center was open every day but I'd figured if the proprietors were ever going to make an exception that would be the day. When I'd asked other shop owners if they were open all year. "Yes, we are," they would boast. I learned to ask. "Even in January?" They'd looked at me with wide eyes. "Well no, not in January." But apparently the proprietor of the arcade meant what he blockprinted on his sign. I vowed to finish my walk before visiting the arcade—and maybe the fudge shop next door.

I took an isolated walk south on the promenade and made two brief stops. The first was outside convention hall (to recall the envy and inadequacy I felt watching ballroom dancers cover the floor with a grace and ease I could never equal). The second stop was even shorter: a brief rest in the gazebo at the south end of the Boardwalk. I trudged across the beach to start the return trek along the water's edge. My gait was slowed by soft sand and head winds. How had I forgotten the wind when taking such a lengthy stroll with the gusts at my back? I plunged my gloved hands into my pockets and bent forward into the relentless bluster. My eyes burned from flying sand and watered from the harsh wind—even with my sunglasses in place.

Beach tags weren't an issue in the winter, although George had offered me one before my walk. He just wanted the opportunity to lament that the beach tags he had purchased for the last years of the twentieth century weren't good for the entire twenty-first century. I didn't mention that we weren't going to be good for the entire twenty-first century either.

The surf, although not particularly high, was dense. Waves broke as far as a hundred yards from shore. The noise of crashing surf, combined with a howling wind, made the day seem even colder. In the freezing air, I found it hard to believe that the wooden frames had ever been stocked with beach chairs and umbrellas and that the sand had been packed with customers who wanted to use them. That day no one else ventured outside without the excuse of a dog. Since no one was violating the dog ban on the beach, I was alone.

As I squinted into the wind, I saw a familiar figure. I'd kept a close enough eye on Wallace Gimbel that I would have recognized the rotund form anywhere. The man was lurking at the north end of the row of arcades. I recognized the topcoat and the fedora and ever-present camera. Periodically, he pointed the camera across the beach. Mr. Gimbel must have seen something in his viewfinder that I didn't. I saw flat sand and low surf—and an occasional flock of birds.

The birds appeared impervious to the weather. None of the flocks I passed along the water's edge gave any indication of noticing the cold—or me. They did not appear to mind my intrusion. They all faced in one direction—at attention—as if facing a ornithological Mecca somewhere to the northwest. What would happen if the birds turned around? For one thing, the wind would wreak havoc with their feathers. For another, they would have faced Mr. Gimbel's camera. What lenses and filters could he possibly have to make his shots worthwhile? I hoped I would never find myself invited to view Wallace Gimbel's vacation slides. Unlikely, I supposed.

When I glanced over my shoulder, I saw that I was being tailed. Sand swirling just above the beach's surface resembled an angel of death. I shivered but not from the cold. As I turned back, I checked. Gimbel hadn't moved. He alternated between staring at the sea through his sunglasses or through his viewfinder. I hoped for the sake of the friends and neighbors who would view these photos that he had a powerful zoom lens.

As I plunged ahead, I was struck by one thought. Earmuffs were a great invention. I wished I owned a pair. My wool hat kept rolling to the top of my skull. I regretted leaving the warmth of the Parsonage.

When I saw them ahead of me, I realized one of Claude's theories was shot. The sun might not have been extremely bright at the moment but the glare was certainly strong enough to zap vampires. The Cummings were alive and on the beach in daylight. Wrapped in their customary black, they were talking to a similarly attired woman. The three stared at the Parsonage. Whatever the conversation concerned, it was short—the length probably dictated by the weather. The woman trudged northward on the beach.

It wasn't unusual for New Yorkers to run into friends in Cape May at any time of year. I'd resented *my* New York friends' discovery of Cape May. As a native Philadelphian, a group that most likely annoyed New Jersey natives with possessiveness toward South Jersey, I claimed the southern part of the state. The New Yorkers could have the north. When my friends in the city started slipping away for weekends in Cape May, I was jealous. Why? Possibly because given its reputation as romantic retreat I had limited opportunity to focus on the town. This weekend, however, I was discovering that Cape May wasn't just for lovers, although as cold as it was, an extra body to cuddle with wouldn't have done any harm.

I would have stopped for a chat with the Cummings but, alone again, the couple, possibly understanding some detail of vampire's capability to withstand the rays of the sun, settled onto the cold sand. Their interaction appeared too intimate to interrupt. I headed for town.

As I tramped across the beach I saw waving arms. They were Hank's. He gestured for me to move faster. With the sand slipping from under my feet I couldn't add any speed to my gait.

"Okay, Okay." I called out but I knew he couldn't hear me above the wind.

As I approached, a shaft of sunlight broke through the clouds and bathed Hank in a sea of light. He smiled. I swear I saw his teeth glimmer. Hank extended a hand in my direction. Few women would have resisted. Hank pulled me close, wrapped his arm around my waist and spoke close to my ear. "It's our guy. He called. Would you like to meet the handsome young man in the blue Honda?"

Of course I would—after I stripped off a few layers of clothing.

Chapter Twenty-One

I was willing to bet that Guy Fleischman was the incredibly handsome man slouched over the far side of the Ugly Mug's bar. "What do you think?" I asked Hank. "A stallion?" I mimicked Jack Beaumont's assessment.

"He said he was five-nine with black curly hair and green eyes."

All we could verify at this distance was that the sitting man had black hair I wouldn't have called curly. What would I call the black mop? Wavy—but more significantly greasy. I assumed—I hoped—that Guy cultivated the wet look.

"He's the only man with black hair I see in here." Hank started around the bar. I followed.

As we approached, the man glanced up and waved us over. His gesture didn't seem to please the blonde and the redhead hovering near his barstool—two attractive women whose flirtations were apparently unnoticed by Guy Fleischman. With Hank and me in the picture, the two women turned their eyes to the football game that held the attention of most of the bar's patrons. I had the feeling they weren't really sports fans, and that a balding blond fellow across the bar was about to get lucky.

We took adjoining stools with me seated between Hank and Guy. I couldn't help noticing that Hank and I were joined at the hip, shoulder, knee and ankles. I glanced at Hank. If the intimate gesture meant anything to him other than a way to move closer to Guy, he didn't let on.

With short stubby fingers that belonged with another body, Guy was cuddling what appeared to be a double scotch. His hands might have been small, but from his handshake I knew they were strong. As he reached across me to shake Hank's hand, I sniffed. Guy might have looked good, but he sure didn't smell good. I studied his clothing. The black pants and white shirt emitted an odor that any outfit might—if a waiter had already worn the clothes to work and to bed for two or three nights. I hoped he planned on changing before tonight's shift or his tips weren't going to cover the cost of gas money.

After introductions, Guy's first action was to apologize. "I didn't mean to scare you today. I didn't understand what was going on with Celia. Teddy phoned me and let me know you were asking questions."

I flashed a weak smile at Hank that asked, "What were the odds...?"

"We had no way of knowing..." Hank let that thought trail off. "If you were so concerned about Celia, why didn't you come to the Parsonage?"

"If she was there and...I mean if she...I didn't want to interfere. I just wanted to make sure she was okay."

"Why are you worried?"

"Gimbel took Celia out to dinner. She was supposed to be at work Friday night. I couldn't imagine why she didn't come back."

"What time did you expect her?"

"After the first show. Another girl does four shows a week."

"Did she tell you she was going to the Parsonage?" I calculated that Gimbel had plenty of time to take Celia to dinner anywhere and return in time to pick up his wife for the trip to the B&B.

"I used the redial button in Gimbel's office."

I wanted to ask how a waiter got into the general manager's office to use the redial button, but Hank appeared more interested in Guy's concerns about Gimbel.

"Have you reported her missing?"

Guy downed half his drink before he answered. "You're not allowed to until the person's been AWOL a couple of days. You know that. Plus, I don't think Celia would like my calling the cops. I mean, Gimbel is her boss. I don't have any real proof. We didn't exactly trust Gimbel. It took him a week to talk Celia into meeting him for dinner. She finally agreed to Friday night. She was supposed to call me on Friday but she never did. When she was late, I got worried. I took an order to Gimbel's office, checked his redial, and got the Parsonage. I knew Celia wouldn't be registered under her own name so I described her. The owner said no one of that description was there." The guy's hands shook so badly, he had trouble lighting a cigarette.

"Why didn't you ask for Gimbel?" Hank's question made sense to me.

Guy had trouble answering. "I didn't want to blow…I wasn't supposed to know…even Celia didn't know." He shook his head and downed the second half of his drink.

Well, that cleared that up. Whatever his reason, he wasn't going to share his motives with us.

Guy returned to his lament. "Celia just got bumped up from the chorus. She worked hard for that promotion. She wouldn't blow it. I'm not saying her relationship with Gimbel didn't help but believe me, she was qualified. Celia is talented…and she was due. That weasel Tom Russo—he's the entertainment manager—he never liked her because she wouldn't put out for him. Celia told me. She needed Gimbel to get what she deserved. That was the only reason she let him…you know. I gotta go to the can." He appended the last sentence so quickly that he was gone before I realized he'd finished talking.

Hank turned on his stool to watch Guy as he made his way around the bar to the men's room. He never took his eyes off the door while Guy remained inside.

"Hank, there's got to be more to this story."

"You know, Meg, I'm beginning to think you're not as flaky as I thought."

"Thank you." I could think of no other response to his comment. "You've been humoring me all day?"

"Pretty much."

I had to give the guy credit for honesty.

"Let me take it from here." Hank squeezed my arm. He asked the bartender to refill Guy's glass and had the drink ready when Guy reappeared—wiping his nose on his sleeve.

Hank gave Guy a reassuring pat on the back as he returned to his barstool. "Look, Guy, if what you're worried about is whether or not she left you for Gimbel, trust us. She isn't with him."

"No. I'm not worried about that...well maybe a little...I was...but no, not really." He downed the refill.

"What I don't understand..." Hank shook his head and plastered a confused expression on his face. "I don't understand why you think Gimbel would hurt her."

Guy's face displayed a combination of surprise, panic, and fear. Even I could see that with my untrained eyes. I wondered what Hank saw.

"It's missing that performance—that's what worries me. Maybe she'll show tonight."

"Look, do me a favor." Hank wrote a number on a cocktail napkin. "Give me a call. To let me know if she gets back. Either way. Call."

"What do you guys want with Celia anyway?" Guy knew to target the weakest link. His eyes turned to me.

"I...I...Hank, why don't you explain."

Hank did—without hesitation. "Did you realize that Celia had an aunt with a small fortune?" His eyes twinkled.

"No."

"Well, I don't think she realized it either. My guess is she didn't know she had an aunt. I can't say too much. Although isn't it a bizarre coincidence that my old friend Meg would be staying where you expect to find her. That amazes me."

"Yeah." Guy was so busy thinking about the fortune that the implausibility of Hank's explanation didn't occur to him. Possibly because Guy was really stupid. Possibly because Hank was an awesome liar.

"So you'll call me when Celia returns?"

"Oh yes. I'll keep in touch." The dollar signs rolled in his eyes like sevens on a slot machine.

"And we'll have Celia call you if she happens to visit the Parsonage." Hank cleared his throat. "You know, Guy, if you think there is any chance that Celia knew she wouldn't be back...if you believe she might have run off...you should check her things."

"No. I was being...well maybe...she might not have had time to let me know." With a mumbled thanks, Guy shook both our hands and headed home to wait for any word from his heiress girlfriend.

Hank leaned closer—which was almost impossible. His arms and legs pressed hard against mine. "There's more to this. I'm not saying that your murder scenario is true, but I am convinced that Guy is not being straight with us."

Chapter Twenty-Two

"Well, what do we do now?" I turned on my barstool to face Hank. He caught my knee between his. I didn't fight to free myself—nor did I make any positive response.

"You realize that this isn't a full-time job. No one is paying us to investigate this."

"Oh, come on. You're having a good time."

"I didn't say I wasn't. I enjoy a caper as much as the next guy." His tone suggested the next guy didn't enjoy capers that much.

"It's fun."

"For you maybe. I do this for a living. You should have some other varieties of play when you're here. Let's do some sightseeing."

The word sightseeing might have thrown panic into my heart but I knew that I'd visited Cape May during the brief period that the lighthouse closed for an abbreviated winter season. Climbing to the top of the lighthouse involved at least five times the steps as the climb to my New York apartment. I seldom arrived at my own front door without looking flushed and sweaty. At the top of the lighthouse? My appearance was something I didn't want to see and I certainly didn't want Hank to see. But Hank wasn't interested in physical activity.

"Do you know that Sunset Beach is the rare place on the East Coast where you can watch the sun set over water?"

"I guess I do now."

"Have you been there before?"

I nodded. I didn't explain that I had watched the sun set from the front seat of my old flame's car while he talked to his office. "It's a convertible, for God's sake, Meg. The sun is big enough. I can see it from here." The sun, yes, but not the wild life. He would not climb out of the car to watch the dolphins frolicking fifty yards offshore. "I've seen fish before." I didn't bother telling him dolphins were mammals.

"Do you want to go again?" Hank's words called me back to the present.

"I've never been there in winter. The sunset might look different than in summer."

First difference: in January, the competition for the best parking space wasn't as stiff. Hank pulled the Porsche into one of the best spaces—a slot that faced the beach and the western horizon directly. "Good, we can watch from here."

"Don't you feel the need to experience the sunset fully?"

My friend Mary and I made a religion of chasing sunsets. Wherever we were, we'd rush out of business meetings to a spot that offered a view of the sun sinking over the ocean, the mountains, the desert—or even a skyscraper or two if that's what the local geography offered. We, however, were not adverse to watching those sunsets through windows. Apparently, Hank was.

"It's a visual experience. I can enjoy the sunset from here." I patted the leather seat.

"Don't you want to feel the change in the air?"

I shrugged. "Not really." The air was only going to get colder.

"You're being a weenie, Ms. Daniels."

Oh no. Was I sounding like David? Of course—but with an explanation. The month was January—not August. I had a good reason for staying in the car. Sixty of them. All points that were not registering on the thermometer.

"We could sit on the porch of the Sunset Beach Grill." He pointed to a building that had been abandoned since the fall.

"I like that place—when it's open."

"You're being snide again." Hank pulled a blanket and a comforter from behind my seat. "Come on. Button up. It's gonna be cold out there."

I retrieved a few layer of clothes that I'd dropped on the floor of Hank's car before making my appearance at the Ugly Mug. I struggled into them and dutifully followed the cop through the coarse sand. He selected a position close to the concrete ship, the *Atlantis*— a vessel built during the steel shortage of World War I that has been slowly sinking off Sunset Beach for years. Hank shook the blanket open then folded it in half and laid the woolen square on the cold, damp surface. "Sit." He faced me but nodded at the blanket.

I glanced around. "Did you bring your dog with you?"

"Ms. Daniels." An unctuous intonation was designed to mock not placate me. "Would you care to have a seat?"

"Thanks." My answer was chipper. I lowered myself into a cross-legged position in my assigned spot at the center of the blanket. Hank sat behind me and wrapped his legs around mine. He wrapped the comforter around the two of us and tucked the corners of the comforter into my lap. I marveled at the nonchalance with which he secured the blanket in spots not many strange hands had touched. Surely, a serious come on lay in my future.

I didn't have much else going on. Okay, I didn't have anything else going on. Nonetheless, I couldn't muster a lot of interest. I hated to admit it but my heart still longed for Andy Beck. I was depressingly monogamous; I was being faithful to a man I wasn't even dating. I vowed to work up an interest in Hank. He was handsome. He had a great smile. He was handsome when he smiled. I searched for other sources of attraction and came up empty. Well, nothing wrong with good-looking, is there?

Wasn't cuddling with Hank romantic? No. Obviously, too obviously, he was not executing those moves for the first time. Or the tenth time. I put my money on somewhere around the hundredth time. And, he'd done so fairly recently. I sniffed the blanket. Eternity by Calvin Klein. I was sure. Maybe he'd gotten lucky with the last visitor. I myself preferred a slightly less polished romantic technique, but who knew? Maybe I'd change my mind. Maybe Hank would change my mind.

Hank squeezed me to indicate we were all settled. "Isn't this cozy?"

"Absolutely toasty." I leaned back to take advantage of what heat his body offered. And, I was sure that was what I was cuddling for: the heat. It wasn't that Hank wasn't nice. He was…pleasant.

With a wait-and-see attitude, I reclined against Hank's chest. He ran his hands through the sand. "Maybe I can find a diamond for you. I bet you don't know about Cape May diamonds."

I didn't tell him I did. I let him explain. The story kept the conversation moving.

When he'd finished his lecture on the best place to find the diamonds (in the low waves near the cement ship), the most effective process to polish the diamonds (tumble the quartz stone for at least a week), and the nicest way to use them (his grandmother's engagement ring was a Cape May diamond), I told him not to worry if he couldn't dig one up for me. The gift shop had a wide selection of rings, earrings, and pins. I assured him I'd be happy to accept store-bought. He appeared less happy to buy than to uncover in the sand. He wrapped his arms around my waist. I knew he was getting a better feel than that. He didn't have to snuggle his arms under two of my layers. But then again, maybe he, like me, was only cuddling for the heat. I waited for his next move. And waited. Maybe he was waiting for dark. The sun was sinking at a snail's pace.

"What time is sunset tonight anyway?" I noted an inappropriate impatience in my words.

"Soon." He tightened his grip. "Don't tell me you're cold."

Comparatively speaking, I wasn't. There wasn't much wind, just a light breeze. Okay, a light breeze that froze my cheeks. The gentle lapping of the waves lulled me into a feeling of comfort. I tried to remember other, warmer sunsets.

Although most sunset-seekers were content to watch from the warmth of their vehicles, Hank and I were not alone on the beach. What lured the other intrepid souls out to watch the sun set over the Delaware Bay? Who they were, I had no idea. Those who passed in front of us were simply silhouettes against the orange sky. When I turned to check out those behind us, their faces were obscured by large spots as my eye retained the image of the sun.

The path of orange across the water began to grow weaker and weaker—the only sign that the sun was sinking. Five minutes passed before I detected action on the part of the sun. The huge orange globe threatened to land on a tanker navigating the bay. The tanker moved in the nick of time.

Hank's strong arms squeezed me. "You okay up there?"

"Yep. Just enjoying the sunset. Really. I am."

Suddenly, a wave slapped the jetty hard as if the bay were crying out for a share of the attention. A lithe young woman dressed all in black leapt agilely out of its spray. Her dance was silhouetted against the sky as a series of small explosions of light decorated the horizon.

"What do you think? A seven on a scale of ten." Hank's lips touched my ear as he asked. I assumed he meant the sunset—but maybe he was rating the woman.

"Oh, let's give this sunset an eight. That nice little fireworks display at the end moved it up a few points." As I turned my head to speak, my hair brushed Hank's cheek.

He brushed the strands aside gently—and with a smile. Then he slapped his hands on my shoulders. "It's gonna get cold as hell here in a few minutes. We don't have to stay until the bitter end." With that Hank leapt to his feet and pulled the comforter from around me. The rush of cold air propelled me to a standing position.

"Jump." Hank commanded and I did—off the blanket which he folded systematically as he walked towards the car. I trudged through the sand behind him, glancing up only when I heard his greeting to a figure that camera in hand advanced awkwardly across the sand. "Wallace Gimbel. Hank Bergman here. You're a little late for the sunset."

Mr. Gimbel raised his hand to shield his eyes. He squinted to verify our identities. "Oh, yes. From the B&B. Wife decided at the last minute she didn't want to come." He glanced towards the water's edge. "I can still get a couple shots off. Excuse me." He held the camera to his eye. "Yep. There's still time."

I remained planted in one position watching Wallace Gimbel as he hurried, in the fashion of a totally out-of-shape man of middle age, across the beach.

"For a couple on a romantic getaway, the Gimbels sure spend a lot of time apart."

"You've never been married, Meg. When you are, reconsider that comment."

I smiled and checked over my shoulder. Based on his awkward movements, even I had to admit Wallace Gimbel made an unlikely murderer.

Chapter Twenty-Three

It wasn't like I invited Hank to visit the arcade with me. As far as I was concerned he could take his incredible face and form elsewhere. Instead, he stood by complaining.

Hank leaned close to make himself heard over the clamor of the arcade machines. In the days of electronic games, the sounds competed with the cacophony of the Atlantic City casinos. Not that skeeball was a silent pastime—but its wooden components had an old-fashioned charm. At least I thought so.

Hank saw skeeball differently. "What thrill do you get throwing an old wooden ball down an alley into a hole."

"Not into just any hole. This is a game of skill, you understand. I'm trying for the hole marked 50."

"Wouldn't know it by watching."

I might have been starved for love, but Hank wasn't offering any romantic nutrition. I was missing Andy Beck. Andy never questioned my love of skeeball. Andy accepted my devotion to the sportish activity. Andy played skeeball with me. Yep, Andy was perfect. Or at least he seemed that way as long as he remained fifteen hundred miles away. I was seeing Hank, not even fifteen feet away, a little too clearly.

And hearing him a little too clearly. "Why are you doing this?" Hank was persistent.

"Because I like it."

"Why?"

"I saw a great rubber snake over there that has my name on it. I just need 10,000 points to make it mine."

"How many do you have now?"

"Let me put it this way. If you want to be here for the prize presentation, you might want to have a seat."

"My wife loved skeeball too." These words didn't come from Hank's mouth. They came from the mouth of a man notable not for his mouth but for his eyes. They were brown and sad. And big. Big, brown eyes coated with tears. I liked skeeball but it had never moved me to tears.

"Is your wife here with you?" I asked although I knew it was unlikely he'd be standing here weeping if she were.

"In a way, yes." He rocked on his heels a few times. "Are you staying near here?"

"Not too close." Hank answered for me. I recognized the alarm in his voice.

"Nice place?"

"Nice enough." Hank's behavior could be termed downright proprietary. He moved closer.

"Are the people friendly? Do they talk to you?"

Hank took my arm. "We really have to get going, dear." Happy for an excuse to drag me away from skeeball, he pulled me towards the door.

"I have three balls left." I protested.

"Forget them."

"I left tickets at the alley."

"Forget them."

"What about my rubber snake?" I broke free of Hank's grasp but not for long.

He grabbed my arm. "I'll get you a real one."

We had made our way through the blinking lights and ringing bells and were out the door before I had my coat on. My protests escalated.

Hank held my coat open and I slid my arms in; I was already shivering.

"Listen to me. I'm a cop. That guy had an agenda. Better to get away from him—fast."

I guess my face showed my annoyance at being dragged away, because Hank quickly said, "Look, I'll put on a sportjacket and take you to dinner." His words sounded a bit as if he were fulfilling an obligation. Hank was really beginning to annoy me.

I didn't respond to his invitation. I could tell that my hesitation surprised him. This was a man who did not expect rejection. After allowing a brief frown to cross his face, he flashed one of those wide smiles. It wasn't the smile that swayed me. Okay, it was the smile. But not because Hank was succeeding in wooing me. He was manipulating me in a slightly different way. Knowing raw sex appeal wasn't going to cut it, he added a touch of pathos. After considering my other options— none—I agreed to accompany him to one of the few restaurants open in January.

◆ ◆ ◆

Back in my room, I searched for an outfit. I wasn't as interested in style as in warmth—but I did want to avoid the day's heavily padded look. I dug through my duffel bag and came up empty-handed. I stood with my hands on hips in the center of the room. There it was again. Noise. More unwanted clamor from the Gimbels' room.

Like the night before, the sound was moaning. But unlike the night before, the only passion involved was sadness. I didn't care what Hank said. Mrs. Gimbel was not enjoying a weekend on her own. Could I be of help? Okay, that's what I wanted Mrs. Gimbel to think. My actual motive? I was wondering what information an emotional woman might let slip.

I ventured down the hallway hoping that Marvella Gimbel's sobbing could be heard through the door. That's what I wanted the crying woman to believe. It might be dangerous—for me—if the Gimbels realized how easily sound carried into the bridal suite. As I came to the entrance to the Gimbels' room, I was happy to hear that the sound could be heard—if one passed an ear within inches of the door.

I took a deep breath and knocked. My tap was tentative but the woman had to have noticed—unless her tears drowned out the knock. I tried again with a firmer hand. The sobs quieted. I waited for the sound of footsteps to the door. I heard nothing but muffled sobs. I decided to give it one more try. "Everything okay in there?" I called without identifying myself. Again, no answer.

I felt relief rather than disappointment. Maybe letting the Gimbels know of my interest in their problems wasn't wise. I scurried back to my room and closed the door quickly.

I put on thermal leggings and a chenille sweater with a outdated collar that provided a lot of warmth. I didn't look stylish, but at least I no longer resembled the Michelin tire man. And, I consoled myself, I *knew* I was dressed badly. To my mind, that's what separated me from the other guests at the B&B.

Cape May is home to many small, charming restaurants—most of which close for the winter. Each restaurant in Cape May appeared to define winter differently—but no matter what their definition of the season each included the weekend I visited the town. The exception was the restaurant that sat atop the Marquis de Lafayette hotel.

I'd never visited the dining room before. David had a favorite restaurant in Cape May and, variety not being a big thing with my ex, we ate there on every visit. Every visit that is until the owners, much to David's dismay, decided to move to warmer climes. Luckily, David exited my life about the same time the couple exited Cape May. I only had to listen to him complain briefly—and then he was packing for his new life.

Okay, there was one point in Hank's favor: he hadn't complained about picking a restaurant. Not that the job was a tough one. As I said, not much was open.

Hank parked his Porsche across the street from the purple and white building. Arm in arm we ran across the street through the lobby and into the elevator. We moved so quickly that I barely noticed that cold. We didn't stop running until we hit the restaurant's bar.

Dinner was uneventful except for meetings with the other Parsonage guests. Mandy Blandings, in a heather-green wool skirt and sweater ensemble from the late sixties, greeted us effusively as we entered the restaurant. Actually, she greeted Hank effusively. She made continuous eye contact with my kind-of-a-date while I labored to make small talk with her husband. What really amazed me was Hank's reaction. As we walked to our table he wrapped an arm around my shoulder, but his eyes remained glued to the table Mandy shared with her husband. I felt like his Seeing Eye dog.

During the meal Hank remained attentive, although I did wonder what he was watching when he glanced at the small mirror behind my seat. If his eyes roamed, so did his legs, arms and hands. The only difference was his limbs had to stay at our table. He pushed his knee to meet mine. He extended his arm to brush mine. He offered his hand to squeeze mine. All the while keeping an eye on the Blandings. Or rather, I suspected, on Mandy Blandings.

I didn't get the attraction. The features on the woman's tiny face were too pointy. Her bland coloring cried out for makeup but, like me, the happy wife apparently didn't have time to apply any—except for brash red lipstick constantly smeared by her husband's attentions. Her hairstyle and glass frames were left over from high school days—her mother's. And *where* did she buy her clothes? I grew so preoccupied with the mysteries of Mandy Blandings' charms that I barely made intelligent conversation until the couple left the restaurant—passing Neil and Lulu Cummings on their way in.

Neil stopped by our table to say hello. Lulu stopped by to stare. I made introductions but apparently Hank had met the couple on earlier visits. Neil greeted Hank politely but, I perceived, a bit nervously. The twosome couldn't seem to get away from us fast enough. I watched in the mirror as they refused the table the maitre d' offered. I didn't know if they felt the need to be closer to the kitchen, or just farther away from us.

Hank watched too, but I didn't believe he was as interested in the couple's selection of a table as he was in Lulu's selection of clothing. She wore a black dress of a material more likely to be found in a hardware store than a fabric shop. Cost would not have been a consideration, since so little was required to make the dress. Two strips of black vinyl hung from her shoulders to the top of her thighs, accented with clear vinyl portholes. Apparently, word of the cold spell hadn't reached her.

"Can you imagine how that fabric holds the cold?" I caught Hank's attention but not his gaze.

"She's wearing boots," was his defense. I dropped the subject.

The Gimbels were at the bar while Hank and I were on dessert. "George must give all the guests the same recommendation," Hank mumbled when he spotted the couple in the mirror. No question the man was a cop. Nothing escaped his attention—not even the activity reflected in the narrow mirror.

Mrs. Gimbel teetered on emerald green high heels that matched yet another cocktail dress from her collection—although the cut of this evening's ensemble suggested it had been purchased within the last decade. Nonetheless, Mr. Gimbel seemed no more pleased by the outfit than any other his wife appeared in. His face displayed its usual scowl.

"I'm surprised to see those two together."

Hank smirked. "Well, now that his girlfriend is dead what else does he have to do?"

I glanced quickly around the room to see if anyone had heard. "Don't make light of it. She may really be dead."

"Oh, I'm not making light, Meg. You can take my comment at face value."

Hank proved his point when he pulled into the Parsonage lot. I quickly discovered why he bypassed an empty spot to park next to the Gimbels' minivan.

"You know," he packed a lot of meaning into the two words, "the Gimbels are still at dinner."

"Yeah, I know. I was there."

"And apparently they walked. Their car is here."

My main reaction was to wonder how Marvella Gimbel walked anywhere in those shoes. I didn't raise the issue. I wanted to see where Hank was headed. "Yeah?"

"And the van might be unlocked."

"So, you could search it. Hank, you're a real pal."

"No. I'm not. I can't search it. A civilian, however, might be able to take a look-see."

"A look-see?"

"Sure. To check for anything odd about the interior—rips, tears, blood stains, bodies."

"You're telling me to break into their car."

"I'm a cop. I would never tell you to do a thing like that. I just said that the car is here and might be open."

I eyed the green minivan. "I never did think that the Gimbels were the minivan type."

"No kids. No grandkids." Hank confirmed my thought.

"You'll stand guard?"

"I can't be an accessory. I might happen to be standing nearby. Naturally, I will greet anyone who happens by."

"And I..."

"And you could saunter over and maybe happen on an open door."

"I didn't bring bail money." I hesitated with my hand on the door handle.

"You won't go to jail. Trust me. No one is going to spot you." He commented on my hesitancy, "You started this investigation. Now that it appears there might actually be something to investigate, you're going to chicken out."

"Chicken out" did it. I pushed the door open and climbed out of the Porsche.

Immediately, a dog's barking propelled me back inside.

"What?" Hank sounded impatient.

"There's a dog out there. It's that Doogie dog. As soon as I got out of the car, he started barking."

"He's in the parking lot?"

I didn't have any idea where the dog lived. "I can just hear it."

"I don't think he's going to tell the Gimbels." He gave me a playful push. "Go ahead."

When I opened the door, the dog's barking began anew. I remember George's example. "Shut up," I yelled and Doogie did. I waited for the clamor to resume but either the dog had lost interest or his master had summoned him inside. After verifying that the parking lot was empty and that no one was watching from the Parsonage, I tried the van's driver's door. It wouldn't budge. "Locked tight." I was halfway into the passenger seat next to Hank when his hand stopped me.

"The other doors open with a key. Maybe Gimbel opened one and forgot to lock it. You could check." He pushed me back into the night air. "Oh, and Meg, remember that internal lights can be turned off either on the roof or on the dashboard. Just a helpful hint." Hank wasn't finished. "Another piece of information you might find useful: I dropped a key ring with a tiny flashlight on it. You might check around for it somewhere—like on the seat you recently vacated. Of course, you would not want to take your gloves off to do so."

I picked up the key ring that harbored one key and a tiny flashlight. I squeezed. An eerie red glow lit my the palms of my gloves. "This light won't be much help."

Hank shrugged.

I slammed the Porsche door behind me and the noise sent my heart into my throat. Maybe I wasn't such a natural at this investigating thing after all.

Casting nervous glances in every direction, I tried the back door of the minivan. Like the driver's door, the hatch was locked. I glanced to my left. Hank was out of his car and watching. "Try the slider." He leaned against the side of his sportscar.

As I moved across the gravel, the crunching sound reverberated in the night. Loudly enough to interrupt the Blandings? Nah, a nuclear blast couldn't interrupt the Blandings.

I twisted the handle. To my delight, and dismay, the door moved. "It's open." I called to Hank in a stage whisper.

"So…?"

"I'm going. I'm going." I slid the door and froze—not from the cold. "Did you hear that?" I called to Hank.

"People in North Wildwood heard, so you'd better move fast." Hank spoke normally—in volume and manner. He didn't appear concerned we would get caught. Of course not. We wouldn't get caught; I would get caught.

I climbed onto the back seat of the minivan. The temperature of the air trapped inside the van made the air outside seem tropical. I had no idea what to do next. Hank had said to search for something odd—something out of place. "No light." I whispered to myself. The news made me skeptical but happy. Shouldn't a light come on when the van door opens? What did the Gimbels need to hide?

I knelt on the floor and shone the little red light over, around and under the bucket seats in front. Nothing had been left in the car. No maps. No glasses. No half-eaten meals from McDonalds. I checked on and around the seats and in the side panel pouches. To me, that degree of neatness appeared suspicious.

I found the glove compartment and immediately understood. The van was a rental. I held the agreement up to what little light came through the windshield and shone the red light on the paper. The car was rented on Friday night using the VISA card of Wallace T. Gimbel. Nothing suspicious about the transaction. But why rent? Why a van? Why not take out an ad that said, "I need to move a body."

"Meg. Move it." Hank's words interrupted my contemplation. I assumed his hand closed the side door.

I climbed into the very back. Wasn't the car supposed to have a third seat? I crawled across the carpet moving the small light from right to left checking for spots and stains. "Ouch." I screamed as my knee slid into the opening designed to hold the legs of the back seat. I froze. No one, even Hank, appeared to hear me. I had just resumed my search when I heard him.

"Mr. Gimbel—you certainly finished dinner quickly," Hank said loudly. I lay flat on my stomach.

Wallace Gimbel grumbled a response that had something to do with Marvella's losing her appetite. Mr. Gimbel appeared to be running out of sympathy for what he called her "relapses."

Apparently Gimbel asked Hank what he was doing because I heard him say, "Waiting for Meg. We're going to go for a walk."

"Well, I've got to get going. Nice talking to you." Gimbel's gruff tone suggested that chatting with Hank was anything but nice.

I heard the crunching of feet on gravel and then a door opening. It was the front door of the minivan. I rolled as close as I could to the back seat and buried my face in the rug, adhering to the "if I can't see them, they can't see me" rule.

Hank resorted to ridiculous chatting—but at least he conducted the conversation calmly. Gimbel, however, made it clear he had no interest in Hank's pointless discourse. He made his point first by turning on the ignition, then by putting the van in gear, and finally by slamming the door in Hank's face—which is what I wanted a gander at as Gimbel backed the vehicle out of its spot. I did not, however, attempt a peek. I clamped my eyes shut and focused on clinging to the back seat.

Luckily for me Gimbel was an overly cautious driver. When he brought the car to a halt, he did so slowly. I didn't have to worry about rolling back and forth on the rug. The sound of his blinker gave me plenty of notice before turns so I could tighten my grip. I felt confident that I could avoid making a clamor. I hoped Gimbel would turn on the radio but even if he didn't I would be safe—as long as he didn't check the back of the van.

Just in case Wallace Gimbel did discover me, I formulated an excuse. Okay, any explanation was going to sound dumb—there was no good reason for hiding in the back of a stranger's minivan. The best I came up with was that I'd hopped in the van to play a trick on Hank. Then, I'd fallen asleep. Dumb? Yes. Believable? Not really— but I could always throw in a few lewd overtones. Gimbel seemed to be the type to fall for that approach.`

If my intellect remained calm, my stomach didn't. I could say my nausea was the effect of rolling around in the back of the van. The truth, however, was I didn't do much rolling. Our route was fairly straightforward. We'd made a left, two rights, another turn at an angle I couldn't figure out, and a final left and ended up on a long, flat, straight stretch of road. I didn't know where we were headed but I did know it was too far to walk back.

Wallace Gimbel mumbled as he drove. What did he say? I had no idea. I picked up only isolated words. "Bitch," predominantly. Mr. Gimbel demonstrated some standard displays of anger. He slammed his palms on the steering wheel. He punched the radio buttons. He hammered the passenger seat. Never, however, did he allow his anger to influence his driving.

My false complacency was shattered when Mr. Gimbel made a wide U turn. Slowly and inexorably the weight of my body pulled me from my position beside the seat. My grip was barely strong enough to hold me. My feet swung towards the back door. Their weight turned me from my hiding place. I didn't attempt to move back to a position parallel with the back seat and its shadows. A method actor to the end, I kept my eyes closed and feigned sleep as Gimbel continued to wherever it was we were headed.

It was no more than ten minutes after we'd left the parking lot when Gimbel brought the car to a cautious stop. I heard him grumbling in the front seat. Though my eyes were closed, I could tell when he turned on the overhead light. I clenched my eyes even more tightly and stuck with my sleeping act. My breathing became so labored, I just knew he could hear it. Maybe Gimbel would have noticed the sound had it not been for what I recognized as his attention to a cell phone. I heard the unmistakable pitch of dialing. Whomever he called apparently didn't answer.

"Damn!" Gimbel threw open the front door. I heard his footsteps on a flat surface. He was pacing back and forth beside the van. Back and forth. Back and forth.

Why didn't he spot me? Or did he see me? With my eyes held tightly shut, I didn't know.

Suddenly, Gimbel released a rash of expletives. I heard the driver's door slam. I wasn't sure if the driver was inside or outside the van. The door opened again. I heard a click and sensed the light go out before the door banged shut. Pushed or pulled? I listened. Aside from my hammering heart, there was no sign of life inside the minivan. Outside I heard footsteps moving away.

I opened my eyes and checked. I was alone in the Gimbels' vehicle—but not for long. I had to get out and fast. I had scurried only halfway to the side door when I heard it. I lay flat on the floor and listened to the whistling ("More Than a Woman," from Saturday Night Fever). The sound grew louder. I heard the snap of the handle and what I recognized as Hank's voice at the same time. His exclamation came too late to stop the action. The side panel slid open. Slowly I raised my eyes. I stared straight into the face of Will Pankenhurst—*aka* Will Parker.

Chapter Twenty-Four

Since I was already inside the van, I was the one put on the defensive.

Pankenhurst, whom I figured was in no position to throw stones, didn't buy my first explanation that I'd fallen asleep while waiting for Hank. He swallowed my second story that my being in the van was all part of an elaborate trick I was trying to play on Hank only because I added lewd overtones to make the claim convincing—at least in Pankenhurst's eyes.

"Will you two stop fighting and get away from that van. Gimbel is headed back this way." Hank gestured from the heavy wooded area lining the route where Wallace Gimbel had parked. We were somewhere in the forest that covered much of South Jersey. That part of the road was lined largely by pine trees. What road? I had no idea. Without explaining his unexpected appearance, Hank took control. Interrupting my whispered bickering with Pankenhurst, Hank shoved the protesting man towards the woods from which he'd just emerged. He jerked me out of the van and dragged me behind him. When the three of us were out of sight of the road, we huddled together. Hank hissed at Pankenhurst. "Where is your car?"

Without protest, Pankenhurst led us to the late model Cadillac. Just my luck. Cape May is full of farmland and forests. Gimbel had to stop in a wooded area filled with pine trees choked by a thicket of pointed leaves and prickly branches. As we picked our way through the rough terrain, those well-armed branches and leaves slapped our faces and poked our bodies. The only sounds were the crunching of branches underfoot, Pankenhurst's heavy breathing, my thumping heart, and the distinctive sound of my parka ripping on a particularly sharp branch. I didn't complain—at least not aloud. Although I wanted to ask where we were, a quick glance at Hank's face warned me not to. I read his expression as anger. Anger? Whose idea was my climbing into the van anyway? I had the impression that this fact had already slipped the cop's mind.

Pankenhurst had parked his car fifty yards behind Gimbel's in a clearing that I suspected had not existed before the Cadillac pulled in. Hank pushed me into the back seat. I didn't comment on his manners or lack thereof. Pankenhurst did as Hank propelled him onto the seat beside me. Nonetheless, when Hank demanded his keys, he turned them over immediately.

Hank drove us to the clearing where he had parked his Porsche. The clearing Hank picked appeared to be an actual opening in the woods. Moving his sports car would not cause the ecological disaster moving Pankenhurst's vehicle had. Hank pulled the keys from the pocket of his bomber jacket and tossed them to me.

"Follow us."

"Hey…she was the one who was in the van. I just heard a noise…"

Hank interrupted Pankenhurst's protest. "Look, all I did was ask her to follow us. If she doesn't, it's grand theft auto. I don't think Ms. Daniels is up for a felony charge."

Hank's assumption was correct. I wasn't. I dutifully followed the Cadillac to a parking space on Carpenter's Lane.

I was becoming a regular at the Ugly Mug although I had been in town for a mere twenty-four hours. We took the corner table that I thought of as mine and ordered beers. I drank mine sheepishly and let Hank assume the lead.

"I don't know what you two are up to," he said, lumping me in with Pankenhurst, "but I think we might benefit from putting our cards on the table and speaking honestly and confidentially. All of this is off the record."

That worked for me—and apparently for Will Pankenhurst.

"Look, I'm hoping to avoid dealing with this matter on an official basis, but before I can decide to overlook this little episode I need to know what's going on. Let me see some ID—both of you."

I offered my driver's license eagerly. Hank smirked before he passed it back to me. "Nice photo."

"Snide." I responded under my breath.

Pankenhurst was clearly not eager to produce ID.

"Got a problem with that, Pankenhurst?" Hank accented the name with irony.

"This is really off the record?" Pankenhurst ran his hand through his thick red hair.

"I've got no interest in pursuing this. As a county official, however, I've got to cover myself. Make sure nothing untoward happens."

Pankenhurst shook his head nervously. "I just happened to be driving by and I heard a noise in the van."

"You were driving by and heard a noise in Gimbel's van?" Incredulous would not adequately describe Hank's tone.

"Of course not." Pankenhurst sputtered. "I...obviously I was walking when I heard the sound."

Obviously? Nothing was obvious except that Pankenhurst was, as my grandmother would have said, full of soup.

"What kind of sound?"

I guessed that Pankenhurst had been busy devising a reason he was walking by the car. He seemed surprised by Hank's question. "What kind of sound?" He repeated the cop's words.

"What did you hear that made you open the van door?"

Pankenhurst leaned forward and wrapped his hands around his mug. "Look, I was keeping an eye on Gimbel all weekend. I'd been waiting for an opportunity to check inside that car. I was searching for information. I was working, actually." His voice became suddenly calm. "I'm not up to anything." He pulled a worn leather wallet from his back pocket and laid it open on the table. I only caught a glance of the Pennsylvania driver's license. "My name is Will Parker. Believe it or not, I'm an accountant."

I believed it. Would anyone mistake the man for a secret agent? Fat chance.

"I wanted to take a peek into the Gimbels' car," he continued, searching Hank's eyes for a reaction. Hank's expression said he wanted more. So, without ever questioning how Hank had happened to find us in the van, Pankenhurst/Parker talked...and talked...and talked. I noted that he shared at least one trait with the woman who loved him.

In more detail than I found interesting, Will explained that he worked for a marketing consulting firm. My ears remained attentive but my eyes kept wandering to the television screen mounted high above the crowd. Football replays. I watched number twelve fake a pass, go right, and cross the goal line at least ten times from four different angles while Pankenhurst/Parker explained that he headed the department that audited the marketing activities at Gimbel's operation. I waited to hear that Gimbel was embezzling, but in the course of his monologue Parker indicated that Gimbel didn't need money as long as he had his wife's. No, he was investigating something more sinister— something for which Gimbel received no monetary reward—something that made Parker's life hell—and threatened the firm's contract.

Over Parker's head number twelve scored yet again. Around the bar, the patrons once again watched attentively and then expressed their delight with the outcome. What did they expect?

"The guy is doing this for pure spite. He's undermining his own business to make our firm look bad. Unless he is on the competition's payroll—which I wouldn't put past him. I wouldn't put anything past the guy."

My eyes remained glued to the screen as if on this replay the quarterback might stumble or fumble. He didn't. His play concluded with the same jubilant dance—not a particularly spirited one. I figured quarterbacks were in no way competitive when it comes to end zone theatrics.

"Someone, I think it's Gimbel, is leaking the statistics to competing casinos," Parker continued. "Say we want to have the winningest slots—we always just miss. We, say, add tables. The competition adds tables. We say add shows. The competition adds shows. We run specials. The competition runs specials. It's like the competition knows. Someone's talking."

"You're sure of this?" Hank took advantage of Gimbel's need to take a breath.

Parker nodded knowingly. "Oh, I know. I know. It's impossible that every year we come so close and then miss. And every year the powers-that-be come to me and give me grief because they don't like the data I give them for marketing purposes. Like, shoot me...I'm only the messenger."

Hank tried to hide the doubt in his voice. "Why would Gimbel do it? It would make him look bad."

Will shrugged. "That is why he is such an obvious choice. It makes no sense."

I agreed with the last statement.

"I suspect he had a plan for moving the marketing services." Will offered.

"When did you start following Gimbel?"

With an involuntary action, I leaned forward in anticipation of Parker's answer.

"I met him for the first time this morning."

I could tell by the look Hank flashed me that I had groaned out loud. Parker didn't seem to notice.

"I lost him on the mall this morning. Later, he went up to Staples to pick something up. I didn't see what it was."

Apparently, he didn't see us following Gimbel either—or if he did, he didn't mention it.

"The next time I saw him leave—alone, that is—was when he drove out to that road."

I noticed Parker omitted his afternoon surveillance in the woods. I wondered what else he had neglected to mention.

"I have no idea if that's where he was really headed or what he's up to. If you hadn't interrupted, I might have seen where he went."

"If I hadn't interrupted," Hank made no attempt to hide his anger, "he would have caught you nosing around his van." Hank might have said our conversation was off the record but he was clearly playing the cop. "While watching Gimbel, have you noted behavior that appears illegal or suspicious?"

"Nothing, so far, but I'm not finished digging. You see, I'd never met Gimbel. I talk to him on the phone but a big muckety-muck like him would never meet a peon like me. So I decided to come here and watch him, get to know him, investigate him a little." As he explained, Parker's southern accent and good-ol'-boy bravado faded.

I checked the television. Hockey had replaced the playoff replays. Apparently the crowd was comprised of football fans. One by one they made their way to the door.

Hank's attention remained riveted on Parker.

"Have you been to the Parsonage before?"

"No, I've never even been to Cape May before."

"When did you make your reservation?"

"On Monday."

"How did you know he'd be here?"

Parker stuttered. "He might have mentioned his plans on the phone."

"Parker, tell me exactly how you knew he'd be here?"

Parker didn't answer. The lone hockey fan at the bar cheered. If Parker or Hank noticed, they didn't let on.

Hank leaned forward and said quietly, "Parker, look, I have no interest in whether or not Gimbel is leaking information. I don't think your claim makes sense but I don't know your business." He paused. "What I do know is what I would do. If I had illegal wiretaps on any phone, I would remove them as quickly as possible." He cleared his throat. "Atlantic City isn't within my jurisdiction but if I did know that a crime was being committed—which I don't know, but if I did I would have to report the situation to the proper authorities—which would be the feds since he's in New Jersey and you're not." His voice assumed a hostile edge. "Another thing I know is that I don't want any-one's right to privacy violated in my jurisdiction, got it?"

Parker nodded his head eagerly.

"And that goes for both of you, got it?"

"I was only trying to keep…I mean, have a little fun." I forgot which story I was using.

Hank silenced me with a stare.

"Look, Parker, I don't mean to sound harsh." Hank transitioned from bad cop to good cop. "I can see that Gimbel would be the type of guy you might not like. He's kind of a blowhard. Kind of a ladies' man."

"You don't know the half of it." Parker implied that if Hank played his cards right, he could know.

"Lucky guy, eh?"

"Luck ran out this month. Some bitch has her screws in him but good. He got one of his cuties pregnant and she ain't letting him off easy"

Motive!

Hank smirked. "Wonder how Mrs. Gimbel would handle that if she knew."

"Oh, she knows. And she is royally pissed about it."

I went with my intuition. Mr. and Mrs. Gimbel had done away with their problem—as I had suspected. "Are you getting good at this or what?" I congratulated myself silently. Wouldn't Andy be proud?

What did it matter? Andy would never know.

Chapter Twenty-Five

"Is Hank with you? Of course, he can stay." George rolled back the door to the drawing room and stuck his head out. I could see that he wore gray striped pajamas under a maroon dressing gown. The robe was as attractive as the pajamas were ugly.

"No. No Hank. Sorry to disappoint you. He dropped me off and headed home." I didn't mention he dropped me off after an evening chockablock with bumping, rubbing, and touching but no overt indication of interest in me. I knew George would be disappointed. I wasn't. Puzzled, yes. Disappointed, no.

"Did you…" George believed his shrug completed the thought.

"Did we what?"

"You know." As he whispered lurid tones curled around the words.

"No, George, I don't think I do know." Although I wondered if I did.

"Find any…you know." He nodded up the steps.

I followed his gaze up the staircase. "Oh, evidence. Did we find any evidence? Yes, we…" I lowered my voice from a stage to an actual whisper. "I should let Hank tell you the rest." I didn't know how much information Hank was willing to share. I could, however, assure George that he and I were not necessarily out in left field.

"Well, tomorrow is another day. We'll meet early and plan our approach." George appeared to seek an expanded role in the investigation.

I was in my room only five minutes when I heard a discreet knock at the door.

"You probably thought I was Hank. I'm sorry to disappoint."

I stared at George with a furrowed brow. I had never thought for a moment my visitor might be Hank. "I am not at all disappointed."

"Well, I had to tell you something I just this minute thought of." George resorted to nonverbal communication, a nod over his shoulder, to indicate he had more information about the Gimbels. "It didn't occur to me before."

With theatrical gestures, George pointed toward the fireplace and indicated I should follow him into the bathroom. The room shared no contiguous walls with the space the Gimbels occupied. Nonetheless, George took precautions. Once we were behind closed doors, he turned on the water in the sink, dropped the toilet seat lid, and made himself comfortable. "Have a seat." He pointed to the narrow edge of the claw-footed tub. I chose the floor instead—actually the small rug with embroidered pink flowers. The tile floor could cause frostbite.

George leaned down to whisper to me. "The Gimbels were supposed to come last weekend. Too bad they didn't. The weather was gorgeous—uncommonly warm for this time of year. Just amazing. Anyway, when Mr. Gimbel called to say they were coming, I offered to clear the bridal suite—this is the room they generally stay in. And Mr. Gimbel said no, he would rather be on the west side of the house in the winter. I didn't get it, but actually his request made it easier for me. I didn't have to evict anyone. Anyway, they ended up canceling…"

"Why?" I interrupted.

"I have no idea but that isn't my point. My point is that when they called, they rebooked for this weekend. You hadn't booked yet, so I offered them the bridal suite and Mr. Gimbel said no. They wanted the room down the hall. He went on about the winter and seasonal affect disorder or whatever the condition is when you get depressed in the winter and wanting the afternoon sun which doesn't make sense because it seems to me that if you're going to be depressed, you'll be depressed and need help getting out of bed in the morning which would be either this room or the one directly across the hall that has the southeast exposure."

I exhaled when George finally took a breath.

"So?"

"So, at the time I didn't think about it but now with your little accusation…"

"Theory," I corrected him.

"Your theory." He shrugged. "Whatever. I think it's significant that he booked that particular room."

"Why?" I whispered eagerly.

"Because the balcony provides access to the roof of the shed which has a fire staircase."

"And they could sneak in and out."

"Bingo."

I lay on the cold tile and stared at the ceiling. Of course, that's what I saw on Friday night. Mr. Gimbel removing the body of his lover. I remembered the tender kiss. Perhaps he regretted the murder but that didn't help Celia. She was still dead. Gimbel had a motive to murder the lover we assumed to be Celia Chaney, and it appeared he had a way of disposing of the body. "Maybe I'm not nuts after all."

"Little girl," George's southern accent was as thick as I'd ever heard it. "I don't think you have a wacky brain cell in that entire head."

Chapter Twenty-Six

I lay in bed worrying about what the Gimbels had observed about my interest in them. They couldn't possibly have overheard the conversation in the bathroom. And if they had? They had killed once. I was sure of it. Why would they hesitate to kill again?

Maybe my relationship with a private investigator had left me overly suspicious. Maybe there was an easy explanation for the Gimbels' odd behavior. And, it was odd. And getting odder. When I heard the click of the door, I tiptoed across the room to kneel at the peephole. Shoes in one hand, camera in the other, Mr. Gimbel was sneaking down the stairs.

I leaned back on my heels. Why was Mr. Gimbel slipping out without Mrs. Gimbel? Where was he going? Evidently, Will Pankenhurst/Parker/whatever wondered, too. Moments after Mr. Gimbel disappeared down the steps, I heard another noise, and looked out to see Will following him. His surveillance technique really needed work. I bet he didn't realize he was whistling "Secret Agent Man."

I pulled a card from the pocket of my parka and tiptoed down the stairs to the phone in the hall. "Hank, you said I could call at any time."

"I meant anytime I was awake."

"Oh, no. You were asleep?"

"Not really. Sleep isn't something I get a lot of."

"Well, I just saw Mr. Gimbel leave."

"It's after eleven." He yawned pointedly.

"It's 11:02 and it's Saturday night, Hank. When was the last time you stayed up late with the big boys."

"Didn't you have enough of an adrenaline rush for one night?"

"What could happen? I'll be safe in your car—if you agree to come over, that is."

"What do you think we'll find out?"

"If I knew, I wouldn't be on the phone asking for help, would I?"

"Do you know where Gimbel went?"

"No."

"So how do you expect to follow him? He'll be long gone before I pick you up."

"You're the cop, you figure it out. Besides, we're searching for two cars. Pankenhurst is on his trail as well."

Grudgingly, Hank promised to pick me up in five minutes. I would need that long to climb into all my clothes. As I dressed I wondered. Wondered why Hank was doing this for me. Wondered why I wanted him to do it. Wondered why I bothered to do it. I shook off the introspection and got ready.

In a modified version of my Michelin man outfit, I tiptoed down the steps and peeked into the drawing room. Neil and Lulu Cummings sat facing each other on separate sofas. Motionless, they responded neither to me nor to each other. In their matching black uniforms, the two assumed identical positions. Straight backs. Legs planted firmly on the floor. Eyes pointed directly ahead staring. At what? I wasn't sure.

Feeling like an intruder, I backed into the dimly lighted hallway to wait for Hank's car to pull up. I jumped when Neil's head popped out of the drawing room.

"Lulu and I...could we have a word with you?"

"Me?" I pointed to my chest for verification.

Neil smiled. "Yes, you."

I shrugged. Why not? I had a few minutes to kill until Hank picked me up.

"Hello." Lulu's greeting was as cold as the night. She was perched in the center of one of the sofas that in the Victorian style offered support at either ends but not in the middle. Her back was locked straight in a posture that I'd been taught in school but never quite achieved.

"You should have interrupted us…" Neil waited until I'd entered the drawing room to follow me in. "We were meditating," he explained.

"Yes. Yes. I didn't want to disturb you. You looked…" How could I possibly end that sentence? "Weird" didn't sound appropriate. I groped for another word.

Neil spoke before I found one. "Please sit down." He pointed to the chair opposite the one I thought of as Claude's. "Lulu and I had a few questions. About your exploits last night. We've had some adventures at the Parsonage ourselves. We stay up late and sometimes we notice things."

My heart jumped. Did he know something about Celia Chancy?

"Like you, we've found ourselves locked out. There are some unusual things going on around here."

He was telling me? I kept quiet to learn what he had observed.

"Do you think someone," he cleared his throat nervously, "or something, locked you out of your room?"

"I was alone in my room." And what was he thinking, *something?*

"Are you sure?"

"I didn't check the closet or the bathroom but I'd used both earlier and no person," I paused for emphasis, "or thing, was there."

"How did the door fall shut?"

"It didn't fall shut. I let the door close behind me as I stepped onto the balcony."

"Did you hear a click or feel a rush of air when the door closed?" Neil was shooting questions at me as if he were a cop and I was the suspect—in some horrible crime.

"All I felt out on the balcony was rushing air."

"Were you suddenly cold?"

Suddenly cold? "I stepped into six degree weather."

Neil didn't catch my astonishment at his question. He continued. "When you locked yourself out, did you notice anyone else on the property?"

What was at the root of Neil's questioning? What was he digging for? "No. Well, wait I saw the Gimbels...." I stopped dead. I didn't believe that I had really seen the couple but I wasn't ready to let the Cummings in on my suspicions. "The Gimbels were on their balcony."

"Alone?" A trick question.

After searching for an appropriate reply, I answered truthfully. "I only saw two people."

"And they were the Gimbels?"

"Well...yes...I assumed...it was their room and their balcony." I cleared my throat nervously. "Was there someone in particular you thought might be on the balcony?"

Neil considered his answer carefully but when he finally spoke his attitude was dismissive. "No, no one."

I was afraid to mention Celia Chaney's name. "Would this have anything to do with the woman who's been getting phone calls?"

Neil answered that question easily. "No. No. She...no phone calls would be involved. I'm sure of that."

I waited for Neil to fire another question. Instead he turned to Lulu. They eyed each other with what I interpreted as disgruntlement or maybe frustration.

"Did you see something unusual last night?" I took up the interrogation.

"No." Neil sounded disappointed. "We didn't see a thing."

"Nothing." It was the first word Lulu had uttered since hello.

The couple's responses had the force of truth and the ability to confuse. "What was that about?" I asked myself as I ran down the steps to Hank's Porsche.

As I jumped into the front seat, my attention had shifted back to Gimbel. I flashed an appreciative smile at Hank, "I owe you."

"Big time" was his answer. Despite his proclaimed dissatisfaction with our mission, Hank had formulated a plan. "We'll drive down the road where Gimbel parked this afternoon—although I have the feeling he just stopped there to make a call. Then we'll check a few places that are open, Cape May Point, and Sunset Beach. Those are the places where we can most easily spot a car."

"Two cars," I reminded him.

I filled Hank in on my talk with George. "So now I view Friday night differently."

"But you didn't think the figure was a corpse at that time."

"Of course not. I don't generally think: what a cute couple—I wonder if one of them is dead. Necrophilia isn't a big issue in my life."

"All I'm saying is your memory might be influenced by what George said."

I knew that was possible. By that point, I thought anything was possible.

"The other odd thing is that the Cummings, Neil and Lulu, were asking me if I saw anything last night. When I mentioned the Gimbels, they didn't appear to have much interest."

"What were they asking about?"

I shook my head. "Wish I knew. They said they didn't see anything unusual last night." I described my interaction with Neil.

"Those guys are flaky. They never talk to anyone. They stay up all night meditating. I think to arouse the Cummings' interest, a person has to be dead." In response to my shocked expression, he added. "For a minimum of one hundred years. That's my theory anyway. They never say boo about what they are doing."

Ghosts? If the Cummings were searching for ghosts, maybe they should keep an eye out for the spirit of Celia Chaney. I'd have to think of a way to ask if they'd noticed any new specters hanging around.

Chapter Twenty-Seven

"Oh, boy. This is way too easy." Hank pulled into the parking lot at Sunset Beach and almost sideswiped Gimbel's van. "We have to assume he's seen us and pretend we meant to come here."

"Why would anyone come here at this time of night?"

"Remember high school?"

I recalled my school days. "We're going to dissect a frog?"

"Right. You go catch the frog—if frogs are dumb enough to come out on a night like this."

"Frogs are too smart—only humans are dumb enough. Where's Parker...Pankenhurst...Whatever."

"Apparently he's not as smart as the average frog. I think we passed his car about 100 yards back. I suspect that a figure I saw along the perimeter of the parking lot a minute ago is Parker. Apparently he doesn't scare easily. I'll take another shot at intimidation tomorrow. I've done more than my share for tonight."

Hank parked in the same space we had taken at sunset. "Here," he wrapped an arm around me and pulled me close. "Lean your head on my shoulder."

Hank threw himself into his acting. I doubted that Gimbel would care where the cop's hands rested but apparently, Hank was going for authenticity. I didn't protest. How could I? His hands hadn't landed anywhere they shouldn't; they were just a few degrees off.

Hank's hands may have been on me but his eyes focused on his side mirror.

"Is he in the car?"

"I can't tell. I don't see a profile but with the dark glass..."

"Oh no." I interrupted. "Here he comes."

Hank froze. "Where?"

"He's walking over from the porch of the grill. He's going to pass right behind the car."

Hank nuzzled my hair with his nose. "Do you have a clear view?"

"Yep. He's only about ten yards away and he's watching the car."

"You'd better kiss me then."

Hank initiated the kiss. A real kiss. My mind raced but I never thought about Gimbel. I thought about lips, tongues, teeth—the whole enchilada. Hank didn't have to kiss me so deeply if the display were for show, did he? His hand moved up from my waist under my jacket. His left hand was suspiciously close to my breast. Was Hank a method actor? Was he under the impression Gimbel could see that action? Was he going to pursue his initial efforts?

Hank pulled away and kissed my forehead lightly. "Where is he now?" He whispered.

"I...I don't know...I had my eyes closed."

"Meg. You were supposed to..."

I never knew what I was "supposed to" because there was a light knock on the window.

"Thank God, it's you," Gimbel said good-naturedly as Hank lowered his window. "Would have been damn embarrassing if the two of you turned out to be strangers. I thought I recognized your car. Just wanted to make sure you were okay. I can see you are. Don't want me to take a picture of this happy occasion, do you?" He brandished the camera.

"I can't speak for Meg but I'm not likely to forget this moment. No picture needed." Hank flashed that smile.

Gimbel raised both eyebrows. "You know, Meg has a room."

Hank made a great effort to appear sheepish. "Acting like teenagers, aren't we?"

"A man needs that once in a while." Gimbel reached in the window and squeezed Hank's shoulder. With that he disappeared into his van.

"What do you think?" I relied on Hank's expertise.

"I think Gimbel was right. The two of us look like teenagers sitting here. I'm lucky my granddaughter didn't show up in the next car."

Granddaughter? In describing his devotion to his daughter, Hank had omitted the information that his daughter had a daughter. "You never mentioned you had a granddaughter."

"I didn't?" He flashed that smile. "That's odd. It's not one of those things I would hide." He kept a grin plastered on his face.

I forced the corners of my lips upward. What were those things that he would hide? I didn't ask. "What I meant was why do you think Gimbel came over and talked to us?"

"I think he recognized my car, which in and of itself is interesting, and wanted to find out what we were doing here. I think he's satisfied he knows."

"What about Parker?

"If we sit here for a few more moments, I think Parker will be convinced of the same—although buying this story and your minivan/joke story might be a stretch. I'll search him out tomorrow and find out what he saw."

"He probably thinks I have a thing about doing it in cars."

Hank let my comment pass.

"So, you're the cop. What do you think Gimbel is up to? Do you really think the photo opportunity was good enough to warrant coming out in the middle of the night?"

"It is a full moon."

I gazed at the small circle high in the sky. "Possibly the moon was impressive when we were at dinner. Looks pretty ordinary to me now."

"Let's hang around and see what happens." Hank adjusted his position including moving a hand onto my thigh. A casual hand. A friendly hand. A stationary hand. I had no clue about his intentions.

"Gimbel could have been dumping the murder weapon."

"Gimbel could have been doing a lot of things. Like taking pictures." His sigh told me Hank was settling in.

"I doubt it. Shouldn't we walk the beach and check...for something...for anything?"

"Something? Anything? That would be easy."

"You're being snide."

"I'm being sensible." Hank was not about to budge from the front seat of his Porsche.

"Where's that flashlight you had before?" I displayed my impatience.

"You never gave it back."

"Oh." I paused. I vaguely remembered dropping the light on a table in my room. "Do you have another one?"

"If I did, I would keep it in the glove compartment."

I found a flashlight and hopped out of the car. "I think I'll take a look-see."

Chapter Twenty-Eight

Maybe Hank was willing to concede that Wallace Gimbel was so devoted to photography that he dragged himself out in the middle of a frigid night to take pictures of black seas and skies, but I certainly wasn't. Okay, the moon was full but so high in the sky that the chance for striking photos had passed hours before. The moon would have photographed the way I did in vacation snapshots taken by my mother: a tiny figure who at that distance was indiscernible from my sister, my Uncle Al, or the Washington Monument.

With the light of the moon I didn't need the flashlight. Navigation was easy—or would have been if I'd had the vaguest idea where I was headed. As I found my way across the beach toward the gentle lapping waters of the Bay, I wished I'd put on a few more layers of clothing. The breeze wasn't strong but the cold didn't need the assistance of a fierce wind to make its point. According to the weatherman on Channel 3, almost a decade had passed since the region had experienced such a cold snap. Why did I choose to be on the beach when the thermometer plunged?

Why? Because Wallace Gimbel did not convince me that he was a photography buff. There had to be more. I turned my back on the bay and studied the beach. Nothing moved. Yet there had to be something, or someone, there. I eyed the patio of the Sunset Beach Grill. That was the obvious place to start but in darkness the deck appeared frightening. Menace was everywhere.

I was about to return to Hank's car when he blew the horn. I turned the flashlight on myself and held up a hand to signal one more minute. We'd come this far; I had to check. With purposeful strides,

I headed for the restaurant porch. Okay, my first ten strides were purposeful—if clumsy in the sand. As I grew closer the fear returned. What if someone was lurking there? If Gimbel had an accomplice, that person was capable of murder. Maybe the purpose of the meeting was to pass the murder weapon. Then the accomplice would not only be capable of murder but armed.

I moved slowly as I approached the front of the deck. I ran the flashlight along the porch. The space appeared empty. I focused the light on the floor and leaned forward to study what I saw. I was crouched with my head under the rail, when I felt the hand.

I never knew I could scream so loud. Never had the need before, I guess. But at this moment I had two incentives: pure unadulterated terror at the hand's touch and sharp unimaginable pain at my head's contact with the wooden railing.

"Oh, I am sorry." Hank made an effort to console me but I warded off his embrace.

"Why did you do that?" I held the back of my head.

"Do what?"

"Sneak up on me."

"I didn't sneak up on you. You knew I was here."

"I knew you were in the car."

Hank stopped protesting. "How's your head?" He reached towards my wound but I waved off his touch.

"It's one of those horribly sharp pains—but the discomfort won't last." Largely thanks to my ugly wool cap.

"What were you studying down there anyway?" Hank took the flashlight from my hand and ran the beam along the porch surface.

"Cigarette butts. See. Gimbel doesn't smoke."

"We don't know if Gimbel smokes or not. We haven't seen him smoke. George and Claude run a smoke-free house."

"So why would a smoker come back repeatedly? I bet Gimbel met an accomplice here. Maybe a female. Some butts have lipstick on them."

"Meg, do you know how many people might have visited this spot in the course of today? We don't even know if these butts are that recent."

There Hank went with that logic thing again.

"But they could be...from tonight...from a few minutes ago."

"Yes, and they could be from the Mesolithic era...or at least yesterday. Let's go." He reached for my hand.

I was reluctant but couldn't think of anything else to be accomplished on the porch. With regret, I let Hank pull me back to the Porsche. Or rather I let Hank believe he was dragging me away. The truth? The cold was killing me.

Chapter Twenty-Nine

I slid the key into the lock. It turned easily. To avoid waking the house, I eased the door closed as slowly as the cold permitted— which wasn't very. The wind chill had to be below zero. I was anxious to get indoors.

There were no signs of life in the B&B. I slipped out of my boots and tiptoed across the hallway. If Neil and Lulu were pursuing their nocturnal activities, they were doing so elsewhere. I moved up the stairs slowly. I was certain step five would get George and Claude's attention; I was willing to bet step nine would wake the entire house. I stopped and listened. No one stirred. I continued up the stairs.

I repeated the cautious entrance at the door to my room: turning the doorknob slowly, easing it open, closely it gingerly behind me. The room was as dark as I'd left it. I had taken only three steps on my tiptoes when I heard the sound. Once again, I froze in place.

I don't have great hearing and even I heard it. Turning my head slowly, I determined the direction from which the noise came. Then I noticed the light under the bathroom door. I heard water running. Not only had someone broken into my room, they had the audacity to use the facilities. Any fear I had was driven away by outrage. What was the person doing in there? Washing up? Oh sure, and drying with my clean towels. Great. If I hadn't returned when I did I might never have known.

The cessation of running water snapped me to my senses. Whoever the visitor was, the person was ready to come out of the bathroom. I searched for a weapon, any weapon. I located decorative items in the darkness but couldn't destroy such valuable objects. After considering the alternative, the intricately cut English crystal no longer seemed so valuable. With the neck of the vase in my fist, I crept across the room, wedged myself between the bathroom door and the tall mahogany wardrobe and waited. For added mobility, I wiggled out of my jacket. I adjusted my grip on the vase. I was ready.

Even though I knew the moment was inevitable, the door's opening shocked me. I felt the fear clear down to my toes. I tightened my hold on the vase. In my entire life I'd never hit another person. Would I do it? Could I do it? Apparently I could.

As the frighteningly large figure emerged from the darkened bathroom, I raised my arm and swung the vase above my head in order to make contact with the back of the intruder's skull. Only as the body slumped to the floor did I wonder why the man wore boxer shorts.

I stood over the figure but could discern only that he was male, tall, and well built. And heavy enough to make an extremely loud thump when landing on thick carpet. I stood guard over the reclining figure pondering what to do next. Nothing came to mind.

"In here." I called in response to the sound of feet rushing down the stairs. I remained frozen with the vase in the air watching for any sign of life. Of course, at that point I would have considered any sign of life a bad sign.

"Meg. Meg, dear. What's wrong?" George's voice came through the door.

"George. Thank God. Help me." I backed towards the door aiming the vase like a 45 Magnum. I need not have bothered. The figure on the floor lay completely still.

After fumbling with the lock, I fumbled with the doorknob.

"Let go of the knob, sweetheart." George's intonation betrayed as much annoyance as concern. "Let go of the handle and let Claude and me in."

Relief flooded through me. Claude and George had come to my rescue. "I will. I will let go." I said I would but I didn't. Fear controlled my grasp on the handle. I was helpless to release the door.

"Meg, what has happened? Open the door."

It wasn't George's command but the moan from the man prone on the floor that made me let go of the knob. "Oh my God, he's moving."

So was I as the door flew open; the force pushed me across the carpet.

"Sorry, darling." George offered an arm to steady me while his eyes searched the moonlight-lit room. It didn't take him long to locate the body. "Oh my God, Meg. What have you done?"

"What have I done? That man was in my bathroom." Shock and indignation infused every word. I was the victim. Why was George acting like the intruder had been wronged? The innkeeper's arm dropped from my shoulder. He ran to the moaning man and knelt at his side.

"Mr. Beck. Mr. Beck. Andy. Are you okay?"

"Andy?" I felt suddenly nauseous.

I walked towards the figure as George turned him onto his back. Slowly the truth was revealed. The classic profile, the handsome face. "Andy." There was no question. I'd just knocked out Andy Beck, the best shot at romance I'd had in the past year.

"Andy." As I shoved George aside, I thrust the crystal vase into his hand. I knelt and gathered the reclining figure in my arms. He didn't yet have the strength to open his eyes. God, would he ever?

"Andy. Speak to me. Are you okay?"

His only response was a groan.

"Oh God. I killed him. It was an accident. I swear. It was an accident. I didn't recognize him. His hair was never that blonde."

Andy's eyes opened and he squinted in my direction. "Meg, what happened? My head..."

"You had a nasty fall, that's all." The kiss I placed on the top of his head evoked a grimace. "Oh, I am sorry. You hit your head."

"I'll get ice." Claude picked his way through the crowd to reach the hallway. For the first time I realized that virtually all the guests had joined us—that is, except the Blandings whom I assumed were otherwise occupied.

I glanced over Andy's head. Thank heavens Mr. Gimbel had sent his wife to investigate. Judging from the look of shock on her face, she'd been told about the position her husband had found me in less than an hour earlier.

"There's no problem here." George reassured the guests. "Ms. Daniels had a surprise guest and it appears that he had an unfortunate fall. In the dark and all. Trying to surprise Ms. Daniels." He waved to disperse the group. They filtered out of the room reluctantly.

"You came here to surprise me?" I kissed Andy's forehead. Although the gesture didn't appear to thrill him, at least he didn't groan.

"Where's here?"

Oh, oh. The situation was bad. Andy's memory was gone—at least part of it. Would he remember that he liked me? "Oh Andy, you are so sweet." I stroked his cheek. "You're really here." I clarified. "At the Parsonage bed-and-breakfast in Cape May."

He nodded weakly. "I remember now. Did I fall?"

I nodded and shook my head in one gesture. "Well...kind of...yes...you fell."

"I heard him..." George paused for emphasis, "fall. Claude and I came running downstairs. We couldn't imagine what had happened." He eyed the vase meaningfully.

I nodded towards the table from which I'd grabbed the ersatz weapon.

If George understood my nonverbal order to return the crystal ornament to its original position, he didn't let on. He twirled the vase in his hands. "Andy had a nasty fall. Maybe we should take him to the emergency room."

"I don't think that will be necessary." Claude wedged himself between George and me. He ran his fingers through Andy's hair. "Let's see where that bump is. Whoa!" His fingers halted their search. "I think we've located the source of your problem." He laid the ice pack on the back of Andy's head—on the left side where the vase had landed. "What the hell did you hit on the way down?"

Andy shook his head before realizing the action caused pain. "I was in the bathroom. I was going to climb into bed and get ready to surprise Meg. I remember brushing my teeth, combing my hair, putting on cologne..."

"You did all that for me. You're so sweet." I turned to smile at George. The glance he shot me silenced me. He still twirled my weapon in his hands.

"I wouldn't miss your birthday. You know I wouldn't." For the first time Andy smiled.

"Meg." It was George's voice. "You didn't tell us it was your birthday. Is Sunday the big day?"

I ignored his question. I was wracked with guilt. I didn't deserve a birthday celebration. How could I do this to such a sweet man? How could I hit him with a vase? Knock him unconscious? Lie to him?

"Okay. Okay. I admit it. I did it. I hit him." My eyes met Andy's. "I hit you. I'm sorry. But I thought...I mean...how could I have known..."

Andy stared back at me with a puzzled expression.

"This man traveled over twenty-four hours to surprise you for your birthday and this is the greeting you give him." George shook his head.

"George, how could I have known Andy was in my bathroom? You certainly didn't give me a clue. I mean, just a few hours ago you were fixing me up with Hank."

"You fixed Meg up?" Andy held his own ice bag. "George, why didn't you tell me?"

While George sputtered, I clarified for Andy. "He didn't actually fix me up. He *tried* to fix me up."

"Tried? You weren't here when I arrived—and that was after one o'clock in the morning."

"I was out on business. With Hank. He's a cop. Okay, and a friend of George's. With whom I think George hoped—*hoped*," I repeated the word for emphasis, "to fix me up."

George waved his arms and addressed Andy. "If I'd known you were coming...but I didn't know...I had no idea." The innkeeper finished sputtering; he was in defensive mode.

"Would you please quiet down? This man may be injured." Claude proceeded to ask Andy a series of questions about his health.

I quizzed George with a puzzled expression.

"He's volunteer EMS."

My features further contorted.

"I know. He doesn't seem the humanitarian type, does he?"

"Would you two mind?" Claude laid a hand on his mate's arm. "Come on, George. You've caused enough trouble for one day."

"*I* did?" George protested. "When we found out Meg wasn't in her room, I left a note downstairs. A cryptic note, mind you. A note that would alert her to a surprise without ruining it."

It was my turn to protest. "Where? I didn't find a note."

"Will you two please stop competing for the 'most defensive' award. Just calm down so we can make sure this man is going to be okay."

"I'm going to be fine." Andy pulled himself into a sitting position. "In my line of work, I've had a lot of experience with bumps on the head. As far as lumps go, this one isn't too bad. Thanks for the ice." Andy smiled at Claude.

"My name is Claude Middleton. I am George's partner and your other host for the weekend. Let me state at this time that it is the most fervent desire of the management of the Parsonage that your first impression of the establishment will be overridden by much more pleasant experiences." Claude offered Andy a hand and helped him to his feet.

Andy staggered. He leaned on Claude as our host led him across the room and helped him onto the tall bed.

"Now Meg." Claude turned towards me. "Can we safely assume you will not be assaulting your visitor again tonight?"

"It was an accident," I protested. Claude's sharp look compelled me to change tacks. "No more violence. I promise."

"And George," Claude turned his attention to his mate. "Can we assume that you will not be admitting any more unexpected visitors to the guests' rooms?"

"I left a note." George restated his defense. Again, Claude's glance produced a end to the protest. "I won't even answer the doorbell if it rings—which it won't because I turned the bell off for the night, as always."

"Andy," for the first time the trace of a smile touched the corners of Claude's lips. "Do you feel safe with this woman after what she's admitted?"

Andy shrugged. "I can take her two out of three. I'll be okay."

"Then let us say good-night." Claude tugged at George's pajama sleeve.

George opened his mouth to speak but thought better of it. He sighed and murmured good-night, then followed the elegantly pajamaed Claude from the room.

I closed and locked the door behind them. Afraid to face Andy, I fumbled with the lock longer than necessary.

"Come here, Meg."

I turned but didn't move.

"Meg, I'm not angry. A little sore but not angry."

I was worried. He hadn't called me Maggie, his affectionate name for me.

He sighed. "This isn't exactly how I pictured your birthday surprise coming down. I took four taxis, two buses, a boat, a seaplane, a prop plane, a jet, and a train to get here. Somehow, I didn't figure the trip ending with your knocking me out. Figuratively, maybe. But literally, no."

"Are you sorry you came?" I slid onto the bed and reached my hands out to touch his tentatively. He wrapped his fingers around mine and pulled me towards him. "The least you can do is hold the icebag in place for me." He slipped the cold bag into my hand and turned onto his stomach.

Balancing the ice on the swelling, I lay beside him. "I am so happy you're here. I never dreamt, never, that you would do something like this for me."

He rolled his head until his eyes met mine. "Maggie, you know that I would do anything for you." He closed his eyes. "Anything," was his last word as he drifted off to sleep.

"Now I do," I whispered without knowing if he heard.

Chapter Thirty

"Andy, are you okay?"

"Hhrmm." The pleasant tone suggested he was.

"Are you awake?"

"I'm trying not to be. I traveled for over thirty-six hours and arrived after one o'clock. I got knocked unconscious and didn't get to sleep until after two. Right now the time is...?" He squinted into the bright sunlight pouring in the windows.

"Seven forty-five."

"I'm tired, Meg. I am very happy to see you, but I am exhausted." He wrapped an arm around me and clutched my hand.

"Are you sure you're okay?"

"You can stop asking." He checked for the lump on the back of his head. "My head is sore to the touch but I'm going to live. If my condition changes, I'll let you know. Why were you acting so paranoid anyway?"

"Paranoid? I don't think reacting to an intruder in your bedroom is acting paranoid."

"I kind of thought you'd remember me." Andy sounded more sarcastic than bitter.

"Don't be ridiculous. I remembered you, I just didn't..."

"Recognize me? Somehow, I thought you'd recognize me."

"Through the door?"

"Okay, but you didn't have to hit me. You could have asked George and Claude for help."

"Makes sense—hearing you propose it in the light of day. Unfortunately, the thought never occurred to me." I sighed. I was beginning to punctuate my conversation in George's fashion. "I guess I got a little caught up in the mystery that's going on around here."

"Mystery?" Andy stretched and ended up with his other arm around me. "What mystery?"

"Well," I leaned on his shoulder and whispered in his ear. "I think the people in the next room murdered someone."

"Anyone in particular?" Cynical hardly described his attitude.

"Yes." I feigned true exasperation. "Someone in particular. Celia Chaney."

"Should this name mean anything to me?"

"Does it sound familiar?"

"Not at all."

"She was a dancer in Atlantic City. She's missing."

"How long has she been missing?"

I turned and checked the clock. "Thirty-six hours."

"Thirty-six hours? Over the weekend? A long weekend? Maybe she went away. And, don't you think you should refer to her in the present tense?"

"Well, yes and no." I recited the whole story to Andy, this time punctuating my sentences with tiny kisses and no mention of Hank's role. The mood was definitely romantic when I made a fatal mistake. "So last night Hank and I went out to the Ugly Mug to see her boyfriend."

I felt the tension grip Andy's body and tried a preemptive strike. "Hank is a much older man." I didn't mention he was actually a somewhat older fellow who resembled Robert Redford. "He's a cop who was willing to help—a friend of George and Claude's."

"The guy George tried to fix you up with?"

"Not really. We just wound up collaborating...on this...mystery...kind of thing."

"Until two in the morning?" His cynicism mixed with hostility but he didn't pull away.

I ignored his implications and explained the previous night's activities concluding with Hank's dropping me off at the door.

"You seem pretty involved with this Hank character."

"I've only known him for..." I checked the clock, "twenty-four hours."

"That you've spent with him. Excuse me, Meg, but it seems to me that you are fully involved with this man."

I understood the emphasis Andy placed on "fully involved."

"Andy, I accept that you don't know me that well. You do, however, know me well enough to realize that I do not get 'fully involved' with many people. Least of all people I've known less than twenty four hours." I forced the anger from my voice.

Andy responded with a pout that his mother had probably coped with thirty years earlier.

"I missed you," I said.

His sulking expression turned to a smile—slowly.

"Really missed you. You realize that, don't you?"

His only response remained the purposely pained expression that few people other than a mother could love.

"Really, really missed you." I waited a few seconds for a response. None was forthcoming. "And," I spoke in soft, loving tones, "if I were you, Andy, I wouldn't push the pouting act too much further or I could get over missing you real fast."

He wrapped both arms around me and held tight. "You sure you and this guy...you didn't...?"

"Andy, I am very sure. He wasn't with me when I came in last night, was he?"

Andy shrugged.

"Now, if you don't intend to discuss what you've been up to over the last six weeks, I suggest you drop the topic and become fully involved with me. Okay?"

Something I said—maybe the threat—worked. The pout disappeared. In its place, a tender expression emerged.

Andy kissed me high on the cheek.

"Does this mean you believe me?"

Andy moved his lips lower on my cheek.

"Are you going to make me beg?"

Andy lips lingered just above my upper lip.

I pulled away and gazed into his green eyes. In them, I saw amusement tinged with apprehension. "Are you playing hard to get?"

"No. It's just I feel like those cherubs on the mantel are watching." He shifted his eyes to the carved fireplace.

"They've seen worse." I forced my face into his line of vision.

Andy leered. "But have they ever seen better?" The time had come for the occupants of the bridal suite to disturb the Gimbels for a change. I certainly gave the effort my full attention—and full volume until I remembered I didn't want the Gimbels to realize how easily sound traveled through the wall.

As an exhausted Andy lay back in the bed with one arm around me, I marveled at how the weekend was improving. I judged by his smile that Andy felt the same, but didn't disturb his rest to verify my opinion. When he finally spoke, his voice was gentle. "You certainly convinced me that you missed me." He paused. "I didn't recall…I mean were you always so…so…vociferous?"

Oh-oh—had the Gimbels heard? "I was just loud for that one moment." I patted his hand. "Right?" I anxiously awaited his answer but he didn't provide one.

"Don't get me wrong. I'm not complaining." He squeezed me tightly. "I hope you don't mind if I ask you something."

"What?"

"Are you always covered with bruises and scratches?"

I had been when Andy first met me; I was now because of my adventures on the roof and in the woods. "I haven't told anyone." I related the story of my late night descent from the balcony to the ground. Andy's reaction had never occurred to me. I was so preoccupied worrying about my own aberrant behavior that I hadn't given serious thought to Neil and Lulu's. Maybe Andy was right. Maybe they were up to no good.

"George says they've been here before." I didn't add that I'd verified this information with Hank. I didn't think I'd be mentioning the cop's name a lot for the remainder of the weekend. "They always sleep the day away and stay up most of the night."

"Roaming the house in the dark?"

"I didn't ask." I explained the events I had witnessed that night and the night before.

"Maggie, there may be a mystery going on here, but maybe not the one you think."

"It doesn't matter. Now that you're here I don't think I'll have time for one mystery, let alone two. I'd rather stay busy with you. You know I'm the winner of a romantic weekend getaway. I really feel obligated to live up to the responsibilities of my office."

"And I intend to offer my full support of all your efforts."

Andy could be counted on to come through in a clutch.

Chapter Thirty-One

Andy and I were moving towards a third attempt to disturb the Gimbels when the summons came through the door. "Get up. Get up." The voice belonged to George. I assume the fist that was knocking did, too.

"Go away, George." Given my cozy position in Andy's arms, my voice was muffled.

"Trust me, you don't want me to go away." George's intonation teased us.

"George, trust her. She wants you to go away." Andy wrapped his arms more tightly around me.

"Well, she'll be sorry." George drummed his fingers on the door.

Andy's eyes met mine. I shrugged. "I've only known him for thirty-six hours but I have the distinct impression he isn't going away."

"Do you have your key to let yourself in?" Andy's approach was pragmatic.

"No." George sounded indignant. "You'll have to let me in."

"I'll do it." Exasperated, Andy climbed into a pair of oversized shorts and T-shirt and padded across the flowered carpet. "This better be good, George."

The instant the door opened a crack George burst inside knocking Andy off balance. Without apology, George charged across the room and climbed onto the high bed in the spot Andy had vacated. "This bed is comfortable don't you think?" He bounced on the mattress.

While I commented politely on the comfort of the accommodations, Andy fought his way back into the bed. "Do you make morning visits to all the rooms, or is this a treat reserved for the bridal suite?"

"You didn't tell me he was sarcastic." George bristled as he snuggled against a down pillow. With a frown on his face, he stared at me huddling under the covers. "Are you naked under there?"

"George," I responded. "Remember how you told me Claude thinks you sometimes overstep?"

"Now?"

I nodded.

"Well, I asked for a reason. Possibly you folks have had enough amour to hold you over for a couple of hours. Plus, you'll have plenty of time for romance tonight. Claude and I have big plans." He ignored Andy's furrowed brow. "Well, we'll be out at a dinner party but...you'll have to wait and see."

Andy pressed George to make his point. "Assuming you have one."

"I heard the Gimbels talking. Talking, what am I saying? They were bickering. Bickering, what I am saying? This was more than bickering. This was a fight. And the upshot is...they are going to get rid of it. Then Gimbel started talking about a suitcase. That was what they said."

George glanced from Andy to me and back.

"George, despite your judgment that I've had enough, I'm still feeling romantic, so if you want to go do whatever..."

"Meg, sweetheart, you're missing my point. They say they are going to dispose of it—the suitcase."

"The suitcase?" Andy's lack of interest was evident. "Why would we care if they are getting rid of a suitcase?"

"Because," I answered for George, "the Gimbels have something in that suitcase they need to hide." I thought for only a few seconds. "I see three possibilities....for what's in the bag. One, Celia Chaney's personal effects. Two, the murder weapon. Or," the thought sickened me, "Celia herself."

Andy interrupted. "You two are out of control. Maybe they're taking a suitcase to Goodwill. Since when is there a law against disposing of unwanted property?"

"Since when do you take the Cape May-Lewes ferry to Goodwill." George's tone could only be described as smug. "I wouldn't normally disturb my guests, but I thought Meg would kill me if she didn't know."

I felt torn. I yearned to catch up on romance in the bridal suite, but if we didn't follow the Gimbels we might not get another chance. "Andy, we owe this to Celia."

"Celia, whom I would like to point out I have never met nor heard of until an hour ago, is probably enjoying a romantic weekend somewhere—which is what I had kind of planned on."

"Andy." I employed my sweetest voice. "It's my birthday. This can be my present—not that your flying and boating and the rest isn't a great gift…it is…trust me…it's the best, but this will be a lark. George is right. We'll have plenty of time to celebrate, but if we don't…" I peered out the window at the clear sky. "It is a good day for a boat ride."

"It's ten degrees out."

"Exactly, I don't know about you, but in this cold I'm not up for the usual Cape May activities—biking, birdwatching, kayaking, whale watching, or even a ride in a horse-drawn carriage—today there isn't a blanket warm enough. A ferry ride is perfect."

Andy wasn't responding—at least in a positive fashion.

"Plus, compared to yesterday the weather is equatorial."

Andy did not crack a smile.

"We'll sit inside. The ride will be lovely. We'll…"

I didn't have to finish my thought. Andy was across the room and pulling a pair of jeans out of his suitcase. "Okay, okay. I could have been floating in a sailboat on rolling waters in 80 degree temperatures watching bikinied beauties floating by, but no, I have to take a three-hundred-foot ferry in choppy forty-degree waters. The most skin I'm gonna see is somebody's nose."

Was my nose cute enough to hold his interest? Only time would tell.

Chapter Thirty-Two

Despite George's best efforts to slow them down, the Gimbels were finishing breakfast by the time Andy and I arrived. Mrs. Gimbel was as usual dressed for the cocktail hour in a royal blue brocade sheath and jacket. Her high heeled shoes were dyed to match. Apparently, Marvella Gimbel developed her style watching 1950s television. She must have been glued to the screen as an infant; her fashion sense was developed long before *Nick at Nite* premiered. I studied the tight dress with the plunging neckline. TV pioneers would have been proud of her. Abbie Lane. Edie Adams. Milton Berle.

Wallace Gimbel stared at Andy and then turned to me with a confused expression all too obvious on his face. "Wallace Gimbel, I'd like you to meet Andy Beck. Andy is an old friend of mine. He surprised me last night."

"I bet."

Andy didn't miss his meaning. Nonetheless, he launched into a round of male bonding with Gimbel. From the way he subtly interspersed questions with tales of his time in Antigua, I could tell that Andy had joined the investigation. My guess: not because he wanted to, but because he needed to outdo Hank whom he hadn't yet met. What would happen then? Andy was a guy; maybe he wouldn't notice that Hank was good-looking.

The Blandings arrived next—in a cloud of giggles. They made only perfunctory greetings. They had better things to do—together. What did it matter if I found the Blandings an unattractive couple? They found each other very attractive. Extremely attractive. Intensely attractive. "We've been married twelve years and are as hot for each other as we were the moment we met," Mr. Blandings spoke to no one in particular as he nuzzled his bride's neck with his rather round nose. Mrs. Blandings fascinated her husband with her conversational skills and aroused him with her physical attributes, none of which were obvious to others—at least they weren't to me. The good news was that the two were so involved with each other that with correct positioning I could pretty much ignore them.

Will Pankenhurst/Parker, who arrived immediately after the Blandings, was more subdued than I'd ever seen him. His clothes were not. He had a real affinity for orange—this morning the shade didn't complement his red hair.

If the Gimbels had the fifties covered, Pankenhurst/Parker handled the seventies. His lapels were wider than my hips. So was each pant leg. His belt was only slightly narrower. The wide leather strap emphasized a belly that he patted periodically—and proudly— almost as if he were forcing his bulk forward to impress us.

I made an effort to see the man from Nanette's point of view. What were the advantages of dating Will Parker? Wearing the fluorescent colors he favored, he wouldn't get lost in the dark. The synthetic materials meant his clothes would never need ironing. Beyond that I couldn't see the appeal.

Will's eyes met mine only briefly. Quickly his expression flashed through guilt, surprise, skepticism, and suspicion. Apparently, he had no idea what I was up to—or how to react. Will greeted Andy politely with a concerned question about the well-being of his head. Andy made a similarly low-key response before leaning my way. "Is every guest supposed to dress as their favorite anachronism?"

I eyed the crowd. The assembled group was amazing for its fashion sense—or lack thereof. There was a trend in the B&B: stay stuck in a year from at least a decade earlier. How about me? I attempted to catch my reflection in the glass but couldn't. In what time period had I locked myself away? Wouldn't I be the last to know? "Remind me to buy a copy of Vogue while we're out." I whispered to a puzzled Andy.

Hank arrived as the Blandings lingered, fondled, and smooched over coffee. Nonetheless, Mandy Blandings took excessive note of Hank's entrance. He squeezed her shoulder as he passed their table and made a great show of greeting Bob Blandings who seemed oblivious to Hank's attention to his wife. Okay, alleged attention. Anyway, I couldn't worry about Bob Blandings' marriage; I had a problem of my own.

"Old?" Andy whispered through gritted teeth. "Robert Redford is old, too." Apparently the resemblance existed in reality as well as in my mind.

I shrugged. "But he has brown eyes." My protest was weak. Andy's expression told me so. I hoped Andy would find my smile disarming. I suspected—make that strongly suspected—he did not.

Andy muttered under his breath. I had to struggle to hear him. I hoped no one else could. "I see what's going on here. I wondered why anyone would take your cockamamie theory seriously. Now I see he didn't. He only wants one thing from you, Meg. Isn't that obvious? He doesn't buy all this mystery stuff."

With a forced geniality I made the introductions, filling Andy and Hank in on each other's backgrounds. "Smoothly" was not a word I would choose to describe my progress. I was relieved when George swept through the room. His statement—"spaceshot is moving"—mocked the secret service-type code he had assigned to the Gimbels.

Hank didn't understand.

"We'll explain in the car." George handed him a muffin. "I'll drive. You eat."

Andy seemed momentarily taken aback that Hank was joining us but didn't complain. Hank, on the other hand, made no attempt to hide facial contortions that challenged Andy's presence.

Claude put down his paper. His voice betrayed strain. "If you persist in stalking the guests, George, would you at least try to be discreet about it?"

George mumbled a terse "Of course," grabbed a coat from the front hall, and tore back into the breakfast room. We followed him through the kitchen, out the back door, and into the jeep. "Check this." George thrust a ferry schedule over the front seat. This time of year, the choices were limited. Assuming George had heard correctly, we easily identified the boat the Gimbels had targeted.

In the front seat, Hank and George squabbled about George's driving as we headed out of town and towards the ferry dock. In the back seat, Andy stared out the window. I wanted to think he was sightseeing, but I was pretty sure he was sulking.

"I am not breaking the law," George protested. "Everyone knows that speed limits are approximate. Fifteen miles over the limit isn't speeding."

"You know they have special cops who just patrol the road. They're just waiting for someone like you." Hank shook his head despairingly then grew animated. "You can't pass here."

"Hank, the lines are actually…"

Hank held up a hand to silence George. "Please, George, I don't want to know…Just remind me not to ride with you again—ever."

"Hank," I tried to distract the cop from his argument with George. "Do you have that photo of Celia with you?"

"You put the picture in the inside pocket of your jacket when I returned it," George volunteered.

Hank grumbled as if reaching inside his coat required months of cross-training. I thanked him profusely, if somewhat facetiously, for the effort.

"Andy, this is Celia Chaney. She's the one we think has been… you know." I handed him the picture.

"She get much work?" As Andy stared at the headshot, a frown spread across his face.

"You don't like her either, do you?" I asked eagerly.

Andy shrugged. "She's nice enough looking. She just lacks...something."

"Gimbel helped her get a promotion. Otherwise I'm not so sure she would have made it out of the chorus." Hank threw in his opinion.

I studied the picture as we drove. Could I let my personal dislike of a five-by-seven glossy stand in the way of my quest for justice? Maybe if Celia Chaney had lived to meet me...maybe we would have been best friends. Nah. I didn't like her. It was that simple. But I didn't like the Gimbels much either. They shouldn't be allowed to get away with murder.

The trip to the ferry slip was remarkably short—thanks to George's speed and much to Hank's dismay. In the brief time span, Hank and Andy talked of formulating a plan. Actually, they played a game of one-upsmanship under the guise of making a plan. I rode silently and let them bicker.

"We'll see what's up and play it by ear." George and I were in agreement.

"I got a call from Guy this morning." Hank spoke over his shoulder to me.

"A mutual friend?" Andy asked with forced casualness.

"Guy is the fellow I told you about last night, Andy. The man Celia Chaney was living with." I turned my attention to Hank. "What did he say?"

"He obviously doesn't trust Celia as much as he pretends to. He checked her closet and drawers and found out she'd packed stuff for the weekend. She took her camera, a bathing suit, a tennis racquet..."

"To come to our place?" George was cynical. "Unnecessary unless Claude's been doing a lot of construction behind my back."

"She didn't know where Gimbel was taking her. He said that. But…Guy made it clear that she believed she was going out for dinner. Now it sounds like she knew she wouldn't be back for the second show. Why would she pack a bag to go out to dinner?" I couldn't guess her motive.

"Maybe she was going to have dinner and then do the show and meet Gimbel later." Hank shrugged.

"Why lie to Guy? He seemed to know what she was up to."

"Seemed." Hank murmured.

"Or maybe she wasn't meeting Gimbel at all. Maybe she went somewhere else."

I discounted Andy's remark. "Possible, but I'm not going to bet on it."

As we drew close to the ferry terminal, Hank shook his head. "I can't believe we're doing this. We definitely have too much time on our hands." He snickered. George and I joined his laughter. A silent Andy didn't seem to be having a very good time.

"It's leaving; it's leaving." George screamed as he followed the signs to the foot passenger parking. "The boat is leaving." He pointed to his right. "No cars. No cars. There are no cars in line."

"He's right." I shrieked in Andy's ear. "Let me out." I grabbed George by the shoulder.

He jerked the jeep to a stop in a no parking zone along the terminal wall and snapped his seatbelt. "You fellows park the car and catch up. Meg and I will buy tickets."

As I ran behind George, I heard Andy's voice. "Meg. Wait." I turned to see Andy run around the back of the jeep. Hank, still belted in the passenger seat, called out the open driver's door. Whatever he said stopped Andy in his tracks. I responded to George's exhortations to hurry up. Glancing back again, I saw Andy climb into the driver's seat. I heard the screech of tires as he and Hank went in search of a parking space.

George ran into the building and make a sudden stop. I slammed into him and realized we had arrived at the ticket desk. "Four adults." He pulled a fifty dollar bill from his wallet.

"You'll make it—if you run." The woman behind the desk thrust the tickets at us.

I followed George out a door and towards the boat. As we ran, I checked over my shoulder for Andy and Hank.

"Don't worry about them. They're in great shape. They'll catch up. We have to make sure that boat knows we want to board." In response to a loud bell, George waved the tickets in the air.

A uniformed official waved us away from the foot passenger entrance. We headed for the car ramp that stopped moving upward. With a loud creaking and grating noises, the ramp was lowered. I didn't notice who pushed open the yellow gate at the foot of the ramp. George and I sped by ignoring the stop sign. As we reached the boat, George and I leapt onto the deck—and into the rear bumper of a white Toyota Camry. We heard the ringing of a bell and the creaking of the ramp as it jolted into action. A leather mesh gate was wrapped across the rear deck. A loud blast of the horn signaled we were moving.

"But we have two more." George, who was not at all out of breath, protested to a man in an orange windbreaker. George searched the area between the terminal and the dock. "Yes, there they are." He pointed to the two men rushing around the terminal building from the parking lot.

"Sorry. We waited for you. We're on our way." The man pulled our boarding passes from the envelope that George brandished. "They can catch the next one—although that might be hard since I suspect you have their tickets." He affected an apologetic smile and shrugged.

"Well, we really don't need them, do we?" George nodded at the duo running across the staging area. We watched helplessly as the boat left them in its wake—at least metaphorically.

"Nothing we can do." I offered.

"Let's move up a deck so we can get a better look at Hank and Andy. We can wave good-bye."

We picked our way through the cars on level one in search of stairs to the upper deck. George led me up two levels. "Better view."

When we ran to the back deck, we saw Andy and Hank involved in animated discussion with the officer who had waved us on board. I waited for Hank to pull out his badge but he didn't. The two men stepped aside. From a position in front of a merry-go-round deserted for the winter, they searched the boat's decks. Andy spotted us first. He cupped his hands and yelled something at us.

"What's he's saying?"

"I can't really hear but I suspect he's giving advice—something like, 'Don't do anything stupid.'" I shrugged. "Just a hunch."

We waved at Andy and Hank as they ran down a long dock— keeping pace with the departing boat. "Keep waving. It will calm them down," George wore a forced grin.

George and I waved—first from the back and then from the side as the boat backed around.

"Isn't this romantic?" George waved as broadly as he smiled. "I feel like I'm sailing on the *Titanic*."

"Me, too." But my smile wasn't so broad. I was contemplating the finale of the 1912 voyage.

Chapter Thirty-Three

"Where do you think they went?"

Did George mean Andy and Hank, or the Gimbels?

"Andy and Hank."

As the ferry cleared the jetty, we'd watched the two men confer and run back towards the ferry terminal. I shrugged. "They can't possibly meet us at the other side." The drive to Lewes would take at least twice the time of the ferry trip. "Do you think they'll call us?"

It was George's turn to shrug. "Are you carrying a cell phone?"

"No, you?"

He shook his head. "Then I'd say he won't call us. It's unlikely he'll contact the captain. Hank knows where to draw the line when he's not on official police business. Just in case he experiences a lapse in judgment, keep an ear open for the PA system."

Actually the intercom was currently in use. Announcements about our seventy-minute voyage were being made. Given the echo, I had no idea what the voice said.

"At least today is a nice day for a ferry ride." Through temperatures marginally warmer than the previous day's, George led me from deck to deck of the M/V Twin Capes.

I determined from the diagram that the ship had five levels; I could never had figured that out myself. The ferry appeared huge—more like a cruise ship than a shuttle. "This is so much nicer than the last time I made this trip."

"And that would have been…?"

"With my parents and sister when I was about twelve."

"Well, times have changed, Meg, my dear. This ferry is the pride of the fleet." He waved at a sign in the stairwell. "Oh Meg, a Lido Deck. Just like the Love Boat. Let's go. What is a Lido Deck anyway?"

Never having taken a cruise, I had no clue.

George and I inspected as many public areas as we could locate. In some instances, the effort required was significant. We found no sign of the Gimbels. By level five, I was growing frustrated. George, however, was enjoying the ride. "We could cruise to the Bahamas on this ship."

"If we brought sleeping bags."

"Exactly. We'll bring the jeep and sleep in the back." He leaned on the rail and threw his head back to enjoy the sunlight. "It's funny, but without any wind, it's almost warm."

He turned the corner and stepped back immediately. "I found the wind. Whatever you do don't turn that corner."

"No problem." I was already shivering.

"We should have brought a camera." George had clearly forgotten our mission. "Let's go pose, you know, like on the *Titanic*."

"If we find Gimbel, we can ask him to snap a quick one. He never goes anywhere without his camera. Just don't scream 'I'm king of the world,' okay?"

"Meg, I can't make any promises." He paused at the top of the stairs. "Ah, smell that." He inhaled deeply. "French fries. Forget photo ops—let's find the snack bar."

We made our way down an indeterminate number of stairs and through innumerable doorways in search of french fries. At the entrance to the snack bar, I plowed into George who had stopped dead. He pushed me back against the wall.

"They're here."

"The french fries? Where else would they be?"

"The Gimbels." He peeked around the rounded corner toward the booth where the Gimbels were enjoying the ride and a snack. "I can't believe he's eating. We just ate. Didn't he like breakfast? You must have noticed."

"George, do they have a suitcase with them?"

"Negative from what I can see from here. Should we say hello?"

I suggested we remain out of sight and follow the couple if they made a move.

"Do you think one of us should go through their car?"

George voted against searching and for surveillance. "You know. The more or less legal activity."

He led me to a booth that provided a perfect vantage point for checking on the couple—which George did with a periodic backward tilt of forty-five degrees. George sighed. "I'd feel a lot more comfortable if I knew the New Jersey and Delaware stalking laws.

To my mind, George's comment raised an invalid concern but an interesting question. Why were the Gimbels crossing a state line? Didn't that make the crime all the worse? Didn't the ferry ride open the investigation up to the feds? Could any criminals be so stupid? I figured Mr. Gimbel was the brains behind the plan. How could a man so successful in business be such a failure at crime. Of course, as far as we knew he was new to criminal activity. Still, he could not have done more to call attention to himself and his wife if he had hired one of those planes to tow a banner along the beach announcing, "We Killed Celia Chaney."

I didn't have time to consider Gimbel's need for remedial criminal instruction. "They're moving." George's whisper reverberated throughout the room.

Without noticing they had us in tow, the Gimbels headed for the car deck. Wallace Gimbel strode confidently to the hallway; Marvella followed tentatively in her trademark spike heels. Both Gimbels exercised extreme care on the steep stars to the parking level.

George and I waited on deck two until we heard the door below slam. Then we ran down the steps to the lowest level of the ship.

With theatrical gestures, George signaled me to wait before he slid the door open and tripped through the opening. Only a hand ventured into the stairwell to indicate I should follow.

As I stepped onto the deck a earsplitting screeching noise greeted me. I froze in place wondering how we had set off sirens. George mouthed, "Car alarm."

I breathed a sigh of relief. George started to slink down the wall. I tugged on his parka. "Don't you think our behavior appears a mite suspicious."

"Right." He strode purposely towards the front of the ship— for three strides before stopping dead in his tracks. "Reverse, reverse. Quickly!"

I headed for the stairwell but George pushed me past the door. "Hide around the corner."

"Did he have the suitcase?" I whispered once we were safely out of sight.

"He has a pink bag—a pink flowered satchel, sort of a duffel bag."

The small bag I saw on Friday night. And, the contents? The murder weapon. I was sure of it. "He's gonna toss the murder weapon. I'm positive. We've got to stop him."

I waited until George gave the all clear. Then, we ran up the steps.

"Maybe we should split up. We'll circle the front deck. You take starboard. I'll take port."

George hesitated. I gave him a shove towards the right side of the boat.

Chapter Thirty-Four

It was when I saw a tape of the news that I got a good description of what happened next. The source was a bystander interviewed on Channel 3 from Philadelphia. She provided a far better account than my memory.

"My husband and I were sitting inside on Level 2 at the front of the ferry. I sorta noticed this couple, the older couple with the flowered bag, when they stepped outside. I noticed because I thought the temperature was far too cold to ride outside. It was very chilly yesterday and on the boat with the wind...Anyway, suddenly I heard the sound of running feet. You know feet are noisy on the deck. It's metal. It was this blonde girl, a woman, excuse me, and she ran towards the couple, then she leapt and grabbed this post, like a column, and jumped up on that metal rail and then the top of the railing. She just went right over." The eye witness smiled knowingly—a smug expression. She spoke with authority. "I thought she was a nut." She chuckled. "A dead nut." The reporter indicated that determination was yet to be made. So far my fall appeared to have been accidental.

Hank and Andy told me the fall took only a second. If so, I must think really fast. I had time to realize that I was falling, to remind myself to keep my eye on the flowered bag, to decide I should break the water in a diving position, to visualize being sucked into the big engine, to worry that the boat would pull away without me, to calculate how long it would take to swim to shore, and to figure out it all didn't matter because I was not going to survive the fall. And, on the off-chance I did, hypothermia would kill me before the ferry could circle around to rescue me.

I didn't feel the rush of the water but I heard it. A sharp sound followed by muted gurgling as I sank ever more slowly into ever darkening waters. Not until the downward thrust ceased did I feel the icy sensation around me. The realization—that if I didn't reach the surface quickly I would freeze inside a block of ice—hit me like my head had hit the water. Hard. I'd never gone swimming in a winter coat before; an item for my mental list of activities never to repeat. I fought my way out of the jacket. I kicked upward with my heavy boots as I struggled with the coat. Holding my breath seemed so natural that until I pulled my arms free I didn't grasp that I might not have the breath to make it to the surface.

I felt them seconds after my head broke through the surface. Hands. Many hands. I resisted their grip because of the severity of the hold and the hardness of the surface they dragged me across. But it didn't matter. The hands were stronger. They slipped under my arms. They yanked on my sweater. They grabbed the seat of my pants. And finally they grasped my feet. When they let go I fell onto a cold, hard surface. I rolled onto my side coughing and spitting water only to be yanked onto my back. Someone leaned against me.

"Get her clothes off." A voice commanded.

While someone obeyed and pulled my jeans off, a mouth covered mind. I pushed hard. "Get away from me." I opened my eyes to find Andy bending over me.

"Andy, I realize I put you off this morning but this is hardly the time..." I noticed the words came out in a jumble as I convulsed in shivers.

"I guess the mouth-to-mouth isn't required."

My eyes turned toward the voice and I saw Hank throwing my jeans aside. He was jamming my legs into a huge navy sweatshirt. "Get her blouse off. She can wear my jacket."

I didn't fight as Andy removed the remainder of my clothes. It was no time for modesty. He rubbed his hands across my skin to warm the surface as Hank pushed my arms into his jacket. When I was, in a fashion, redressed, Hank gave a wave to the stalled ferry and gunned the engine. "Keep her down out of the wind and cover her head."

Andy pulled off his jacket and then his sweater. He wrapped the sweater around my head like a turban and pulled his jacket back on. Then he pushed me flat on the deck of the boat and lay on top of me. "You'll be fine. Don't worry." The possibility that I wouldn't be never occurred to me. "You scared us to death, you know. Hank figured in this freezing water you had two minutes—tops."

"Two minutes for what?" I pushed the words through my chattering teeth.

"Two minutes until hypothermia killed you. But thank God..." He didn't finish his thought. Caught in his grip, I couldn't move but neither could I feel the cold as we bounced across water that seemed far less calm in the small motorboat.

"Andy," I whispered directly into his ear.

"Yes," He answered softly.

"Do you think anyone noticed?"

Chapter Thirty-Five

At the ER, people asked why the shock of hitting the Delaware Bay in January didn't kill me instantly. "I can't believe she wasn't sucked into the engine." "I can't believe she came to the surface with those boots on." "I can't believe she didn't get knocked unconscious on impact." "I can't believe she's not dead." Some of the questioners—especially those associated with news organizations—didn't bother hiding their disappointment at my unlikely survival—which had something to do with the Gulf Stream and the unseasonably warm winter we'd had until two days before.

Hank summarized, "Meg took the kind of plunge that might kill you but cannot be relied upon to do so."

Kill me? The fall barely startled me. I didn't even have to stay in the hospital overnight, although I probably wouldn't have been able to escape except that a) Hank was a cop and b) George, who arrived at the hospital after a return ferry trip with the Gimbels, swore that he had a nursing background. Luckily, no one asked for his license. "It's a gay stereotype. Why not take advantage when possible?" He sighed. "On the upside, I also told them I was a good dancer and they bought that, too."

George's perspective on my fall was unusual. "I can't believe you left me alone with those two. You know, the Gimbels. And," he affected a dramatic pause, "didn't I feel like a fool on that boat after you—how shall I say it...*disembarked*. People noticed. They knew we'd gotten on together."

I was more interested in hard news than George's emotional condition. "What did the Gimbels do? What did they say? What did they tell you?"

"Tell me? Don't you mean what did I tell *them*? I had to ride back with those two. I was stuck providing them with an explanation. If they ask, you and Andy had a fight over Hank. You and I took a ride so you could clear your head. I like this story because it explains why the boys were following us in a boat as well as providing a psychological context for your aberrant behavior. I think I'm getting good at this detective stuff." He paused to pull a plastic bag from the large pocket of his parka. "When I heard you were okay, I bought you a gift. A little memento of our ride."

To avoid sounding ungrateful, I didn't tell George that a memento of the day's ride could be categorized as overkill. I thanked him before I peeked into the bag—not after. "George!" My reaction was harsh.

"I thought you could wear your gift at the press conference." He unfurled a T-shirt with *Cape May-Lewes Ferry* scrolled across the front for Andy and Hank's inspection.

"There isn't going to be a press conference." I refolded the shirt.

George raised a single eyebrow.

"Really. I'll lay low for the rest of the day. The press will lose interest." Suddenly a horrible thought hit me. "No one got a picture of me in the water, did they?"

George shrugged. "Not that's surfaced yet."

"You know Gimbel is always walking around with that camera..."

"Oh, yes," George interrupted. "Mrs. Gimbel was miffed he hadn't brought it. She figured they could have sold a photo for a few bucks."

"I thought she was rich?"

"How do you think she stays that way?" George bounced on my hospital bed. "Not very comfy, is it?" He turned to Hank and Andy. "Now tell me how you boys happened to be waiting for Esther Williams here to take to the water."

Hank did the talking. Andy perched on the edge of the bed squeezing my hand—the one without the IV. George had settled on the other side.

We all watched the foot of the bed where Hank provided an explanation. He had the same fear about George that Andy had about me.

"And that would be?" George asked skeptically.

Hank cleared his throat. "Maybe you have a little too much zest for life—and this mystery of yours."

"Meaning you were sure one of us would do something dumb." George feigned indignation.

Hank nodded.

George shrugged. "Fair assumption. Go on."

Hank and Andy had concluded that they'd better keep an eye on us. "We didn't expect to fish one of you out of the water. We just wanted to catch up with you in Delaware." After wracking their brains for a way of catching the ferry, Hank recalled a friend who managed a marina along the Delaware Bay about fifteen miles north of the ferry stop. "He generally keeps two or three boats in the water all year. We picked the fastest one and set out across the bay. We were about to pass the ferry when we saw someone go in the water. We weren't even sure who we were saving—although Andy had his suspicions."

Andy squeezed my hand. He remained strangely quiet.

"I guess this means you guys saved my life."

"You owe us big time," Hank smiled broadly.

A silent Andy squeezed my hand.

"Before you sign off on your first born, Meg, remember there were tankers nearby. They could have sent a skiff to pick you up." George minimized the twosome's heroics.

"To retrieve the body," Hank interrupted. "She wouldn't have survived if we had reached her a few minutes later."

Andy was squeezing my hand so hard it hurt...but since he had recently saved my life I didn't feel I should complain.

"Okay. Okay." George waved his hands in surrender. "You guys are heroes. But don't forget I was the one putting up with the Gimbels—who have gone back to the Parsonage, by the way."

"What was their position?" Hank asked.

"Mrs. Gimbel got a fair amount of sympathy among the passengers for being so obviously upset by what was clearly an accident. Mr. Gimbel got far less sympathy with the attitude, 'That girl is nuts. Did you see her? She just jumped.'"

I was sure there were those in the crowd who agreed with Mr. Gimbel. Let's face it. The other passengers don't generally think highly of the ones who fall off the ferry—especially when the rescue slows the trip.

"Did the cops inquire as to why Gimbel happened to be dropping items off the ferry?" I asked the question.

"He said the bag was resting on the rail and he simply lost his grip. Things can fall off the ferry, you know." George shot an ironic glance in my direction. "Accidents happen."

I wasn't about to argue that point.

Chapter Thirty-Six

When we returned to the Parsonage, Claude was waiting at the back door. He tried to hide his concern but even though I'd only known him for about twenty-four hours his efforts were transparent to me. I didn't let on, though, that I'd stopped buying his misanthrope act.

"George told me the entire story over the phone, and I must admit I have a number of questions for you—several involving the laws of physics." Claude's tone was cynical but his behavior was solicitous. He relinquished his usual chair so I would be closest to the fire. He knelt to tuck a blanket around my legs. He produced another cover for my shoulders. "Indulge me and stay bundled up. Your system has had quite a shock. Now. Tell me what happened." He settled in a nearby chair.

I gave Claude the official line—in case he was asked. "I ran into people I knew from your B&B—the Gimbels. I saw them drop their bag, and in my effort to catch it I fell overboard."

"And you and the bag both ended up in the water?"

"At least, she came back out. That bag never will." Hank interrupted from the velvet sofa he shared with Andy.

"You mean to tell me that I fell off that boat trying to save a bag that we will never see again?"

Hank cleared his throat before he spoke. "Fell?"

I became more defensive. "Yes, fell. What else?"

"Since 1964 that fleet of ferries has transported over twenty million passengers. To my knowledge, you would be the first person to have ever fallen overboard."

I shrugged. "You don't actually know that. You shouldn't make assumptions."

"My point is that it is difficult to fall off a ferry. What about jumped?" Hank colored the verb with irony.

"I didn't jump off that ferry. Do you think I'm nuts? If the fall didn't kill me, the water temperature would have."

"You know that now because I told you." Hank pretended to thumb through a coffee-table book on Victorian architecture.

"Everyone knows that." I made no attempt to keep the impatience out of my voice.

"Everyone knows that now." Hank closed the book and flashed one of the most insincere smiles I'd ever seen.

"Will you two cut out the bickering?" Andy interrupted. "She fell. She jumped. What does it matter now?"

"What matters," Hank was quick with a retort, "is that she thinks I'm dumb enough to believe she fell up and over a four-foot railing and then struck a perfect swan dive position as she headed for the water."

"Okay, maybe, just maybe I contributed to the fall by trying to save the Gimbels' bag. But I slipped." I folded my arms across my chest. "Why the lecture? It isn't like I'm likely to make the same mistake again. What are you thinking? I've got to teach this girl a lesson. The next time she sees a duffel bag stuffed with murder evidence being thrown off a ship in the middle of January, I bet she'll think twice about trying to save it. It happened; it's over."

Hank shrugged. "I just find your behavior fascinating. There were only two probable outcomes. One, you miss the bag and it sinks to the bottom of the Delaware Bay, and two, you catch it and go with it to the bottom of the Delaware Bay."

I started to protest but Andy came to my defense. "Hank, Meg has had a rough day. Don't you think we should cut her some slack?" Andy's tone was unfriendly.

"Sure, if you want me to lie in my report."

"Okay, okay." I interrupted their argument. "Maybe I jumped as a reaction to slipping. I wasn't thinking."

"That sounds reasonable." The cop rolled his eyes.

"Can we discuss the bigger picture?" Andy grew impatient. "I was skeptical at first but I think Meg is really onto something here. We all know the probable crime that was committed on Friday night. The murder that..." he nodded towards the upper floors, "...is going to get away with."

Hank ignored Andy and addressed me. "You know another cop might not have let you off so easily. He might have proven that you were an attempted suicide."

Andy faced Hank to silence him. "May we?" He asked and continued without waiting for an answer. "Gimbel says he and his wife were fighting about her spending habits. He got very angry and threatened to throw her bag overboard to teach her a lesson."

"So she'd have to buy replacement clothes? He's a sharp one." I sighed deeply. "He threw the murder weapon overboard. I know it."

Andy intervened quickly. "Let's think about this. We know that on Friday night Gimbel checked in with a woman who was not his wife, but who was registered as Mrs. Gimbel."

It was Hank who commented. "Based on the testimony of a person who jumped off the Cape May-Lewes ferry."

"Slipped," I muttered.

"Whatever."

Andy ignored Hank's comment. "We have evidence that by the next day the real Mrs. Gimbel had taken the place of the other woman."

Hank had a counterpoint for every point. "Or simply ate too much salt and got swollen ankles."

"*Puh-lease.* There isn't that much salt in the Dead Sea." I wrapped the blanket around me.

Andy continued. "We have reason to believe that the other woman was Celia Chaney—a woman who, according to her boyfriend, claimed to be pregnant by Wallace Gimbel. We know that Celia has stopped showing up for work."

"Two days missed does not exactly make a hard-and-fast case." Hank persisted in playing devil's advocate.

Andy continued with his recitation of the facts. "We know that she packed to leave for more than one evening. We know that she told Guy Fleischman she was only having dinner with Wallace Gimbel. We know that she had been seeing Gimbel previously."

"Why did she take her bathing suits?" I interrupted. "Cape May might be south of Atlantic City but I can say from experience that the water is not appreciably warmer. There was no indoor pool available to her. So, why the bathing suits? Guy clearly said that she had gone away. He told Hank her tennis clothes, bathing suits, and camera were gone. *Why?*"

"Because she was staying with Gimbel for one night until his wife came and then moving on." Hank was impatient.

"So then she should have taken vacation time. There was no need to bring grief on herself by being a no-show."

"Maybe she had a date to swim and play tennis before work." Hank had an answer for everything.

Andy raised another issue. "Why did Wallace Gimbel establish with everyone at the Parsonage that Mrs. Gimbel had been there all the time? The person you'd think he'd want to fool is Mrs. Gimbel. If he had his girlfriend over for the night, he should have hidden her from us—then he wouldn't have to explain anything to his wife." Andy continued. "If his wife saw him throw that bag overboard, she had to know what was going on. She was in on the plan—or at least the cover-up."

"I vote 'in on the plan'!" I spat my response. "She probably did the deed. After all, who had a better motive. Kill the girlfriend. Maybe all he did was help dispose of the body." I turned to Hank for confirmation.

"I can think of a dozen scenarios that work just as well." The cop folded his arms across his chest.

"And..." This time Andy and I spoke in unison.

"And..." Hank sputtered, "and...maybe it's time we concentrate on eliciting hard data from the Gimbels. And from you, Meg. Let's go over in detail everything you heard Friday night. But first let me call Guy Fleischman. I think that if he hasn't heard from Celia, it's time for him to overcome his reticence and report her disappearance to the Atlantic City police."

A crime had been committed. We were all coming to believe that. Mr. Gimbel was one of the sloppiest criminals around. He almost invited discovery. Yet, he seemed poised to get away with murder. I was willing to bet that, like the weapon that killed her, Celia Chaney slept with the fishes.

Chapter Thirty-Seven

After sharing the plan with Claude and me, Andy and Hank went off to discuss the details. We heard their squabbling as they disappeared into the small study across the hall.

"Andy is very nice." Claude laid another—unneeded—blanket across my knees. "I'm glad he showed up. I'm fond of Hank, but I must say I was a bit worried about your spending so much time with him."

"Why? He's been so helpful and supportive."

"Yes, but certainly you noticed..." He let the sentence trail off.

"Oh, I had him figured out early on."

Claude's voice signaled his relief. "I guess I underestimated you. Not everyone is perceptive enough to recognize sexual addiction."

For a moment, I wasn't sure I'd heard him right. Hank—a sex addict? Meaning he had no control? He'd had no problem resisting me. He had laid the groundwork but he had never made a move. He'd had loads of opportunity. What was wrong with me? The fact that I had no interest was beside the point. If he were an addict, how could he have resisted? I was barely listening as Claude went on.

"Anyway I guess you know how to handle him."

"Uh, yeah," I stammered. "I guess so."

"Please don't mention our little talk. George is ever optimistic that if he produces the right woman, Hank will settle down. He was so excited when you arrived on our doorstep. I, on the other hand, maintain that a zebra doesn't lose its stripes—especially in middle age." As usual, Claude picked up a newspaper. I was still staring at the back page when George set a silver tray on the marble-topped table in the center of the room.

Despite his busy day, George served a tea that was worthy of the finest hotels in London. Carefully cut sandwiches, home-baked scones with Devonshire cream and pastry chasers. The spread even lured the Cummings into the daylight.

Teatime revealed Neil to be much more friendly and outgoing when the sun was up. He had a warm personality to match his handshake. Why he had married Lulu remained a mystery to me. She was gorgeous in a stark, downtown kind of way, with a face and figure that any woman would envy, but she had a jaded attitude, a perpetually dour expression on her face, and no discernible personality. Neil on the other hand was demonstrating a contagiously cheerful disposition, to which only Lulu seemed oblivious. What happened to him after dark? I recalled Claude's theory and shuddered. I didn't believe in vampires, but Neil had the required charm. I eyed the couple huddled together on the couch. I bet Lulu had the nastier bite.

"You poor dear." Mrs. Gimbel's actions were solicitous but her eyes were devoid of emotion as she teetered into the room on her usual stiletto heels. "That was very foolish of you to jump just to save that silly old bag."

"I slipped."

I heard Claude mumble, "Whatever."

"It doesn't matter how she got in the water. She did end up in the water. Let's take good care of her." Marvella Gimbel was my new best friend.

"Yes, by all means." Mr. Gimbel's tone stopped just short of sarcastic. I flashed him a weak smile. With any luck, he wouldn't stay long. He had his overcoat folded neatly on the seat beside him with his ever-present camera sitting on top of it.

I was thrilled to see George sweep into the library bearing more scones. "Meg, dear, you're on the radio and the TV. I'm taping it all. By tomorrow I'm sure your story will be in all the papers." His delivery was cheerful, as if he were relating good news.

Mr. Gimbel expressed an annoyance that I found more than a bit inappropriate. "You could have been killed. At this time of year that water can freeze you to death in a matter of minutes. Everyone knows that."

"Apparently." I released a deep sigh and hid my face in my steaming raspberry tea.

"Oh, Meg. I hope you don't blame us." Marvella Gimbel moved to touch the hand that lay in my lap. I switched to a two-fisted hold on my cup.

"It was an accident. I slipped."

"Whatever." Claude never missed his cue.

"*Slipped*, Ms. Daniels?" Mr. Gimbel raised an eyebrow. "You're being too modest. You ran a hundred-yard dash across the deck and made a leap for that bag. I had the bag resting on the rail—and truthfully I don't know what happened. Then all of a sudden Meg—and the bag—were in the water. I'm not saying it's Meg's fault. I'm sure I would have dropped the duffel no matter what." While his voice seemed to make an attempt at warmth, his eyes were cold as ice as he turned back to me. Did he know what I had been doing, what I had been thinking, and what I believed? There was no way he could know—was there?

Mrs. Gimbel took the role of town crier, repeating the story as each couple arrived for tea. "You'll read this tomorrow in the newspaper but Meg here is the woman who jumped off the ferry today."

Each time I corrected her. "Slipped." Why did I bother?

Lulu appeared bored—but I suspected she always did. Neil was full of questions. The Blandings feigned interest, but unsuccessfully. The Pankenhurst/Parker/Whatevers expressed concern, although Will eyed me suspiciously.

Out of the blue—at least from my point of view—George proposed a photograph. I suspected he had an ulterior motive; I just wasn't sure what it was.

"Come on, Mr. G. I'd love to have a picture of this group. I don't think we'll encounter too many occasions to compare with the rather unusual events of today." George grabbed Wallace Gimbel's camera and shoved it in the man's hands. "Please."

"I don't have a flash."

George eyed the camera. "Are you using fast film? You must be with those night shoots you sneak out for."

Gimbel scowled as he nodded.

"So open her up and you'll be fine. Send me the negative and I'll make sure everyone gets a copy."

Andy wandered into the drawing room just in time for the photo shoot. He was the only one traveling in that direction. Everyone else wanted out.

"Well, we'd love to stay but we really can't." Will was on his feet.

I understood why Will Parker didn't want to be photographed. I didn't understand Mr. Blandings' concern.

His wife protested. "It's a snapshot for God's sake. We're not asking you to sit through a session with Annie Leibovitz."

Mr. Blandings was clearly uncomfortable. "This isn't for the newspaper, is it?"

"Trust me, Bob, I will make sure no picture of me finds its way into the newspaper." That day, my interest in being anonymous was as strong as anyone's.

Mr. Gimbel stared at the camera as if he'd never held one before. He didn't want to take the picture but didn't know how to resist George's eagerness.

"George, Mr. Gimbel can't waste his film on us. He probably doesn't have that many shots left." Why did I bother to get Gimbel off the hook? I wasn't interested in sparing his feelings; I sensed quite a few people in the room weren't interested in posing. My perception was in no way an indication of superior intelligence. An amoeba would have reached the same conclusion.

"I am short of film—for tonight—and there's a full moon." Gimbel was apologetic.

Claude finally stepped in—quashing the enthusiasm that blinded George to Wallace Gimbel's discomfort. Keeping his mate's ebullience in check wasn't easy, but Claude obviously had a fair amount of experience. He distracted George with the need for freshening the pastries.

Hank's arrival diverted the group's attention from talk of photo-ops. "You look good." The cop greeted me first. "Considering you jumped off a ship earlier today."

"I slipped."

"Whatever." Claude's voice floated across the room.

Based on how often I saw Andy check his watch, I surmised that Hank had missed his cue. George made a great show of taking his coat and serving him tea. "We have a full house here today but I know you can find a seat."

I wasn't surprised that Mandy Blandings cozied up to her husband to make room for the cop.

"To what do we owe the honor of this visit?" Claude asked with his usual droll delivery.

"Cold afternoon—especially after my unscheduled boat ride." He made a great show of rubbing his hands together. "I knew you'd be serving tea around a warm fire. Or a drink. I am off duty."

"Off duty." George repeated. "So I don't have to worry that you'll haul me in for that murder."

"George." My intonation cautioned my host to keep quiet.

"What murder?" Mrs. Gimbel came to attention.

"Don't listen to them, ma'am. They don't know what they are talking about." I admired the way Hank averted his eyes. I believe he even managed a slight blush on his already flushed cheeks.

"Hank, I'm the one who talked. I found out when I called you at the station earlier this afternoon. Whoever answered the phone forgot to put me on hold." My coy posturing indicated that my statement implied more than it said on the surface.

"I'll register your complaint." Hank dropped three sugar cubes into his tea.

"But I overhead a male officer say they had found a body in North Cape May."

"You did not." Hank put his cup and saucer on the elegant marble-topped table beside him and glared at me. The cop was right on two counts. One: I hadn't heard any officer say anything. Two: no bodies had surfaced anywhere in Cape May and surrounding counties. He'd checked.

Neil leaned forward. "This sounds interesting. Did I hear the word *body?*"

"You did." George was emphatic.

"No. You're wrong." Hank snapped his answer and fixed me with an angry stare.

"If I'm wrong it's only because I misinterpreted some little detail. Face it, Hank. Like it or not the cat is out of the bag." I turned to the Gimbels. "Well, I can only tell you what I overheard…"

"Yes, please tell us." My take on Mrs. Gimbel's request was that despite trying to sound amused, she was frightened.

"Ms. Daniels." Hank interrupted.

"Chill out, Officer Bergman. We've heard your denials." I leaned forward to hold the group's attention. "To allay Officer Bergman's fears and to stop him from interrupting, let's just say that I am writing a story. The story goes this way. Let's say the cops find the body of a young female on a beach. Maybe dumped. Maybe washed up. I didn't hear those details. However, I can say that she was in her twenties, approximately five foot nine with long dark hair."

"Meg." Hank again tried to interrupt.

"Anyway," I ignored the cop. "What I overheard on the phone…"

"Meg." Hank turned the one word into a warning. He acted increasingly incensed.

"Hank, check out this assemblage. Do you see any murderers here?"

Hank stared at his hands and shook his head. "That is not the point."

"Well, what is the point?"

"What you are saying is not true."

"Right." I winked at Mrs. Gimbel. She stared at me with wide eyes.

"I will not be a party to this." Hank made a pretty good actor—although his part did not require a lot of skill. Why? It required no lies on his part. Andy and Hank had carefully scripted the scene that way.

"Meg." Mandy Blandings made no effort to hide the reproach in her voice. "I think you're making Hank uncomfortable." Her hand reached towards him as he rose. To me the action looked like an unconscious expression of yearning. I checked Bob Blandings' face. If he noticed, his reaction didn't show on his face.

"Okay, Hank. You are on the record. You are not a party to this." I grimaced and blew air through my lips as the cop departed. "Are we all in agreement?" I raised my voice to speak to his back. "Officer Hank Bergman wants no part of this story. "

Neil's tone was reassuring. "We won't repeat your account. Right gang?" His statement extracted murmurs of agreement from the crowd.

"Nothing personal, but I'm not comfortable with this discussion." Hank waved my words off with disgust and disappeared into the small study across the hall. "Call me when you're ready to change the subject."

"Good riddance." I shouted after him. "I'm only telling a story." I leaned forward and held Mrs. Gimbel's gaze with my own. "Anyway, I heard them say that they found a body. I heard the word footprints but I didn't hear whose or where. I heard the word fragments. I assumed bullet—but maybe it's really bone fragments. But I did hear body and that there was skin under the fingernails."

"How did she die?" Again the question came from Mrs. Gimbel. My take on the quiver in her voice was that she had bought in. She believed we were talking about Celia Chaney. Mr. Gimbel did not appear ruffled but rather thoughtful. He continued to stare at his plate.

I shook my head. "As I said, I overheard a comment about fragments. I guess bullet fragments. If only I had better ears. You know sometimes I have trouble with my left ear, and—"

"Why do they think it's murder?" Mrs. Gimbel interrupted "Maybe the girl died of natural causes."

"They found a bullet, Marvella. Don't be stupid," Mr. Gimbel grumbled.

"I don't know if they have a bullet or if it is traceable. When you construct a story based on a few remarks, you leave holes."

"I don't know. You're doing okay. Make up more. I'm enjoying this tale." Neil patted Lulu's knee. She revealed no reaction.

Mrs. Pankenhurst concocted the next part of the tale. "Maybe she was carjacked."

"That's good." Mrs. Gimbel nodded enthusiastically. "Kids these day—and even professional criminals…"

"Marvella, don't get into this." Mr. Gimbel's response was inordinately harsh.

George turned to me and with eyes wide with innocence asked, "When was the body dumped?"

"Hmmmm." I pondered his question with great theatrics. "I don't recall the cops saying. Maybe they found a skeleton. We're all making the assumption this is a fresh body." I snapped my fingers. "Must be recent. The corpse still has hair."

"It has to be a fresh body." Mr. Gimbel addressed the group without taking his eyes off his plate. "Why the hell would they worry if the murder happened forty years ago."

"*If* her death was a murder." Mrs. Gimbel chirped up. "It might have been an accident."

"Yes." The comment was Claude's lone contribution in the last ten minutes. "Maybe she slipped off the ferry."

Chapter Thirty-Eight

After tea, the Gimbels retired to their room. George promised to keep his eye on them. At Hank's request, he, Andy, and I set off to Atlantic City with Hank driving George's jeep. Andy rode shotgun. I took the back seat.

Atlantic City was our cover destination—an excuse to drop by and visit Guy Fleischman.

"So what exactly are we doing?" Andy didn't hide his impatience.

"We're just making a courtesy call," Hank said. "Three…friends on an outing to Atlantic City…who are curious—make that concerned—about a missing person. Besides, Meg is a woman."

I didn't get Hank's point. "I'm a woman? What does that mean? You want me to make a play for Guy? To him thirty-four is like Methuselah."

"I thought you were thirty-three."

"Yesterday I was. Anyway, I'm not that strong in the seduction department." Why was I telling these two guys this? After all, they knew me.

"I don't need you to seduce him. If the opportunity presents itself, I want you to sympathize with him—you know those things girls talk about. Girls, and guys who are emotionally distraught, that is. I'd also like you as a female to observe him and give me your intuition. By the way—Happy Birthday."

"And why am I along?" Andy didn't bother infusing his voice with pleasant overtones.

"I don't like P.I.s much, but there might be some, er, dirty work to be done. I may need your help."

Andy didn't answer—audibly.

Guy lived in Ventnor just below Atlantic City. Hank took the bridge to Margate and entered the town from the south. For me, Ventnor aroused conflicting emotions. I mourned the beachfront houses that had given way to motels and rejoiced at the crop of new construction that heralded the return of private residences to the beachfront—even if those houses would need signage indicating that they are not hotels.

Following the seagull signs up the Ocean Drive, I spotted relatively unchanged buildings and stores—familiar scenes that brought back memories of childhood visits to the beach.

Feeling the need to ease the tension between the two men, I chatted. "When I was little I used to come to Ventnor to visit my grandmother. There weren't all these motels then—mostly it was all beautiful houses. My grandmother had a friend—"

"Meg, let's keep focused on the job at hand."

Hank may have been focused on the investigation, but I still found his comment annoying. Checking out Celia Chaney's fate wasn't anyone's job. I could quit whenever I wanted. Or could I? Did a sense of duty or a natural curiosity convince me that it was too late to drop out without seeing the case to its conclusion? I didn't know. I simply accepted that I was in—no matter how annoying Hank's behavior. Luckily, there was Andy. I turned to him. "Remember? I told you about the boarding house."

"Yes, and it sounded great." The smile he tossed over his shoulder was reassuring but brief. He hung his left hand over the back of the seat and held mine. He said nothing more, but his own annoyance with Hank was evident on his face.

I thought back to my early years in Ventnor. When I was no more than six, we would visit my grandmother in a big old-fashioned boarding house that offered an elegant lifestyle I had not experienced since. That way of life had died in Ventnor and the rest of the world at large.

Guy's apartment building also reflected a lifestyle that had passed. The structure he called home was a great place to live—in the forties. Celia and Guy moved in a little too late in the century—actually they were born a little too late in the century—to enjoy the building's glory days. The pale brickwork had held up, but the outside woodwork indicated the extent of the building's deterioration. The wide, marble-floored hallways were devoid of decoration yet somehow still shabby. Even so, the paint and lighting that screamed "dingy" could not prepare us for the squalor of 6C—although the obscenity etched on the door should have given us a clue. Hank knocked on the "F."

Guy seemed happy to see Hank, willing to see me, and reluctant to meet Andy.

"You and Celia lived together?" I asked as I studied the living room.

"Over a year now." The pride in his voice was obvious.

I hate to deal in sexual stereotypes, but I wouldn't have believed a woman had even visited the apartment in the last year. I could see ten or twelve eighteen-year-old boys living here, sure, but one or more females over the age of twelve, no way. "She's been gone since Friday, right?"

"Right."

I shook my head. Maybe the apartment had been ransacked. No, Guy would have mentioned that to Hank. Maybe he'd had a party. No, Guy showed no signs of moving past the tragedy of Celia's disappearance. Maybe he was just a slob.

No one had ever nominated me for the good housekeeping award, but Guy and Celia's residence made my place look neat. I didn't own as many items as were strewn across the coffee table. I was willing to wager that no one had eaten at the dining room table in months; a dozen piles of paper stood over a foot high. Not that I understood how anyone could eat in the apartment at all. Not only was the place messy—it was visibly dirty. When I notice a place is dirty, believe me—it's filthy. On the upside, the smell of stale cigarette smoke masked the body odor I'd smelled when Guy greeted us. I didn't want to know what odor was being generated by the pile of laundry, heavy on black socks, that waited for attention in the corner. To make sure I didn't find out, I didn't push aside the seashell overflowing with burned-down brown filters and lipstick-smudged white filters. The makeshift ashtray served as an air freshener.

Guy cleared newspapers off every chair and cleared beer cans from around their legs, making room for two of us to sit down. Hank and I took the seats—albeit somewhat reluctantly. The cop inspected the cushion carefully before sitting down. I figured what I didn't know couldn't hurt me, so I didn't look.

Guy wore black trousers and an open-necked white shirt that I suspected he had worked in the night before and that I worried he would work in again that night. The clothes' appearance would not be improved by reclining on the sofa, which was what Guy did—even though there was not sufficient seating for all three of us. Andy leaned against the door.

"Who's he?" Guy nodded at Andy.

"A colleague." Hank grabbed a magazine and thumbed through the pages absent-mindedly. "I take it you haven't heard from Celia."

Guy shook his head.

"Have you called the police?"

Again, Guy shook his head. "Celia would kill me."

"Why?" I suspected Hank sounded more harsh than he intended.

"She—Celia…she wouldn't like it."

"Guy, I don't mean to alarm you but there's no way to sugarcoat this."

Sugarcoat, no. Obfuscate, maybe.

"Guy, I am here as an acquaintance." Hank flashed a new variation on his dazzling smile. This version demanded trust. "Although there has been no official investigation, unofficial sources are speculating that there is reason to suspect Celia may have encountered some unplanned event that may have led to an unpleasant fate."

Guy understood what Hank was trying so hard not to say. Maybe he wasn't as dumb as I thought. Comprehending what Hank communicated was no easy task.

Guy buried his face in his hands and moaned—in low tones that grew louder and louder. "Oh, no. Oh, no. Oh, no. It's my fault. I should have stopped her. I should have stopped her."

Guy's was a display of grief that seemed real, and deeper than any I'd witnessed. He ran into the next room—so quickly he neglected to close the door tightly behind him. We overheard the various stages as he got sick. After the nasty noises stopped, Guy remained in the bathroom for several minutes. Whatever he was doing, I was fairly sure he wasn't cleaning up. When the young man finally returned, he was obviously weak.

"Sorry, man. We might be all wrong. We wanted to talk to you before taking this to an official level." Hank handled the questioning. "I didn't understand, Guy. Why did you say you should have stopped her?"

Following Guy's story was difficult. His tale was frequently interrupted by sobbing. "Celia told him she was pregnant. She figured he owed her." Guy fought to bring his emotions under control.

"She was certain Gimbel was the father?"

"There was no baby. All Celia wanted...she just needed some money...from Gimbel. She got false test results...a friend...well, you don't care how...she got a positive...pregnancy test, you know. He...I mean Gimbel...he had...has plenty of money. Everyone knew his wife was...is rich. She belonged to some wealthy New York family."

Was I the only one concerned by his use of the past tense? What exactly had he and Celia been planning?

"Celia and I wanted to move and start over, and she figured if she told him she was pregnant, we could get some seed money."

Sounded a mite like extortion to me.

Guy wiped his nose on the back of his hand and the back of his hand on his pants. Just one more stain added to a formidable collection.

Guy appeared more composed as he continued. "I told her she was overplaying her hand. She decided he had to believe she loved him. He had to be convinced that she wanted him to leave his wife. I was afraid he would do it, but Celia knew. She said there was no way Gimbel would jump off that money train. She figured she would just make him feel guilty by saying she loved him."

"And?"

"I don't know if he felt guilty or not, but he said he wanted to marry her. That was my worst fear. I believed Celia would marry him—for the money, of course." He tried to reassure himself. "I know she loves me."

"Of course," Hank agreed.

I found accepting Celia's fate easier and easier. Celia Chaney wasn't exactly a good person. Except, perhaps, when compared to the Gimbels.

Chapter Thirty-Nine

"I am *not* flirting with Hank. I don't even know *how* to flirt. If I recall correctly, you told me that once." With effort, I climbed onto the antique bed. Alone with Andy in the bridal suite, the last thing on my mind was Hank. The cop had done his best to convince Guy to report Celia missing, dropped Andy and me off at the Parsonage, and headed off mumbling about Gimbel. As far as I was concerned the investigation was in his hands.

"I'm beat, Andy. I had a rough day. I feel a little sore. I know you guys didn't mean any harm when you dragged me onto the boat, but my arms and legs are covered with bruises."

"Well, you may not be that good at flirting, but you seem to be trying pretty hard." Andy dug in his suitcase but emerged empty-handed—and angry.

I waved a hand to beckon him and waited. He wasn't going to come around that easily. I dragged myself out of bed and across the room. "Andy, I...I have no interest in Hank."

"But you admit to flirting with him."

I grabbed Andy's hand and held the back against my cheek. "Claude told me this morning that Hank has a sex addiction."

Andy stared at me silently for a moment. "Is this information about the man you were out with last night supposed to put my mind at ease?" Despite his words he did not pull his hand away.

"No." I wanted to explain. "I felt kind of bad..."

"Because you...?"

"No, I told you, we *didn't*. I just felt bad...Andy, did I ever tell you about my friend Elinor and Wilt Chamberlain?"

"You have a friend who slept with Wilt Chamberlain?"

"No. That's my point. He wrote that book about how he slept with thousands of women. But he was always a perfect gentleman with Elinor."

Andy didn't understand.

"No matter what, she felt like a loser. Like Elinor, I feel bad because Hank never made a play for me. I watched him flirt with Mandy Blandings and Nanette Pankenhurst, and check out women on the street. He was nice to me but I swear he never made a pass— although there were moments I was expecting one." I sighed. "Apparently I am to sexual addiction what Zyban is to smoking."

"So, you wanted him to make a pass?"

"No." I paused. "I wanted him to want to make a pass."

Andy turned his hand to caress my cheek. "Listen, I'm a man, and I can see that Hank has the hots for you. I wouldn't be so jealous if he didn't." He seemed surprised by his own words. "You know I'm jealous, right?"

"You're just saying that to be nice."

"I'm not that nice. Besides, how many times have you accused me of bickering with Hank?"

I shrugged. I was capable of sulking at least as well as Andy.

"And why do you think we were bickering?"

Again, I shrugged.

"Because we were jealous of each other. Trust me. Take his reticence as a compliment."

I stood silently, sporting the same pouty expression Andy had worn twelve hours before.

"Come on," Andy said, giving me a playful hug; I smiled through gritted teeth to disguise the pain. "You're no invalid, and it's your birthday—how about I take you out to dinner?"

◆ ◆ ◆

I didn't have the nerve to tell Andy that the restaurant he chose—George's recommendation—was where Hank and I had eaten the night before. I figured no one was likely to point out the coincidence if I didn't, and that with a little luck none of the restaurant staff would remember me. I was right—and wrong.

I was recognized immediately, but not by the staff. "Oh, you're *that* woman, aren't you?"

I had a horrible feeling I was.

"The woman who jumped off the ferry?"

"Actually, I slipped."

"Whatever." The woman traded the broad smile on her face for a concerned frown. She patted my arm—gently, but the gesture hurt. I smiled with difficulty and moved my arm out of range. "You look fine," she said. "Are you feeling okay?"

"Thanks for asking. I'm fine." I spoke through clenched teeth.

She turned and yelled across the bar to her husband. "Hey, Jack—look! It's the gal who jumped off the ferry!"

He did—and so did everyone else. I could only be grateful the restaurant wasn't filled with a July crowd.

"I slipped," I protested feebly. No one heard me.

Andy and I had a drink in the bar before taking our table. Why not give every other customer time to gossip about us? I leaned close to Andy in the hopes of blocking the gawkers' view. The tactic was fairly successful, but one man in particular managed to see around the blockade. He seemed to be studying me with more than a passing curiosity.

"Do you know that guy behind you? The one in the crew neck sweater. About forty." The man averted his eyes when I met his gaze.

Andy glanced over his shoulder. "With the reddish hair? I've never seen him before."

"He's watching me like a hawk."

"Well, Meg, you are sort of a celebrity around here."

"I know, but he was looking at me like...I don't know—like he knows me. He looks vaguely familiar. Normally it wouldn't bother me but—"

"Let me handle this. I'll be discreet." Andy wandered over, stood next to man and ordered another round of drinks. I watched them exchange a few words. The guy shook his head. I watched as Andy asked a few more questions. After shaking his head a few more times, the stranger took over the conversation. Andy was nodding.

The man appeared upset. He looked into the distance as he spoke. I swore I saw his eyes tear up. Andy consoled him with a hearty pat on the back before he grabbed our drinks and said good-bye.

"So?" I asked as I relieved Andy of a glass of white wine.

"He doesn't know you. Until that woman yelled across the room, he didn't know anyone had jumped—I mean, fallen off the ferry. And he doesn't know Celia Chaney, either. I thought I might as well ask."

"It took him that long to tell you that?"

"Nah, he told me his entire life story. He's having some problems. He's kind of upset and a little bit drunk." Andy seemed nervous, as if he were hiding something.

"That's it?"

"That's it. Let's see if our table is ready."

I glanced back. The guy lounged across the piano. He didn't seem the type to like Barry Manilow, yet the redhead with the pale brown eyes was warbling "Mandy" as we left the bar to take our table.

Chapter Forty

I was thrilled to be with Andy and thought he felt the same way—over appetizers. By the main course, he'd grown silent. I had a bad feeling. My premonition proved correct when he finished his swordfish, wiped his lips, and placed his neatly folded napkin in his lap. He cleared his throat. Big trouble. I knew it.

"Meg, there's something I've got to talk to you about. Please listen to me. I can't be with you under false pretenses."

It was my birthday—false pretenses would do just fine. Bad news could wait until Monday. I would have explained, but I was speechless waiting for the ax to fall. The last twenty-four hours had been too good to be true. I knew it.

"I don't want you to say a word. Just listen."

I nodded. I was numb.

"Remember your comment last night about my not wanting to discuss what I've been doing for the last six weeks." I nodded as he continued. "Well, you're right. It is painful for me to discuss my behavior with you. I know you think that Antigua is full of beautiful, fun-loving women—and it's true. I mean, Maggie, the women are so fit, so youthful, so full of life..." He shook his head in awe. "There are so many *types* of women—anything and everything a man could want. Blondes. Redheads. Brunettes. Tall women. Short women..."

"Andy, I recall that you said I should be quiet, but you've made your point. I think I've got the picture."

"Yeah. Sorry." He took a deep breath. "Anyway, I've had my share of opportunities and I took them."

I'd known that. Okay, I hadn't hired a private detective to follow Andy so I didn't really *know*. Let's say I *intuited* that. Nonetheless, hearing the news, I felt sick.

"I mean, there I was living my dream. I've wanted to live that way for as long as I remember."

"I understand, Andy." I lifted my napkin from my lap and laid it on the table.

"I mean, it was my dream...and you ruined it."

"Excuse me?" My voice was louder than I'd planned. Under the table, my hands clenched the tablecloth.

"You ruined it for me. I mean I would always be thinking, 'Hey wouldn't Maggie get a kick out of this' or 'I bet Maggie would think this was beautiful' or 'I wonder what Maggie would have to say about that.' Always. I would be with this beautiful woman...I mean I'd be laying there..."

"Lying...although maybe what you really mean is laying." I interrupted.

He smiled. "You know what I'm saying...afterward I'd put my arm around...or I'd touch..."

Andy, I prayed silently, please don't go there.

But he did. "I mean the sex would be terrific, absolutely great, and the woman, maybe a really nice girl, would have an incredible body..." He reacted to the expression on my face. "I'm not very good at this, am I?"

"Unless you're trying to drive a stake through my heart, no, you're not."

"Just hear me out. I'd stare at her, this great looking woman, lay-ing...lying there and you know what I would think?"

"I wonder if she's ready for another go round?" I took a stab in the dark.

He shook his head. "Five months ago you would have been right. But you know what I think now at moments like that? I think, 'I wish Maggie were here.'"

"With the two of you?"

"No." He dragged the word out for emphasis. "*Instead* of her...whoever she is. Maggie, I think I have a big problem. I think...I know...I really like you."

He liked me. He really liked me. Andy had taken five minutes to build up to this? Even I knew *he liked me*. Before I produced a snappy retort, Andy was at it again.

"No. I'm lying. It's worse than that. I think I love you. There, I said it. I mean I really don't know because I've never actually felt like this before, except maybe in sixth grade when Cindy Carlson matured...I mean, wow she did *mature*...and I would think about her all the time. But since I've been an adult...nothing like this. I mean I wonder what you're doing and who you're with.... When I got here...and saw Hank...I cursed my luck—my bad luck. I thought I was one day too late."

I couldn't keep the smile from my lips. "Now you know how a girl feels."

"Maggie, be serious. I think it's love. This feeling I have. I think it is. I feel it. I do, I'm sorry, but that's it. I think I love you and I know I'm rushing things but since I don't know when I might see you again...and who knows how long this feeling will last..."

He folded his hands on the table and stared at me. "This is when you're supposed to say, 'Andy, I love you, too.' At least, that's how I rehearsed it."

"Are you *sure* you love me? Are you sure you're not just *homesick*?"

He shook his head. "I've considered this situation from a lot of angles, and I'm sure. I love you, Maggie. I know we were together for only..." He counted on his fingers. The task did not require many digits. "Was it really only two months?"

I nodded. "The same amount of time we've been apart."

"It doesn't matter. I never thought I'd meet anyone I felt so comfortable—and at the same time uncomfortable—with. I guess I shouldn't have gone to Antigua. To tell you the truth, I knew how I felt before I left. I just couldn't admit it."

Andy was watching me for an answer. He wanted me to say I loved him. Did I? I knew that by the age of thirty-four I was supposed to understand these things but I didn't have a clue. I did know that I had a terrible crush on the man who sat across the table from me. Like a thirteen-year-old, I felt my heart flutter when he entered the room.

I felt an undeniable attraction and an inexplicable connection. The unexplained feelings—sensing his presence when he entered a room—okay, maybe not when he showed up in my bathroom in the middle of the night, but at other times. Turning to meet his gaze as his eyes caught sight of me. Knowing he was on the other end of the phone when he called.

"Maggie, aren't you going to say anything?"

I nodded but didn't speak.

"Love" wasn't a word we used in my family, and certainly not a word I used outside the family. I'd spent three years with David and never told him I loved him. Never thought it, either. The lack of commitment didn't seem to concern him. In my mind, love involved full understanding of the other person, years of shared experiences, knowledge of the other person's middle name.

"Andy, what's your full name?"

"Andrew Sinclair Beck. Sinclair is my mother's maiden name. You're thinking you don't know me well enough, right? I think you do. I feel like I knew you the minute I met you."

At last I found something to say. "You talked about all we had in common and how we were so much alike. Well, I didn't see it at first. I mean, I liked you...boy, did I like you...but I thought we were nothing alike. But since you've been gone, I've seen how connected I felt to you. I would know that you would see things my way—that we shared a worldview—and I missed you more and more each day."

"So you do love me?"

I shrugged. "I lose my appetite when you're around. I'm a little scared of you. I'm a little shy when I first see you."

"So does that mean…?"

"I don't use these words lightly, but I've got to admit that there's a pretty good chance I love you, too." Once the words were out they didn't seem so bad. "I love you." I listened to the words hanging in the air.

"So. This is good, isn't it?" Andy leaned across the table and forced my eyes to meet his.

"That's the conventional wisdom."

"I have something else to say—you know I bought a boat…"

I nodded. Of course I knew what took Andy to Antigua.

"I was thinking that maybe you could defer graduate school. They let you do that, don't they?"

Again, I nodded.

"I understand that you'll need some time to think about my request. I'm asking a lot, I know that…but really it's only four, five, maybe six months."

"What is only six months?"

"The time you would have to take off. I thought you might want to come down to Antigua and sail with me to New Jersey where I'll keep the boat next summer. We'll do some ocean sailing and then come up the inland waterway. You can start school in the fall, or maybe the summer semester. I don't want you to answer me now."

"Why?"

"It's a big decision. Don't dismiss my proposition out of hand…"

"But I…"

"No. Please think over what I said and let me know tomorrow. Just promise you'll consider my proposal."

"Andy, I…"

"Promise?"

I sighed. "I promise."

"Okay." He released a deep breath. "So, what do we do now?"

I reached across the table and took his hand. "Andy, I don't consider myself much of a sophisticate, but I've seen enough movies that I've this part covered. Get the check. Fast."

"But it's your birthday. I ordered a cake—well, actually George did. I thought you'd be embarrassed but he insisted."

I glanced across the room. "The Gimbels are here again tonight."

Andy missed the word "again."

"Yeah?"

If Andy harbored any doubts regarding the depth of my feelings for him, they should have disappeared in the moment. I eschewed spying on the Gimbels. Quite a shift in priorities. What I didn't say was that I could think of nothing suspicious about a man taking his wife to dinner—even when the couple was Marvella and Wallace Gimbel. What I did say was: "Send the dessert to their table. Let them eat cake."

Chapter Forty-One

When we arrived at the Parsonage, Hank was waiting in the drawing room. He rushed to greet Andy and me. Actually, he rushed to stop us. He attempted to block our way to the stairs. Unluckily for him, the Victorians favored wide hallways. We didn't have to stop, and we didn't.

"Mrs. Gimbel is ready."

Mrs. Gimbel wasn't the only one. "Great, Hank, we can talk to her in the morning." Without slowing, I flashed a smile best described as perfunctory.

"Meg, you're the one who started this." Hank stared at me with eyes that broadcast disappointment. He was sure to add a little anger to the mix.

Okay. I had to admit he was right. I had started this adventure or episode or caper—whatever our activities could be called. But I had been bored. I was no longer bored. "The Gimbels aren't here. We just saw them at dinner."

"I know. I saw Mrs. Gimbel before she left. We were chatting in the library. I had her that close..." He held his thumb and index fingers together. "If Gimbel hadn't shown up, I know she would have cracked."

"She admitted there was a murder?" Andy asked the questions.

"No."

"She admitted she knew Celia Chaney?"

"No."

"She admitted her husband was having an affair?"

"Almost."

"Almost?" Andy used a sarcastic tone he usually reserved for me. "She said her husband has an avid interest in photography and he's been running out at odd hours to take photos." Hank was obviously impressed with the news. I might have been, too—the night before.

"Okay, Hank," Andy said. "Let me see if I have this. You got Marvella Gimbel to admit that her husband has an avid interest in photography. Give him the chair." Andy nudged me towards the stairs.

"Beck, listen to me. He goes out every night. That means she will be here alone. I know I can get her to talk."

"Well, good luck." Andy guided me closer to the stairs.

"I've got to have support. I need to lure her into a social situation. Gimbel won't let her end up in another one-on-one with me."

"Where are Claude and George?" I checked around as if they had been hiding since Andy and I came in.

"They went to a party. They're no help. I need you, Meg." He cleared his throat—apologetically, I thought. "I need both of you."

"This isn't a good time—it's my birthday," I reminded Hank.

"Look, Meg, who started this whole investigation? You have to finish it."

Good cop? Bad cop? How could I describe a guilt-inducing cop? I wouldn't be coerced into feeling derelict in my duty. I had no obligation. "I was only a concerned citizen. I brought the situation to your attention. You're the cop, you finish it."

The expression on Hank's face—part dejection, part anger, part confusion—convinced me. To feel guilty, that is. "Okay, we'll help you." I included Andy. "But there's something else I have to finish first. When we left the restaurant the Gimbels were on appetizers. They look like dessert eaters to me. Andy and I need a few minutes, then we'll—"

"Rule Britannia" interrupted. "I'll get it." Andy volunteered to answer the chimes only because he was closest to the front door.

Over Andy's shoulder, I recognized the visitor. He was the young man from the restaurant—the Barry Manilow fan. Had he followed us? What did he want? As Hank and I continued our debate, I thought I heard the stranger say he'd come for his wife.

Andy escorted the visitor into the small library off the hall. As he emerged two or three minutes later, I overheard him advising the man, "Wait here. I'll see what I can do."

Andy squeezed my arm as he slipped by me. "I'll see if I can help this fellow and then I'll be right back."

I nodded and asked with contorted features: where are you going? He in turn tried to answer with similarly twisted features. I had no idea what he was doing. I was still in the process of extricating myself from Hank and his demands when I heard the key in the lock. "Here come Claude and George. They can help you, Hank."

With that, the door flew open and slammed into the combo coat rack/umbrella stand against the wall.

"Ouch!" Nanette Pankenhurst/Parker/Whatever threw her hand over her mouth. "Do you think Claude and George heard?"

"They're not here, Nanette." I eyed her suspiciously. "Are you okay?"

"Right...as...rain." She spaced the words evenly before bursting into tears.

"Oh, no," Hank whispered to me. "I'm not good with crying women. Three divorces, you know. They cry; I leave. You handle her, okay?" Superman never moved faster.

One of us had to handle the faux Mrs. Pankenhurst. That, I didn't question, since it was obvious she really needed help. I glanced up the stairs. Andy was occupied—conferring with Mandy Blandings in the hallway. I didn't have time to figure out the link between their consultation and the man waiting in the small study. My hands were full with Nanette. Literally. She wrapped her arms around me and buried her head in my shoulder. I patted her back tentatively. Playing the affectionate type didn't come easy to me.

"Now, now." I attempted to soothe the sobbing guest.

To show her thanks, she wiped her nose on my sweater.

"I'll help you to your room."

"No!" she screamed. "I don't want to see him."

"Did Will hurt you?" I held her at arm's length and studied her face.

"No. No. Will would never hurt me." She sniffed and issued a correction. "He would never mean to hurt me."

"But he did?"

Her sobs told the story. Actually, they let me know there was a story. As much as I wanted to abandon her, I couldn't bring myself to leave the crying woman alone. She needed to confide in someone. "We should sit in the drawing room. No one's in there right now, and we can ask Hank to bring you some tea."

"I'd rather have scotch."

"You've already had some scotch, haven't you?"

"Not that much."

"Hank!" I screamed in a soprano my mother had worked hard to eliminate from my vocal range.

The cop's face appeared around the corner. He'd been hiding in the dining room. He moved slowly and tentatively.

"Could we have some tea, please?"

I felt his relief. Of all possible requests, that one apparently suited him. No crying, no hugging, no deep conversation required. I led the alleged Mrs. Pankenhurst to the sofa. "Maybe Will doesn't know how you feel."

"How could he not?" Nanette blew her nose hard. Thankfully, my sweater was not involved. Someone—Hank, as I learned later—had left a box of tissues on the table next to the couch.

Twenty minutes and as many tissues disappeared while I, as unqualified as I was on both the personal and professional level, provided romantic advice to Nanette. Convincing her that fifteen years of unrequited love was quite enough wasn't difficult. I, however, wasn't convinced the love was unrequited. "Do you think Will invited you here in the hopes that something might happen? You know, between the two of you."

She shook her head and blew her nose simultaneously. "He just needed a cover."

"But you said he's a real ladies' man. He wouldn't have had any trouble finding a date."

"Yeah, but they would have expected attention from him. Maybe a little time together." Despite the box of tissues, she continued to sniffle. I took the Kleenex and held the box in front of her. Absentmindedly, she pulled out a tissue, sniffing loudly without getting it anywhere near her nose.

"Nanette, maybe it's time you had expectations. Maybe he doesn't know you want his attention. Seems to me he took a big chance asking you to come here. He's sharing a very important part of his life with you." Not knowing what she knew, I didn't elaborate. "Why don't you go upstairs and tell him how you feel?" *Please go upstairs,* I prayed silently.

"But..."

"But what? The worst-case scenario is that you find a new job and a new love. You can't continue down *this* road. Road? *What* road? You're not going anywhere."

"He wouldn't want me. Will usually goes with...you know... beautiful women."

I didn't have enough time to turn Nanette into Farrah Fawcett. For that matter, no one did. I tried to conjure up another seventies icon that might appeal to Will Parker. I didn't work well under pressure; I came up empty. "Just be yourself. You have a lot of history with Will. Just dry your eyes, put a little cold water on them to bring down the swelling, and a little makeup."

"Eye makeup. I don't *have* any eye makeup."

I didn't have much but what I did have, I gave to Nanette. I was more anxious for her to confront Will Parker than she was. I'd only been waiting thirty-five minutes for time alone with Andy. Thirty-five *long* minutes. How could she have lived that way for sixteen years?

I had to ask. "Nanette, what is it you love about Will?"

A grin caressed the corners of her lips. Her eyes also smiled as she gazed past me into space. "He is very, very smart...and kind... and honest. He's so earnest, but not serious. Like this whole thing with Gimbel...he told me, you know...he made this...caper—fun... so much fun."

"How so?" I recalled discovering a weeping Nanette on at least two occasions.

"Going to a thrift shop and buying all those ridiculous clothes. I mean, he had never even met Wallace Gimbel. There was no chance Gimbel would identify him unless he recognized his voice. But Will figured that even if he slipped and dropped that good-ol'-boy accent, Gimbel would never associate the guy in the bright orange leisure suit with the accountant in the conservative Philadelphia firm."

"You're not even from Baltimore?"

"I've never even been to Baltimore—except through the station on Amtrak. Will grew up there. Still has family there—borrowed his cousin's car for the weekend. All to fool Gimbel because he would never tie Will Parker to Baltimore." Her glassy-eyed smile returned. "See what I mean—Will is lots of fun. If we had more time, he would have grown those big muttonchop whiskers."

Sideburns! I should have caught that detail. If Will Parker were as devoted to the seventies as he appeared to be, his hair would have been longer, wider, bigger. I felt relief. I was happier fixing Nanette up with a man who dwelled in the current decade.

Chapter Forty-Two

The entire time I consoled Nanette, Andy shuffled in and out of the library with the young stranger, Mandy Blandings, and then Bob Blandings. Whatever was going on made Mandy Blandings cry and Bob Blandings fume. Hank had been no help in either situation. He had delivered Nanette's tea, eavesdropped on Andy's conference for a few moments, and then disappeared.

I had to wait ten minutes after Nanette ventured upstairs to hear Andy's story. Ten minutes that felt like an hour.

"Maggie, I am so sorry. That was Mandy's husband." Andy slipped onto the plush Victorian sofa and wrapped an arm around my shoulder.

"Ex-husband." I corrected him.

"No. Husband. Mandy is here with her boyfriend. That was the reason Matthew, that's his name, was staring at us at the restaurant. He's been watching the house all weekend. He recognized you." He squeezed my shoulder. "I would have told you but...you felt bad because of Hank's flirting with Mandy. I didn't think you'd want to know there was yet another man who found her irresistible. Matthew told me the entire story at the restaurant. Bob is someone she works with. Matthew is still in love with her and wants her back."

"Mandy?"

Andy nodded.

"Mandy Blandings?"

"Actually, Mandy Mather. She and Bob used the name Blandings because they liked the movie."

"I can't believe all these men are in love with that woman." I shook my head. "But the Blandings kept talking about how they had been married for twelve years and were still crazy about each other."

"Well, that part is true. He's been married for seven; she's been married for five. Just not to each other."

"And her husband wants her back?"

"Desperately."

I didn't get it. I already knew how Bob felt about her. I suspected what Hank thought, and her husband wanted her back. No man had ever swooned over me that way and, if one were to believe the fashion magazines, I should have had several advantages over Mrs. Blandings. But then again, if I believed the fashion magazines, millions of women had advantages over me. Was I jealous? Okay, maybe a little but I was more perplexed. Then I realized: what did it matter? My love life had picked up appreciably since I'd first wondered about the Mandy Blandings' phenomenon. I was only interested in what Andy thought.

Suddenly, another realization hit me.

"Andy, if he's been watching the house all weekend, then he might know something about Celia Chaney."

While Mandy Blandings/Mather/whatever packed her belongings, Andy and I grilled her husband about what he had seen outside the Parsonage. Matthew didn't have much interest in our questions but neither did he have the energy to fend them off.

Without providing guidance regarding the information we sought, Andy took the lead. "During the time you've been watching the house, did you notice anything suspicious?"

"Did I? On Friday night—I remember it was like two degrees—some woman climbed down from the second floor in a nightgown. No coat. No shoes. No underwear." Andy frowned first at Matthew and then at me.

"It was a windy night," I offered by way of explanation.

"Nothing else unusual?"

"Sometimes when I'd be hanging around after lights out, I'd see someone moving on the first floor—but I didn't go up to the window and look in. Whoever it was didn't come out—at least not out the front door. I see some old guy going in and out all the time—sometimes kinda late—but he doesn't do anything odd. Just goes around to the parking lot and drives away. I don't know what type of car; I see the lights. Sometimes I see him come back. I don't know what he does, but he does it fairly often. Brings his old lady sometimes."

"Did you ever see him with another woman?"

Matthew Mather shook his head. "No. I saw them kissing on the balcony one night, but then I started watching that crazy broad on the roof—so I didn't see nothing good."

Great. Our only witness had been distracted by the crazy broad who looked herself out of her room. I saw no reason to reveal the woman's identity.

Chapter Forty-Three

A teary-eyed Mandy—I guess we'd have to call her Mandy Whatever—appeared suitcase in hand shortly after we'd finished questioning Matthew. I had no idea what caused her tears. I suspected her problem had something to do with not having your cake and eating it, too. Matthew greeted her with a soft smile, kind words, and admiring eyes. He took his errant wife's suitcase, wrapped an arm around her waist and guided her out the front door. I watched with amazement. I'd never understand her appeal.

I dropped next to Andy on a soft Victorian sofa. "What do you think of her?" I emphasized the word "you."

He shrugged. "She's kind of cute. She has a certain…"

"*Je ne sais quoi?*"

"Yes, she does." He eyed me with concern. "Does that bother you?"

I shrugged. "It doesn't bother me; I'm flummoxed. And maybe a little jealous."

"I hope that doesn't mean you'd rather be with Bob Blandings or Matthew?"

"Andy, there is no one I would rather be with…"

He grabbed my hand. "In that case, want to make a run for it?"

"I'm there." I let Andy pull me towards the hallway. We'd taken two steps when the doors from the dining room flew open and I heard singing voices.

"I bet you thought we forgot." That voice, the same voice that led the singing, belonged to George. Claude turned out the lights but the room grew brighter. Hank carried a layer cake with many candles— I strongly suspected there were thirty-four. It was the first time I remembered being blinded by the candles on my birthday cake. I knew it wouldn't be the last.

"Count 'em, Meg." George encouraged me as Hank placed the flaming confection in the center of a large marble topped library table.

"I trust you, George."

Andy squeezed my hand and pulled me close. "Need help blowing those out?"

"Not at thirty-four, thank you very much." I proved my point by extinguishing every candle with a single breath.

Any other time, I might have lingered over several slices of the gooey concoction. Given my desire to disappear upstairs, I cut the cake, nibbled at a small slice, and said my thank yous. I was ready to make a run for it when Hank, whom I hadn't noticed disappear, reappeared from the hallway. He wasn't alone. "Mr. Gimbel ran out to take a few photos but I convinced Mrs. Gimbel to join us for cake. Cut her a big piece, will you Meg?"

I smiled through gritted teeth and cut a big piece for Marvella Gimbel and a sliver for Hank. He ushered Mrs. Gimbel to the sofa Andy and I had recently vacated. If the woman knew she was being lured into a trap she didn't let on. Still in the red cocktail dress she'd worn to dinner, she settled into a corner with her red silk shoes dangling six inches above the elegantly worn carpet.

Hank delivered a piece of chocolate cake and a cup of tea, both served in fine china festooned with red roses. "You can have a big piece. You don't have to diet." The emphasis he put on the word "you" made me think that he harbored a belief that someone in the room should watch their caloric intake. I did not dwell on the implications of his remark.

Mrs. Gimbel picked at her cake. I found myself thinking, wouldn't liquor be more effective?—after all, we wanted the woman to spill the beans. I considered my own feelings. No, I'd sell out for a piece of devil's food cake long before a drink tempted me.

Claude took his regular position near the fire. George sat across from him in an identical chair. Andy and I sat on one end of a Victorian sofa and cuddled as discreetly as possible. We all acted as if we had assembled for a social occasion—I wasn't sure if George and Claude were aware we hadn't. Hank had to wrest control of the conversation from the ever garrulous George. Once he succeeded, I had no doubt where the discussion was headed; I simply wasn't sure how the cop was going to get it there.

Hank had taken a position down the couch from Mrs. Gimbel. "Yep, thirty-four looks good to me. How about you, Marvella?' He edged closer and squeezed her knee. Her red satin skirt stopped six inches above the joint. I checked her legs—just in case. They were still twice the size of the ankles I'd observed on Friday night.

"I barely remember being thirty-four." Marvella sounded wistful. She demonstrated no interest in her cake—ostensibly because she and her husband had enjoyed my birthday cake at the restaurant.

"Of course, it's easier for me. Being a man and all. It's not fair, but in the aging game we men get away with murder. Don't we boys?" Afraid to misdirect the conversation, the men in the room nodded and murmured their agreement—even George appeared to have figured out that something was up.

"We men are awful. I've had three wives. Each of them twenty when I married them. It isn't easy for the women."

"No." Mrs. Gimbel's eyes misted with tears. "It isn't. Men have their needs when they reach a certain age. Understanding their behavior doesn't make accepting it any easier." She lay down her fork. She might as well. She hadn't touched her cake.

Hank moved closer to Marvella Gimbel on the couch and lay a hand on her arm. "Mrs. Gimbel, you know that you are free to go, but I have to tell you that we know about Celia Chaney."

"You know…?" Her face grew flushed.

Hank nodded. I figured he couldn't say much because we really didn't know a thing. "We're all here to help you..."

"Nobody can help me." She barely whispered.

"I can...we can help you." He squeezed her arm. Very gently. Very tentatively.

"I don't know...now...once it happened...I know that no one can help me." Her face was as red as her lipstick.

"I thought telling us what happened might make things easier on you."

Marvella's eyes begged Hank for information. "How did you know? The body you found...?"

Hank shook his head. "We know Celia is missing. We haven't found her."

"I've been so upset. I wanted to tell someone."

I waited for tears to fall but none did.

Hank rested one arm across Mrs. Gimbel's shoulder. He placed his other hand on top of hers. Then he flashed a modified version of that smile. That was all it took. Marvella Gimbel clutched Hank's hand and sang like a canary. Through sobs she told us all we had suspected and more. Luckily, Hank had the forethought to place a box of tissues and a wastepaper basket at her side. She had almost filled the trash can before we finished the background information.

"That woman was pregnant. She told Wallace three weeks ago. She was willing to have DNA testing. The baby was Wallace's. He didn't deny her accusation." She sniffled. "I think he was actually a little proud that his...you know was working." She blew her nose noisily and continued. "He came to me and confessed. He said he loved me and didn't want to lose me. It was his idea, you know."

"Killing her?" Hank filled in the words.

"I swear...it was his idea. The whole plan was his. He said she would ruin him. He'd lose his job."

My face told her that I believed her explanation. I didn't.

"She could have sued him for sexual harassment." Mrs. Gimbel grew defensive. "I didn't care. I have money. But Wallace is noble. He said he didn't want to take my money." She punctuated her confession with another loud noseblow. "He planned the whole thing. He would bring her here—as me—so we would both have an alibi all night. Then he would smother her." Her eyes dried as she became eerily calm. "The plan was that I would sneak in and take her place. He would then steal out the back and dispose of the body."

She stared at me. She had something to tell me. I didn't prompt her. When she finally spoke, her tone was calm, almost pedantic. "I know I got jumpy when you talked about our making love that night. Wallace explained the situation to me. There was some hullabaloo and he had to...he strangled her."

"Hullabaloo" seemed an oddly festive word to describe a murder.

"He made the noises himself to cover up the sounds...her cries when he...."

Yeah, right. I wished I owned land to sell to the woman.

"Anyway, when I got there, she wasn't dead. I mean, we thought she was. We were talking and she woke up—like that woman in the bathtub in that movie Fatal Attraction. She was making these gasping sounds..." Mrs. Gimbel replicated horrid, yet oddly subdued noises. In a lot of ways, Gimbel was a dumb criminal, but at least by strangling Celia Chaney, even unsuccessfully, he'd made it impossible for her to scream.

Mrs. Gimbel stopped and shook her head. "It was very frightening."

Especially for Celia Chaney I thought.

"Anyway, Wallace and I were deciding what to do next and she moved. She was trying to talk and sit up. Wallace handed me that flowered bag...the one that you...the one that Wallace...the one that fell overboard."

"Whatever." At last my turn.

"He told me there was a gun in the bag. He had to hold her...that girl...down. He kept his hand over her mouth or she would have screamed." A hint of annoyance crept into her voice.

Yeah, that Celia. I was right about her being annoying. She just wouldn't go along with the plan.

"What could I do? He kept hissing at me. 'Shoot her. Shoot her.' I had trouble getting the gun out but when I finally did, it was all ready to fire. Wallace had gotten a silencer—just in case. 'Shoot. Shoot.' He had to tell me a half dozen times." Mrs. Gimbel's eyes were wide open and glazed. She was reliving the moment. "She was getting stronger and stronger. I had to shoot her. What other options did I have? I shot her. Twice." She shrugged. "What else could I do?"

I'm sure we all had a few suggestions but we simply nodded in agreement.

I never witnessed much beseeching in my life but that's what Marvella Gimbel was doing. She turned to Hank. "They'll understand that this...thing...wasn't my fault won't they? It was his idea. The entire scheme wasn't my doing. I just did what he told me. Wallace makes all the decisions in our house."

Apparently Mrs. Gimbel was stuck in the fifties in more ways than her fashion sense.

Chapter Forty-Four

Hank disappeared to contact the local police, leaving me alone with Marvella Gimbel. I'd won the job simply because I wasn't fast enough—George, Claude, and Andy had headed for the hallway with Hank before I made my move. I also believed that the men suspected there would be comforting involved—women's work.

The cop had not yet formally arrested Marvella Gimbel. I didn't know his plan. Were we waiting for her husband?

In the meantime, I found myself taking care of a murderer. Marvella Gimbel didn't appear to comprehend that she was in trouble—big trouble. She seemed to believe that confessing put her on the same side of the law as the rest of us.

"You know, I always thought it would be so hard…to kill someone, but it wasn't."

I nodded. I didn't have any experiences to share.

"I fired a gun once when I was a little girl and the force nearly knocked me down." She smiled at the memory. "But the other night, it was so simple." Her eyes met mine; her tears had dried. "Can you imagine?"

I shook my head. I really couldn't.

Her eyes glazed over as she remembered the event. "Wallace told me to get the gun. I hadn't touched a weapon like that in years. You can imagine guns don't figure heavily in my life."

I nodded—although I didn't know anything about her life.

"I just pulled the trigger and the action felt so smooth. It was so easy. I stood there and watched that woman die. She just stopped struggling."

I didn't know how to respond.

"I wish we hadn't done this." Marvella was suddenly calm. "I shouldn't have gone along with Wallace. I knew better, but Wallace has always made the decisions in our house."

I nodded sympathetically, while thinking she'd better formulate a better defense for her trial.

"Oh, this has not been a good day." With that she lay her head on the arm of the sofa and fell asleep.

I regarded Marvella with awe, for two reasons. One, I couldn't fathom sleeping under these circumstances. Two, I couldn't understand how her eye makeup stayed in place. Despite her voluminous tears, her mascara and liner remained steadfastly affixed to every spot she had covered. It seemed nothing short of a marvel of modern science.

Hank signaled me to join him in the hallway. "How is she?"

"You mean aside from unconscious? Well, she seems to feel she didn't do anything wrong because the murder was all Wallace's idea. I am, however, a little worried that she will kill again. She kept saying how easy it was to shoot Celia."

"Easy?" Hank seemed surprised.

I repeated the story she had told me about how much easier it was to fire a gun as an adult.

Hank's eyes met Andy's. The two men shared a puzzled expression.

"How was I supposed to respond when she told me that?" I looked from Andy to Hank and back. They didn't notice. They were involved in deep nonverbal communication. "What?"

Neither man answered. Hank's eyes were locked on Andy's. He nodded toward the drawing room as if questioning Andy. Andy nodded.

"*What?*" I became more persistent but to no avail.

Hank headed toward the drawing room. Andy and I followed. Actually, Andy followed Hank. I followed Andy.

The cop knelt beside Marvella Gimbel and shook her shoulder gently. He spoke with a kindness I hadn't expected. "Mrs. Gimbel, I have to ask you another question."

"Do you have to?" She seemed annoyed that her sleep was disturbed.

"I think it's in your best interest."

Hank helped the sleepy woman to a sitting position. She pushed her plump legs together and made an effort to pull her skirt to her knees. The dress wouldn't reach. "Could you describe the gun to me?"

"Well, I don't know guns." She punctuated her statement with an attempt to push loose hairs into her chignon. "Wallace handled all that."

Yes, I thought, and the checking account, investments, and the trash every Thursday night.

"It was a forty-five." She nodded for emphasis. "That's what Wallace told me."

"And would you tell me how it felt to fire the gun?"

"I told you before. Do I have to go through this again?"

"Mrs. Gimbel, as I said I think it's in your best interest. I need to know exactly what it felt like to fire that gun at Celia Chaney."

So Marvella Gimbel told her story again. Her story about how easy it felt to kill another person.

I watched the two men's reactions. Whatever she said far exceeded the sum of her words.

Chapter Forty-Five

"Tell me." I pestered Andy as soon as the Parsonage's front door closed behind Hank, Marvella Gimbel and an array of local authorities.

"Tell you what?" Andy's mind had already moved onto other topics. He reached out and pulled me towards him. Wrapping both arms around me, he nuzzled my neck.

"Don't be coy, Andy. Tell me what you and Hank know that I don't."

"What makes you think we know anything?" Andy wasn't talking. What he was doing was a fair imitation of Bob Blandings.

Despite my aggravation with the Blandings-like behavior, I threw myself into a public display of affection worthy of Mandy Whatever-her-name-really-was. I forgot all about the Gimbels. "I have a room you know," I whispered in Andy's ear.

He grabbed my hand and pulled me toward the stairway. Andy made it to the top in record time. I made it to the middle where—in an overly polite gesture—I stopped to answer a question from Neil Cummings. "What has been going on around here?"

"You're not going to believe this story, although it's not quite over. The whole episode started the night I got here. I locked myself out."

"No!" Neil was still playing amnesiac.

"Well, turns out I saw a crime happening. I'm sure you'll get the entire explanation tomorrow, but I saw Mr. Gimbel carrying a corpse. That's how all this started I guess." I talked fast. I was ready to go upstairs. I had been for several hours. "When I was locked out, I glanced over onto the Gimbels' balcony and I saw a couple. I didn't get a good look at the man but he had the woman scooped up in his arms and she had on a long white nightgown like something from Victorian days and a long shawl-like thing wrapped around her and she had long dark hair…and it turns out she was dead."

Neil and Lulu stared at me with wide eyes.

"Anyway, if you see Mr. Gimbel, you might want to steer clear of him for obvious reasons but he won't get back into the house because the police are outside. So anyway tomorrow we should all know more. Talk to you then."

I ran up the stairs and charged through the door to my room, left open by an eager Andy. Dropping clothes as I went, I made my way to the high antique bed where he waited. I wasn't afraid of appearing overanxious. I'd long since crossed that threshold. If anything, I looked desperate.

"Andy, I am so happy you surprised me. This has been my best birthday ever." In the light of the full moon filtering through the lace curtains, I studied the former P.I.'s face. I stared into the cool green eyes that had mesmerized me the summer before. They retained their power.

"It's certainly been one of the longest birthday dates ever. Did you realize we've been trying to get upstairs for over three hours?" He kissed my forehead and then my nose.

"I have been painfully aware of that, but now—" I paused. "Now we hear a scream." I sat straight up. "What was that?"

"Ignore it." Andy pulled me down beside him and nibbled on my lip with a vigor worthy of the Blandings.

"Gladly." I welcomed his kiss.

The next scream was accompanied by a thud. My eyes flew open.

"Maggie, I know. You'll never know how much it pains me to say this, but someone needs help."

"We could hope someone else helps them."

"Who?"

"Claude and George heard me the night I…you fell." I searched for another solution. "What about the cops out front?"

"I doubt if they heard that. Go get them. I'll check it out." The noise had clearly originated in the Gimbels' room.

"Andy, wait. Maybe we should let the cops handle the situation."

"If they move quickly..."

"I'll get them here fast."

If I had to do it all over again, I would have taken the time to put on shoes. That old twenty-twenty hindsight. The way I saw it, however, was that the faster I got the cops involved, the faster I could head back to my bed—and Andy. So I grabbed Andy's parka—mine was spending the night on the bottom of the Delaware Bay. His jacket just skimmed my knees, providing enough warmth and modesty for a quick run to summon the police. I pulled up the zipper and ran for the stairs. About two strides away from the top step, I became Mr. Gimbel's second hostage—the first, I later learned, having been knocked unconscious after screaming for help. I heeded Mr. Gimbel's advice not to do so. Actually, I heeded the knife at my throat.

"Okay, you're my ticket out of here."

Ticket out of here? This guy spent too much time watching American Movie Classics.

"If we're going out, I should just pop back in and grab my slippers."

"Very funny." He pushed me forward. I resisted—expecting Andy to venture into the hall. He certainly was in no hurry to help the person in the Gimbels' room. Was he heeding my advice to wait for the cops? Why choose this of all moments to listen to me?

At the bottom of the stairs, I strained to see if Neil and Lulu lurked in the dark. Of all nights, they picked this one to take their work elsewhere.

"You know the back way out. Take me there." Gimbel snarled and tightened the grip on my arm. He was stronger than I'd suspected.

"Why don't we go out the front? It's closer." I pulled him towards the heavy double doors. Unfortunately, I was a resistible force and he was an immovable object. My effort failed.

"How dumb do you think I am?" There was a question best left unanswered. "There's cops all over the place."

"Why should that matter to you, Mr. Gimbel?" I feigned innocence.

"Because I think the cops believe that looney-tune wife of mine."

Oh, oh. I guess we should have thought of eavesdroppers. What did I mean we?—Hank was the pro. Why didn't he realized Gimbel was already in the building? Hadn't he checked?

"Move it, will you."

Given the blade at my throat, I moved. Gimbel dragged me down the hall towards the conservatory doors. I prayed that George and Claude had not retired for the night, but the room was dark—and empty.

Making as much noise as possible, I led Gimbel—or actually, let Gimbel push me—through the pantry into the large kitchen. Damn those two guys. They were so neat I couldn't find a single item to knock to the floor. In my apartment in New York, it was almost impossible to pass through the tiny kitchen without knocking at least a half-dozen utensils off the counter.

I hadn't managed to summon help by the time we reached the back door. "Okay, here you go." I turned the latch, threw open the door, and waved Gimbel out. For all I cared, he could go—I had no desire to be a hero.

"You're coming with me."

"I'd love to, but I really can't. My boyfriend's waiting for—"

"This isn't a social invitation. You're coming with me."

Great. I stood firm, thinking he couldn't make me leave without a fight. He brushed the blade across my neck lightly. I moved.

The cold of the brick steps against my bare feet was nothing compared to the suffering the pebbles in the parking lot caused. I cried out at the pain.

"Keep it down!" Gimbel hissed.

"It hurts. Maybe you should leave me here. You can travel faster alone."

"Yeah, right." He shoved me forward. "Move it." He shot an angry look at a hedge on the south side of the lot. "Now you got that goddamn dog going. Every damn time I come by here it's a major pain in the ass. Somebody's got to do something about the bitch."

I hoped he meant the dog.

He dragged me to a dark Lexus.

I hesitated. "What's this?" I didn't ask what had happened to the van. Missing evidence was Hank's problem—not mine.

"My car, you moron. We're getting out of here."

How did Gimbel plan to keep me quiet and coerce me into the car? Admittedly, I was in bad shape, but even a strong man couldn't keep the knife at my throat as we drove. Gimbel didn't have a prayer of doing so. With the weapon out of the picture, I would have a good shot at escape.

When Gimbel opened the passenger door, I figured I was home free. He wouldn't use the knife—he wasn't the type of man who got blood stains on his leather upholstery. Either I was wrong, or he didn't realize that smashing me in the back of the head with an unidentified but heavy object would make my head bleed.

I was never fully unconscious and the groggy sensation didn't last long. We were still in town when I opened my eyes. I wasn't sure if we had arrived at our destination or not. Those cars are amazing. Gimbel's idled so quietly that I couldn't be certain if the motor was running or not. As it turned out we were only stopped at a traffic light. Gimbel stepped on the gas; we continued out of town.

Wallace Gimbel was an unusual killer; he had gone to the trouble to belt me into the front seat. He was, as I recalled both from tailing him and hiding in his minivan, a most cautious driver. Becoming a fugitive didn't change that An intense frown plastered on his face, he clutched the wheel with both hands. He was so focused on the road ahead, he didn't notice that I was conscious. Slowly, I moved my hand along the door panel searching for the lock. Nice car, I thought. I didn't know years and models but the vehicle must have been new. The smell of leather was still fresh. When my right hand found the door handle, I slid my other hand between the seats in search of the seat belt release.

"What do you think you're doing?" Gimbel grabbed my left hand and pinned it in my lap.

"You don't need me. You've gotten away. Let me out." I tried to sound practical, not frantic.

"You'll go when I'm good and ready." Gimbel's grip hurt my hand.

I checked out the car for an item to facilitate my escape. A nail file slipping around on the dashboard caught my attention. "A nail file. You took me hostage with a nail file?"

"Moron. Where would I have found a knife in my room?"

I felt the moron comment was uncalled for. The knife point—or rather the point about the knife—that was a good observation. I wished I'd thought of it ten minutes earlier.

I considered my options—all based on the assumption that I could unlock Gimbel's vise-like grip on my left hand. I could open the door and roll out of the moving car, and then spend the next year in the hospital. I could open the window and scream—at least once until Gimbel got the electric window back up. I could attack him and force the car off the road—but that probably brought me back to the year-in-the-hospital outcome.

Instead, I adopted a wait-and-see attitude. Or at least that's what I convinced myself my lack of action was.

As I settled into the passenger's seat, my foot hit something hard "Oh, I am sorry." I blurted out the words before the concept of apologizing to a kidnapper hit me. "You shouldn't leave your camera on the floor." I reached down and grabbed the equipment.

If Gimbel was concerned or annoyed about my abuse of the camera, he didn't let on. Then again, he did have other, bigger, things on his mind. I had an idea that I might be able to distract Gimbel with a discussion of photography. "Nice camera." I examined the totally manual 35mm equipment. "Had it long?"

Gimbel appeared suspicious, but answered. "Not too long. It was a gift."

"You take a lot of landscapes." I made a statement; I didn't ask a question.

"Ah...Yeah. I guess so." He paused. "I like to position Marvella in the foreground."

I'd never seen him photograph his wife. "Do much in deep focus?"

He eyed me as if my question was a trick, which it was. "I don't know much about technique. I just get something in focus and shoot."

Not with that camera he didn't. I thought of tripping him up with talk of f-stops and speed settings but saw little point. Using photography as a cover for his forays into crime was the least of Gimbel's problems. I decided to be ingratiating instead of confrontational. I chatted. "I used to do some photography but not lately—"

"Look, can the discussion. I've got some thinking to do."

Yeah? Well maybe you should have done more thinking before you came up with your cockamamie scheme. I kept the thought to myself. I sat silently and watched the scenery—as much as the moonlight rendered visible—go by.

We were headed towards Sunset Beach when Gimbel made a sudden left turn into Cape May Point. The residential area was quiet and dark. No one was on the streets. No lights shone in the windows.

I knew only one spot in Cape May Point and that appeared to be where we were headed: the lighthouse. As Gimbel swung the car into the parking lot, the headlight swept the space—deserted except for a green minivan in the corner. I figured that either freedom or death was moments away.

"Mr. Gimbel. You won't get away with this. The police will find you. Your wife has already confessed to the murder of Celia Chaney."

"Celia Chaney?" The wheels of his mind were spinning—visibly. I watched as his eyes reflected all the mental action. He brought the car to a stop and pointed to a woman walking across the parking lot. "Don't be ridiculous. Here comes Celia Chaney now."

Chapter Forty-Six

So this was Celia Chaney. As she walked through the moonlight, I studied the woman who'd been the focus of my weekend. For a dead person she looked pretty darn good—and moved well. In black parka, black leggings, and black flats, Celia resembled a friend of Neil and Lulu Cummings more than a paramour of Wallace Gimbel. She was tall, slender and in the light of the moon appeared to have lovely ankles. When she moved closer, I noted she had a face her five-by-seven glossy had flattered. At least that was my guess. The wind repeatedly tossed her thick brown hair across her rather ordinary features. She fought a good battle to push the hair back but lost.

"Celia Chaney?" I spoke the name aloud. "Well, then," I snapped my seatbelt. "You haven't got a problem in the world. I'll catch a cab back." I hopped out of the car and ran. If I'd had worn shoes, I would have had a shot at getting away. As it was, I was no match for Celia Chaney. God, she had long legs—and a firm grip. I couldn't figure out how she overtook me so quickly.

"What do I do with her, Bunny?" I expected strong legs of a dancer but she had remarkable upper body strength. My struggling to wrest myself from her grasp didn't phase her.

"Just hold her. I've got to think." Gimbel paced the lot next to his car.

I heard sirens in the distance. I hoped they would prompt Gimbel to make a quick decision. For one thing, I was almost positive that Celia was leaving bruises on my already battered arms. For another, I was only wearing one item of clothing and although the night was warmer than the two before, the weather couldn't be termed balmy.

There was one other reason. I was fairly certain I was allergic to Celia's perfume—a fragrance she wore far too much of. "You wouldn't have a tissue on you, would you?"

I read the answer in Celia's glare. If she had a box of Kleenex in her pocket, I wasn't getting one sheet. On the upside, she might wear too much perfume but she definitely smelled better than her boyfriend Guy.

Celia held me with one hand and pulled an elastic band from her pocket with the other. With her free hand, she subdued the swirling mass of hair. How did she do that? It didn't seem the time to ask. It did seem the time to struggle—to no avail. Her fingers held my arm like a steel clamp.

With her hair pulled tight against her head, Celia's face took on a menacing air. "Wallace, tell me what's going on. Who is she? Why did you tell me to come here?" She tightened her already firm hold on me. "I hope it doesn't have anything to with those sirens."

"Would you shut up and let me think?" Gimbel rubbed his bald spot. For warmth, for habit, for luck? If he believed the massage would help his brain generate a good idea, he was wrong.

"Maybe we should think while driving—away from the sirens." Under her breath Celia mumbled, "Putz."

I heard her; Gimbel didn't. I wasn't feeling hopeful about their relationship. Though on the issue of fleeing, I had to side with Celia. Even I was getting impatient for Gimbel to make a decision. My head hurt from the cut on my scalp and my attempts to figure out where this frail looking dancer got her strength.

The longer we stood there the less the cold bothered me. I was sweating. Or at least I was until the realization hit me. These people weren't killers—at least we had no proof that they were murderers. One of the them was actually the victim. I was willing to bet that fact—that Celia Chaney was not dead—was what Hank and Andy had read between the lines of Marvella's confession.

I eyed the portly gentleman in the heavy topcoat. I'd come to think of Wallace Gimbel as a killer, but in fact I'd seen no evidence that he could hurt a fly. Obviously any insect could get away before Gimbel made a decision about his fate.

Someone had to take control of the situation. I figured it had to be me. "Gimbel, the cops want you for killing Celia. If this is really Celia, I don't see what your problem is."

"What?" For a dancer, Celia had some soprano. I wondered if she ever thought of doing Broadway. "The cops. Who brought the cops into this?"

"Calm down. I'm thinking," Gimbel protested.

Not fast enough. The sirens were getting close.

"I'm out of here." Celia released me. "Wallace, you are without a doubt..." If she'd ever harbored any affection for Gimbel (and I bet she hadn't) the emotions had set sail—and sunk.

I don't know why upon receiving my freedom, I determined to restrain Celia Chaney. Full of bravado, I stepped in front of her. "Celia, I'm not sure what's going on here, but I think you'd better stay and talk to the police."

"Yeah, right." She turned and headed for the minivan.

I grabbed the hood of her parka. "I think you should wait."

"You stupid bitch. Why would I care what you think?" Celia broke away and started to run.

I suppose mine was a reflex action. I followed. Without shoes, I hopped across the parking lot like a religious zealot across hot coals. There would have been no chance of my overtaking the surefooted runner had she not turned to check on the progress of the sirens that were quickly approaching. She stumbled. I still had not caught up when, back on her feet, she headed for the Cape May HawkWatch platform.

I think I felt outrage at her willingness to disturb the bird sanctuary. Why? I had no idea. I was no birder. I knew nothing about ornithology. Yet somehow at that point I experienced a burst of energy. I lunged and managed to grab the bottom of her parka. My grasp spun her around.

"You are without a doubt the dumbest bitch..." She ended the sentence with her hand raised.

The words were harsh enough. She didn't have to hit me. I saw her arm pull back and the fist move in my direction. I was so shocked I froze. As her punch landed on my jaw, I was again impressed by her upper body strength. When her knuckles made contact my head flew back. I heard a loud snap. Dazed, I fell first to my knees and then flat onto my face. As I lay on the ground at her feet, I couldn't help noticing. Celia Chaney had really lovely ankles.

Chapter Forty-Seven

At last—police cars. Two vehicles with flashing lights made the turn into the parking area; a third vehicle blocked the exit. One car ground to a halt beside Gimbel's Lexus. The other continued into the lot. Their speed was enough to scare anyone dressed—or almost dressed—in dark colors laying on the black surface at night. I was probably the only person in that category and it frightened me. I scrambled to move out of the way. Crawling didn't do the trick. I rolled across the rough surface—all the time thinking of Andy's question. "Are you always covered with cuts and bruises?"

Safe on the grass, I peeked over my shoulder and saw Andy among those jumping out of the police cruisers. A uniformed cop grabbed Gimbel, who attempted a few last strokes of his bald spot before the officer secured his arms behind his back.

Andy focused on Celia. He pursued her up the ramp to the bird-watching platform. My sentiments were with Andy but my money was on Celia as she headed back to the minivan. With a burst of strength Andy moved within a few feet of the dancer. He stretched his arms forward and lunged at her. He missed but stayed on his feet. Stumbling forward he made contact with Celia as she glanced over her shoulder. I'm not sure how but the two of them become entangled. Celia was the one who went down.

She was some fighter. A uniformed officer ran to Andy's aid. Both men were required to subdue the woman. I guessed Celia worked out when most people stayed home cleaning the house.

"Maggie, are you okay?" Andy called across the parking lot. There was insufficient personnel for anyone to come to my aid.

"I think she broke my jaw." Loud snapping noises reverberated in my ears as I attempted to speak.

"What?"

"She hit me."

"Who?"

"Celia. The person I was so worried about broke my jaw." I poked at the joint in hopes of working the bones back into place. "That's the last time I jump overboard for anyone."

"I thought you slipped." Andy's amused voice floated through the night.

"Whatever."

Chapter Forty-Eight

I returned to the emergency room for the second time that weekend. When the paramedics dropped me off, the night shift didn't recognize me as the woman who had fallen off the ferry. The evening visit was much quieter. No police. No press. No Andy.

By the time Andy was back from the police station, I knew a lot. I knew that my jaw, although not broken, had been dislocated; I knew that Andy had brought the police to my rescue; I knew that I would not be getting involved in any future investigations. I swore that to Andy when he arrived.

"You should be very proud. If it weren't for you, Gimbel would have pulled off his plan." He kissed my forehead and brushed my bangs from my face. "When can you get out of here?"

"As soon as they bring me my clothes. Well, my cloth. Actually, your cloth." I invented the singular term to identify Andy's parka. "They transferred me to this room but your jacket didn't make the move."

"Well, I think you look pretty hot in paper hospital gowns."

God knows he'd seen me in enough of them. "As a matter of fact, since I've known you hospital smells turn me on." He bent to kiss me. "You must be happy knowing the role you played in bringing Gimbel et al. to justice."

"Do you know what would make me happy? I'd love it if every time I moved my jaw, it didn't make a clacking noise." I demonstrated for him.

"I'm sure that sounds a lot louder to you than it does to the rest of the world. Besides, your jaw may not sound good but it looks good. Your face isn't even swollen." He ran a finger over my face with a light touch. "Though you've got a lot...I mean a couple of little scratches on your cheeks."

I explained about rolling across the parking lot to escape the wheels of the speeding squad cars.

"I'm sure we would have seen you."

"Or felt the bump when you ran over me. How did you find us, anyway?"

Before he could answer, the drape was pulled back and Lulu Cummings stuck her head around. "Are you okay?"

Andy reached out a hand to welcome her into the room. "I didn't have a chance to tell you. I ran into Lulu when she was checking out of the hospital. You'll be happy to hear that she's okay."

"Thanks to you, Andy." She wrapped an arm around my boyfriend's waist.

I'd always wanted to see Lulu smile—but not at Andy. Not with a worshipful expression in her eyes.

"You're okay? I didn't know you weren't okay." I tried to draw her attention back to me.

Andy wrapped a friendly arm around her narrow shoulders. "That was Lulu's scream we heard. Gimbel knocked her out when she broke into his room."

"You broke into his room?" I stared at Lulu with wonderment.

She was still gazing at Andy with admiration. "Not really...and it wasn't Gimbel's room *per se*. He just happened to be in there."

Yeah, because he'd rented the room. I eyed the woman with amazement. She was beaming. What had happened to her dour expression? I missed it.

"This is a interesting story." Andy released Lulu and settled close to her—on the foot of my bed. "Remember that little one-minute summary of the murder you gave Lulu and Neil."

"Vaguely."

"Well, that couple you described are Ethan and Abigail Cahill—or at least they match the description of Ethan and Abigail." Andy spoke as if I should recognize the names.

Lulu nodded. "We've been trying to contact them for years."

"I didn't see Mr. Gimbel holding Celia Chaney?"

Neil took that moment to make his entrance—talking. "Well, it may have been, but Lulu claims your portrayal exactly matches the description of her great-great-grandmother who eloped from this house in 1895. How are you?" He swept across the room and planted a kiss on my cheek as if we were old friends.

"Her great-great-grandmother is over a hundred years old?" I accepted his kiss with a question.

"No, she's dead. She was murdered by the man with whom she ran away—although not until twenty years later." Neil didn't miss a beat.

"Neil and Lulu have spent countless nights in the Parsonage, and—"

"Countless." Lulu interrupted Andy.

"They have been trying to contact her. They believe you saw her. Actually, that night you dropped from the roof, they thought they'd found her. They sensed her presence and then you fell out of the sky."

"My hair's a different color."

"Absolutely—but we didn't know what she looked like later in life. Her hair might have gone gray."

I eyed Neil with a mixture of anger and amazement. My hair was blonde, not gray. And what did he mean, later in life? If I had five years on Neil, that would be surprising.

Andy's eyes met mine. He knew what I was thinking. He smiled and shrugged. "Anyway, now Neil and Lulu are convinced you saw Abigail and Ethan. They were so excited—and you may recall that you mentioned Gimbel was out of the building and would be detained by the police on their way in—anyway, they were so excited they went into Gimbel's room. Gimbel, who returned to the house without our knowing, was on alert because he overheard bits of our discussions with his wife. He knocked Neil out cold as they broke in and then grabbed Lulu.

He figured he had to sneak away so he wanted to use her as a hostage, but she wouldn't cooperate so he knocked her out, too."

I looked from Lulu to Neil. "No permanent damage, I hope?"

"We're fine—in fact, the hospital never even admitted me," Neil said.

Andy continued. "Anyway, when I went in to investigate the scream I found Neil and Lulu. Fortunately I looked out the window in time to see Gimbel force you into that Lexus. I ran out and got a police cruiser to follow him, but he had a good head start. For awhile I thought we'd lost you."

"It felt like forever until you got there."

"It felt that way to me, too." He lifted my hand and kissed my fingers—or at least the spots between the bandages.

Neil and Lulu took that as their cue to leave. Neil kissed me goodbye; Lulu kissed Andy. With a promise to see us back at the B&B, they disappeared into the hallway.

"Alone at last." Andy leaned on the edge of the gurney. "The other good news is that they booked Celia on assault charges for hitting you, and Gimbel for kidnapping. They weren't quite sure what to do with him since he was originally wanted for murder and walked in with the corpse."

"You knew at the B&B that Celia wasn't dead. How? Marvella Gimbel confessed."

"No. Marvella Gimbel confessed to conspiracy and attempted murder."

"Are you going to be cute about this or are you going to explain?"

"If you hadn't repeated what she said, we might not have known. As I said, you're a hero."

"Known what?"

"Have you ever fired a gun?"

"No, but if you don't explain things to me soon, I just might."

"Remember when Mrs. Gimbel said how easy killing Celia was? How different it was firing a gun when she was young? Well, that's because she remembered the kick. What impressed her the other night was that she never felt the kick." He watched me to see if I got it.

"I figured advances in technology—"

"No. A gun fires very differently when it's firing blanks. If she had fired real bullets, she would have felt the kick."

"So you're telling me she fired blanks."

"Exactly."

"Why would she fire blanks? That makes no sense."

"It makes no sense if she knew. She didn't know."

Andy let me sit quietly and figure the story out for myself. "Gimbel gave her the gun. Gimbel told her to fire. Celia played dead."

No wonder Gimbel remained so calm in the face of all the questions. No wonder he did things that looked suspicious. He wasn't afraid of getting caught. He knew there was no murder. On the other hand, poor Mrs. Gimbel was riddled with guilt and filled with dread until she'd confessed her deeds to the police. She didn't know.

"They set her up. She thought she and her husband were setting Celia up, but all the time they were setting her up."

Andy nodded.

"This news certainly makes sense of a few of Gimbel's stupid moves. Like the license plate."

Andy didn't understand.

"He had a rental van but the car had an old license plate. He must have switched the plates—not for any valid reason but to impress Mrs. Gimbel with the efforts he made to cover their crime. All the evidence that he was a dumb criminal actually points to his being a savvy deceiver—although it would have been hard to explain to the cops if he'd gotten stopped."

"Wasn't that a hit in the seventies?— 'Savvy Deceiver'?" Andy smiled.

I ignored his remark. "And Guy and Celia were setting Gimbel up."

"Nice bunch, huh? We'll have to have them over for dinner... when they get out of jail." Andy squeezed my hand tentatively. "If it weren't for you and your…curiosity," he chose the word carefully, "the murder would have gone undiscovered because there was no murder. The Gimbels would have gone back to Atlantic City. There would have been some talk about Celia's being missing. I'm sure Gimbel had formulated a plan for handling her disappearance. Soon he would have been off to join her. Marvella Gimbel would have lived the rest of her life in fear of her husband—because he was the only person who knew she was a killer."

I gripped Andy's hand as firmly as my bandaged fingers would allow. "So tell me the entire story."

He started. After about three sentences, I was lost.

"Whoa, boy. I'm not following all this. Give me the chronology."

So he did. "It all started when Gimbel took a fancy to Celia. She wasn't the first woman at the casino he'd gotten involved with. From what I can gather Gimbel was generally rather discreet. Celia was different. Gimbel fell pretty hard for Celia and Celia knew it. She and Guy decided to take advantage of his feelings."

"He got her a promotion."

"Hardly enough for Celia and Guy. I don't think either one of them is particularly interested in working for a living."

"So?"

Andy brushed a strand of hair from my forehead and studied the area about my eyes. Whatever he saw wasn't good; he didn't break the bad news to me. He kept to the topic of criminal activity. "So, Celia and Guy came up with an idea—hardly a new one—to tell Gimbel that Celia was pregnant. They just wanted to raise a little quick cash. Seed money to move to California and start a new life."

"I don't think they call that seed money. Don't they call it extortion?"

"Most would. I don't think Celia and Guy use three-syllable words. May I continue?"

He didn't wait for my answer. "My personal opinion is that Celia actually thought the childless Gimbel might leave his wife for her.

She thought he was loaded. I'm not quite sure where that left Guy—
except out in the cold."

"But what good would it do Celia to snag Gimbel?" I asked about
the crime but I was focused on Andy's eyes. Why couldn't he take
his eyes off my forehead? Just how bad could a few scratches look?
"Gimbel's wife had the big bucks."

"Exactly. And Gimbel was honest about that with Celia. So the
two of them cooked up a scheme to get control of Mrs. Gimbel and,
more importantly, her money."

"She's lucky they didn't just kill her."

"I don't think their decision was a result of any moral position.
Killing Marvella Gimbel was just too obvious. The husband is always
the prime suspect. So Gimbel and Celia came up with the idea to make
Marvella think she was a killer. Then they could extort money from her."

"Not Celia. She'd have to play dead."

"Gimbel had the kind of contacts to get her a new identity. She
has no family to speak of. She wouldn't be missed."

"Except by Guy."

"Yeah. Poor Guy. I don't know if she was going to, but so far
Celia hadn't let him in on the plan. I mean he thought he was in on
the plan. He just didn't know that Celia had moved on to Plan B. She
left him behind to raise suspicions about her disappearance. But
remember, he was under strict instructions not to call in the police.
I'm sure that Celia had some plan to keep him under control."

"You know, if I were Celia, I would have made Mrs. Gimbel think
she killed Guy and then I would have killed him. Then I wouldn't have
had to play dead."

At last the focus of Andy's gaze shifted to my eyes. He stared at
me long and hard. "You're scary."

"I didn't say I would do it. I said if I were Celia, I would have
done it." I didn't think Andy appreciated the distinction.

"Either way, Celia was very nice to Guy." I scowled—first at the
thought of what Celia and Gimbel had planned for Guy and then because
of the pain when my facial muscles pulled my skin tight across my face.

Andy returned to his explanation. "Remember, Celia and Gimbel were off to a life of leisure in the islands. All they wanted was some money. Neither of them were planning a career in their new location."

"How much money was Mrs. Gimbel willing to give them?"

"To avoid being tried for murder? Plenty. She's got tons of money. And, she would have kept paying—possibly in the hopes that Gimbel would change his mind and come back to her. Why she would want him back is beyond me—but I sense that she does—at least she did before his real plan was exposed."

Andy explained how Gimbel had handled his wife. "Because she was the one who actually pulled the trigger he began to distance himself from the crime—to feign remorse. She bought that he was having second thoughts. She actually began to apologize for doing exactly what he told her to do. She even claimed to understand that Wallace Gimbel was having doubts about what they did. She hoped someday he'd forgive her. Gimbel figured he'd go back to Atlantic City, pack up, make a graceful exit—he told Marvella so no one would become suspicious of her—and then go meet Celia."

"And they believed that Guy wouldn't blow the whistle?" My tone said I didn't.

Andy shrugged. "As I said, I'm certain that Celia had some plan to handle Guy. He loved Celia, but I'm not sure he didn't love money more. His financial expectations aren't that high. I bet he could be bought off for a fairly small sum. Gimbel didn't know a thing about Guy. Remember, he still thought that Celia was pregnant and in love with him. He didn't know he'd have to deal with her ex-lover . . ."

"Or maybe just her lover."

"Yeah." Andy considered the possibility. "We'll never know what Celia had planned for Guy. I'm sure she figured she could handle him. I'm pretty sure she could have. And, even given this turn of events, I'm pretty sure she will—as soon as she figures out a plan that works in her favor."

"And when a baby didn't come?" Gimbel wasn't that dumb!

Again, Andy shrugged. "Maybe one would—just a little later than Gimbel expected. If not, that would be easy enough to explain."

"What about Marvella Gimbel now?"

"Mrs. Gimbel is still singing and providing the cops with information. You're right about her attitude. She's been advised of her rights but especially now that she knows Celia is alive she feels like a victim, so she'll tell the cops anything. I think she's over Gimbel. She's already got her eye on Hank."

"Is Guy in jail?"

"Not yet. They've got their hands full with these three."

"What a crowd George and Claude had this weekend! The Pankenhursts aren't the Pankenhursts. The Blandings aren't the Blandings. Seems the only people on the up and up were Neil and Lulu—the ones who appeared most suspicious. Aren't the cops concerned about their being in Gimbel's room?"

Andy shrugged. "Hank handled it. You okay?"

"Yeah…except…you know before I met you I never ended up in the emergency room. I mean seldom…or rarely."

"I know. We have fun, don't we?" He kissed my forehead.

"Right. This is fun." I peered into his green eyes. "You can kiss me. You won't hurt me."

And so he kissed me again. At first tentatively and then longer and deeper. I lay back and pulled Andy onto the bed. His weight hurt but an extra ache or pain hardly made a difference at this point. I opened my mouth wide and welcomed his kiss. That was when he screamed.

"Oh my God." He moaned. "Oh my God." He was holding his face and jumping in place.

"They didn't tell me. They didn't tell me." I protested.

"Tell you what?" A nurse had appeared in response to Andy's screams.

"That her jaw would snap shut." Andy slurred the words. "Oh my God. Oh my God."

I translated for the perplexed nurse. Then, the three of us screamed. Andy screamed in pain. The nurse and I screamed at Andy. I was apologizing. The nurse was begging. "Open your mouth. Let me see. Move your hand."

She pulled Andy's hand from his mouth. "She didn't break the skin. You're fine but I'll admit that sort of bite is painful." She shot a disapproving glance in my direction—as if I'd bitten Andy's tongue on purpose.

"Kay," I read the nurse's name tag. "Will this happen again?"

She raised an eyebrow. "Well, I wouldn't plan a trip to lovers' lane tonight but once your jaw is back in place, you'll be fine." She turned to Andy. "If you're concerned, you might consider a tetanus shot." With that she disappeared into the hallway.

Andy turned to me. "Ah, alone at last." At least I think that was what he said. With his words formed by a swollen tongue, I found him hard to understand. He held my hand with his left hand and his jaw with the right.

"You know, you're right, Andy. We always have fun, don't we?"

He glared at me over his hand.

"Someday we'll laugh at this."

Someday, but not today, I added silently.

Chapter Forty-Nine

The sky displayed the first traces of light when Andy and I returned to the bridal suite. Andy pulled back a lace curtain and eyed the horizon. "If we hurry, we can be on the beach for the sunrise."

I removed my paper hospital shoes before climbing onto the tall bed. I continued to wear Andy's parka over the paper gown. "If we hurry we can be sound asleep before sunrise." I lay my head on the cushion of flowers.

"If I go brush my teeth, do you promise not to knock me out when I emerge from the bathroom."

"Andy, do I look like I want to hit anyone? Trust me, I wouldn't have the strength even if I wanted to." My eyes were already closed. I fought to open them when I felt Andy climb into bed beside me.

"You know, this weekend didn't work out the way I'd planned." His voice sounded almost normal; his tongue appeared to be making a quick recovery. Andy wrapped his arms around me.

I waited for him to rescind his declaration of love from the night before—to tell me that he had been carried away by emotion, given my brush with death. At least he'd waited until my birthday was over.

"But I really had fun."

I released a sigh of relief. "Me, too. I thought I'd be sitting alone in the bridal suite longing for romance."

"Isn't this better? Two of us sitting in the bridal suite longing for romance."

"We may be injured but at least we're not totally disabled."

"No, we're not." He kissed me lightly—on the cheek.

"It's okay." I rolled onto my side and wrapped my arms around him. "You can kiss me. Kissing doesn't hurt."

"Not you...but if that thing snaps shut again..." He shuddered. "That hurt." He seemed reluctant to continue. "You know, Meg, if you're not too tired...could we talk about the proposition...I mean proposal...or suggestion...I made at dinner last night? I respect your decision to devote your life to good works...but, graduate school will always be there. And you'll have your entire life to do good."

"Do you really believe if I wait until the fall to go back to school that the world will be so totally pulled together that I will never have a chance to do good?" I pulled back and gazed into his sea green eyes. They had narrowed with worry. "Let me see if I understand what you're proposing." I rolled onto my elbows and stared down at the former P.I. "On one hand, a very sweet, very loving and I must say very cute man is asking me to follow him to turquoise waters, balmy breezes, and relentless sun so that I can spend the next five months sunning, sailing and...whatever. On the other hand, I can spend those months freezing in winter weather, riding buses to boring classes, writing papers, and taking exams so I can find a job that pays thirty percent of the one I left. And, let me see if I have this right, you think it's a tough decision."

Andy shrugged.

"See. I told you. You really don't know me very well, do you?"

Andy shrugged again. "I'd like to get to know you better."

"How big is your boat?"

Andy appeared puzzled. "Thirty-five feet."

"Oh, I think after five, six months on a thirty-five foot sailboat, you're going to know me a lot better."

Chapter Fifty

George had tears in his eyes when the same limo that dropped me off pulled up to take Andy and me to New York. There was time for leisurely good-byes on the porch given the warmth of the sun and a temperature that had jumped thirty degrees.

"I can't remember the last time I had this much fun. This was the best weekend." George wrapped one arm through mine and another through Andy's.

Claude shrugged. "He said that last weekend. Actually, he says the same thing every weekend." He paused for effect. "But this weekend, I think he's right."

"I think we should have a reunion this summer." George was sincere.

I hated to put a crimp in his plans but any reunion would be a fairly small one. "I don't think the Gimbels will be on parole yet."

"And the Blandings were just a one-shot deal. They no longer exist." Andy discounted one more couple.

"You know what, though. We might be able to invite the Pankenhursts."

I hated to disillusion my host but I filled him in on the Pankenhurst/Parkers—up to and including my advice to the lovelorn the night before.

"Well, Meg, you may well have been successful. They might be a couple. We haven't seen them yet this morning." George was optimistic.

"And, if you have the reunion at night, I am certain that Neil and Lulu Cummings would love to attend." Claude made the recommendation. "They'll probably be here anyway hanging around with Ethan and Abigail."

"Yes, tell Ethan and Abigail to keep the weekend free." As the only potential believer in the group, I added their names to the guest list. "At least Abigail. As I heard it Ethan is a killer."

"He would have fit right in this weekend." Claude was right.

Andy tugged on my arm to let me know we should go.

"George."

He wrapped his arms around me and patted my back with enthusiasm. "You two hurry back." Ever the matchmaker, he whispered in my ear, "I can always free up the honeymoon suite for you if you need it."

A lump in my throat prevented me from answering; I nodded that I would try to return. Then I turned to my other host for the weekend.

"Claude."

I was surprised by the warmth, strength, and length of his embrace. He, too, whispered an invitation to come back soon.

I stepped back to etch a memory of the couple into my memory. I found my voice. "It was really nice meeting you." The words sounded so strange on my lips. I felt like I had known my hosts forever.

"Now, before you are whisked away by that extremely tasteful vehicle," Claude eyed the long white limo with black windows with disdain, "why don't we formalize our plans to meet again."

"Yes." George was beyond enthusiastic. "When will you two be sailing by Cape May on your way north?"

I looked to Andy for an answer.

"May. June. Definitely by June. My friend Steve is going to let me use the dock in back of his house on Long Beach Island for the summer. I want to be there by the fourth of July for sure."

"So, we'll see you as you pass by." George's tone indicated that this was an order—not an invitation.

"As long as we keep on schedule, maybe we can spend a night or two at the Parsonage. And we should be able to make good time if Maggie can promise me one thing." Andy blocked his mouth with his hand and spoke to George and Claude in a stage whisper. "I think given the events of this weekend, you'll understand why I am asking." He paused for effect before turning my way. "When we're sailing, could you suppress any urges to jump overboard?"

I feigned anger. "You guys! You'll never let me forget one little mistake. I'm telling you for the last time—I slipped."

The three men exchanged glances and shrugged in unison. "Whatever."

Don't Miss These Other Great Plexus Books...

PATRIOTS, PIRATES, AND PINEYS
By Robert A. Peterson

Southern New Jersey is a region full of rich heritage, and yet it is one of the best kept historical secrets of our nation. Many famous people have lived in Southern New Jersey, and numerous world-renowned businesses were started in this area as well.

This collection of biographies gives the reader a sense of history about the area through the stories of the people who resided here with the tales of such famous figures as John Wanamaker, Henry Rowan, and Sara Spenser Washington. Some of the subjects would be considered patriots, some pirates, and some Pineys, but they all would be considered people who helped make America what it is today.

Hardbound • ISBN 0-937548-37-5 • $29.95
Softbound • ISBN 0-937548-39-1 • $19.95

OVER THE GARDEN STATE & OTHER STORIES
By Robert Bateman

Novelist Bateman (Pinelands, Whitman's Tomb) offers six new stories set in his native Southern New Jersey. While providing plenty of authentic local color in his portrayal of small-town and farm life, the bustle of the Jersey shore with its boardwalks, and the solitude and otherworldliness of the famous Pine Barrens, Bateman's sensitively portrayed protagonists are the stars here. The title story tells of an Italian prisoner of war laboring on a South Jersey farm circa 1944. There, he finds danger and dreams, friendship and romance—and, ultimately, more fireworks than he could have wished for.

Available: November 1999 • hardbound • ISBN: 0-937548-40-8 • $22.95

KILLING TIME IN OCEAN CITY
By Jane Kelly

After being jolted from a sound sleep by police early in her vacation, Meg Daniels discovers that her former boss has turned up dead near her rented beach house in Ocean City, New Jersey. A series of suspicious circumstances turns Meg into a prime suspect in his murder, and the evidence against her seems to be mounting every minute. Along the way the action shifts from Ocean City to Atlantic City to the Pine Barrens, with Meg frantically hunting for answers while she herself becomes a target of the killer.

The familiarity of the author with the shore areas of South Jersey brings a fun, real-life dimension for the local reader to this suspense-filled "whodunit." You'll be quickly turning the pages from the moment the body is discovered through the book's surprise ending.

Hardbound • ISBN 0-937548-38-3 • $22.95

To order or for a catalog: 609-654-6500, Fax Order Service: 609-654-4309

Plexus Publishing, Inc.

143 Old Marlton Pike • Medford • NJ 08055
E-mail: patp@plexuspub.com